PRAISE FOR

BALONEY
AND FRIENDS

"GREG PIZZOLI DOES IT AGAIN! THESE DELIGHTFULLY FUNNY FRIENDS WILL INSPIRE YOUNG READERS TO WRITE AND DRAW THEIR OWN STORIES."

—DAV PILKEY, **CREATOR OF THE DOG MAN AND CAPTAIN UNDERPANTS SERIES**

"KIDS WILL GOBBLE UP *BALONEY!*"

—BEN CLANTON, **CREATOR OF THE NARWHAL AND JELLY SERIES**

"PORCINE-LY PERFECT!"

—LAURIE KELLER, **GEISEL AWARD—WINNING AUTHOR OF *WE ARE GROWING!***

"WILD EXUBERANCE...WILL DRAW YOUNG READERS RIGHT IN. A SURE BET FOR ELEPHANT AND PIGGIE FANS WHO ARE READY FOR THE NEXT STEP UP."

—*BOOKLIST*

"THE WARMTH, GOOFINESS, AND ACCESSIBILITY MAKE THIS AN EASY PICK FOR TRANSITIONING READERS."

—*THE BULLETIN OF THE CENTER FOR CHILDREN'S BOOKS*

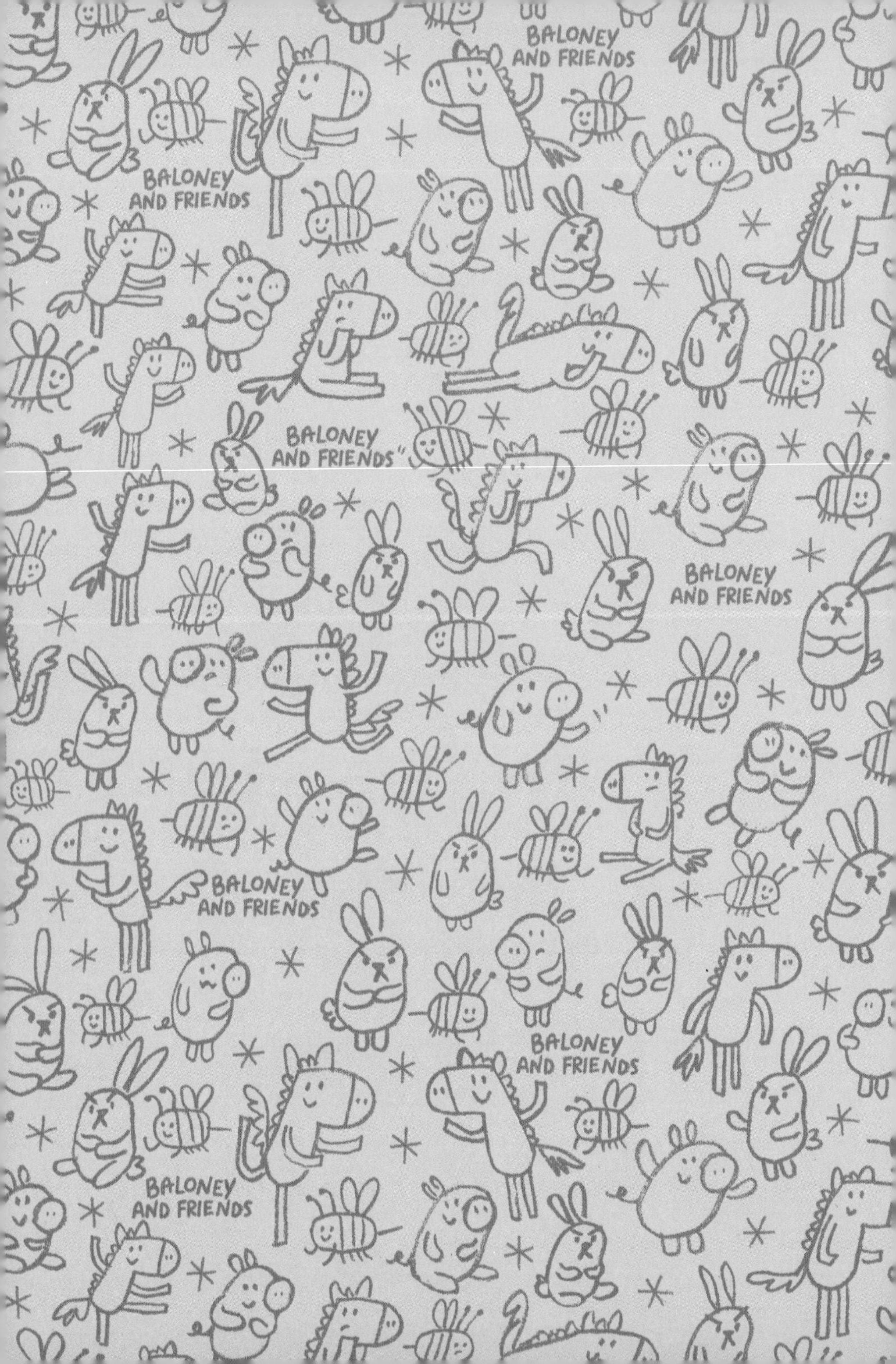
BALONEY AND FRIENDS
BALONEY AND FRIENDS
BALONEY AND FRIENDS
BALONEY AND FRIENDS
BALONEY AND FRIENDS
BALONEY AND FRIENDS
BALONEY AND FRIENDS

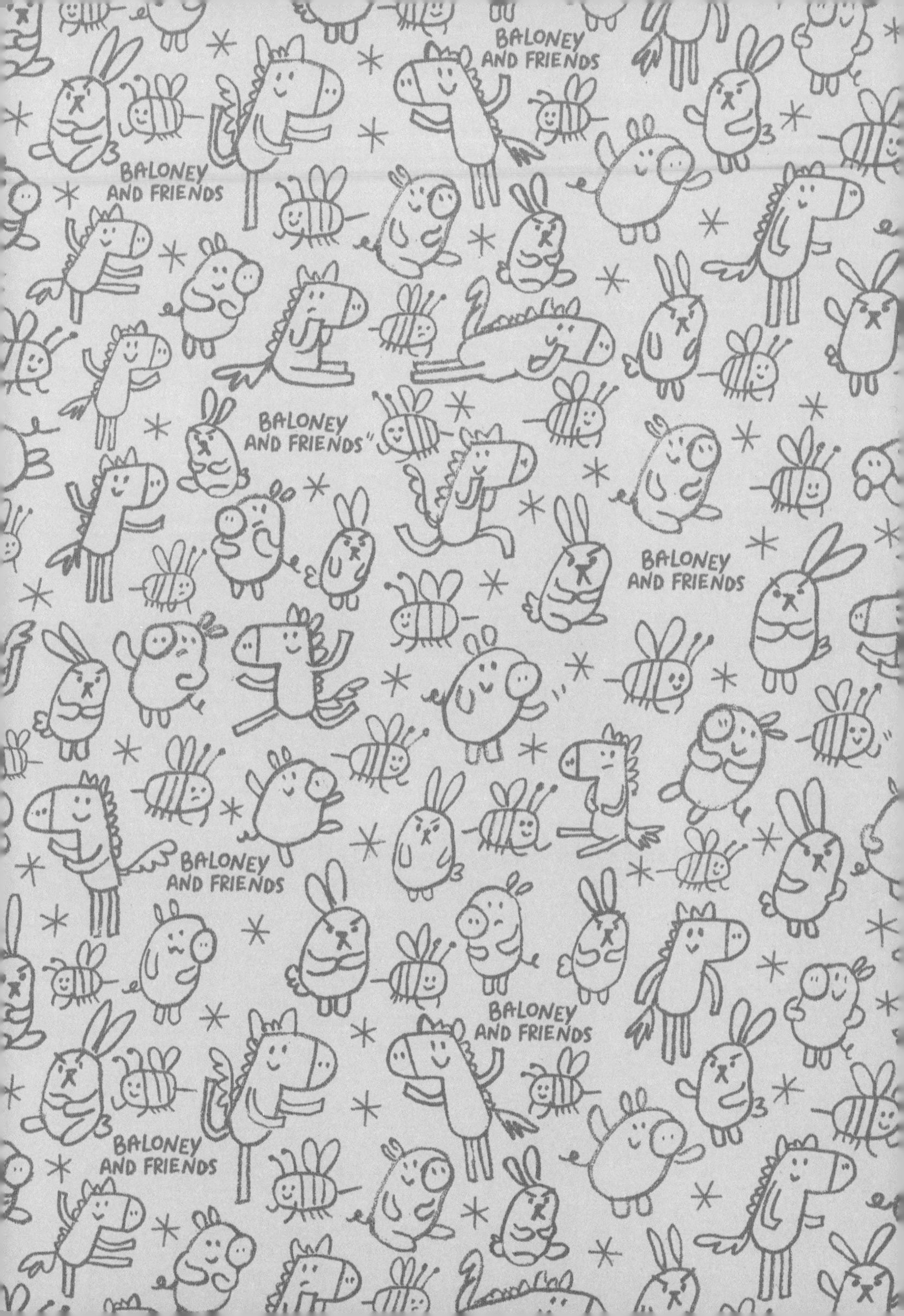
BALONEY AND FRIENDS
BALONEY AND FRIENDS
BALONEY AND FRIENDS
BALONEY AND FRIENDS
BALONEY AND FRIENDS
BALONEY AND FRIENDS
BALONEY AND FRIENDS

GREG
PIZZOLI

LB

LITTLE, BROWN AND COMPANY
BOOKS FOR YOUNG READERS

FOR MANDY, IAN, ASTRID, AND THOR

ABOUT THIS BOOK

This book was edited by Andrea Spooner and art directed by Dave Caplan. The production was supervised by Bernadette Flinn, and the production editor was Lindsay Walter-Greaney. The text was hand-lettered by Greg Pizzoli.

Little, Brown and Company • Hachette Book Group • 1290 Avenue of the Americas, New York, NY 10104 • Visit us at LBYR.com • First Trade Paperback Edition: January 2022 • Little, Brown and Company is a division of Hachette Book Group, Inc. • The Little, Brown name and logo are trademarks of Hachette Book Group, Inc. • The publisher is not responsible for websites (or their content) that are not owned by the publisher. • The Library of Congress has cataloged the hardcover edition as follows: Names: Pizzoli, Greg, author, illustrator. • Title: Baloney and friends: going up! / Greg Pizzoli. • Description: First edition. • New York: Little, Brown and Company, 2021. • Series: Baloney and friends • Summary: "Baloney and friends continue their adventures that include creating a theme song, having a sleepover, using their imagination, and learning to appreciate the meaning of life"—Provided by publisher. • Identifiers: LCCN 2020022080 (print) • LCCN 2020022081 (ebook) • ISBN 9780759554801 (paper over board) • ISBN 9780759554818 (ebook) • Subjects: LCSH: Graphic novels. • CYAC: Graphic novels. • Friendship—Fiction. • Classification: LCC PZ7.7.P54 Bal 2021 (print) • LCC PZ7.7.P54 (ebook) • DDC 741.5/973—dc23 • LC record available at https://lccn.loc.gov/2020022080 • LC ebook record available at https://lccn.loc gov/2020022081 • ISBNs: 978-0-316-33765-6 (pbk.), 978-0-7595-5481-8 (ebook), 978-0-316-59251-2 (ebook), 978-0-316-59253-6 (ebook) • PRINTED IN CHINA • APS • 10 9 8 7 6 5 4 3 2 1

BALONEY

AND FRIENDS

GOING UP!

GREG PIZZOLI

LITTLE, BROWN AND COMPANY

New York   Boston

TABLE OF CONTENTS

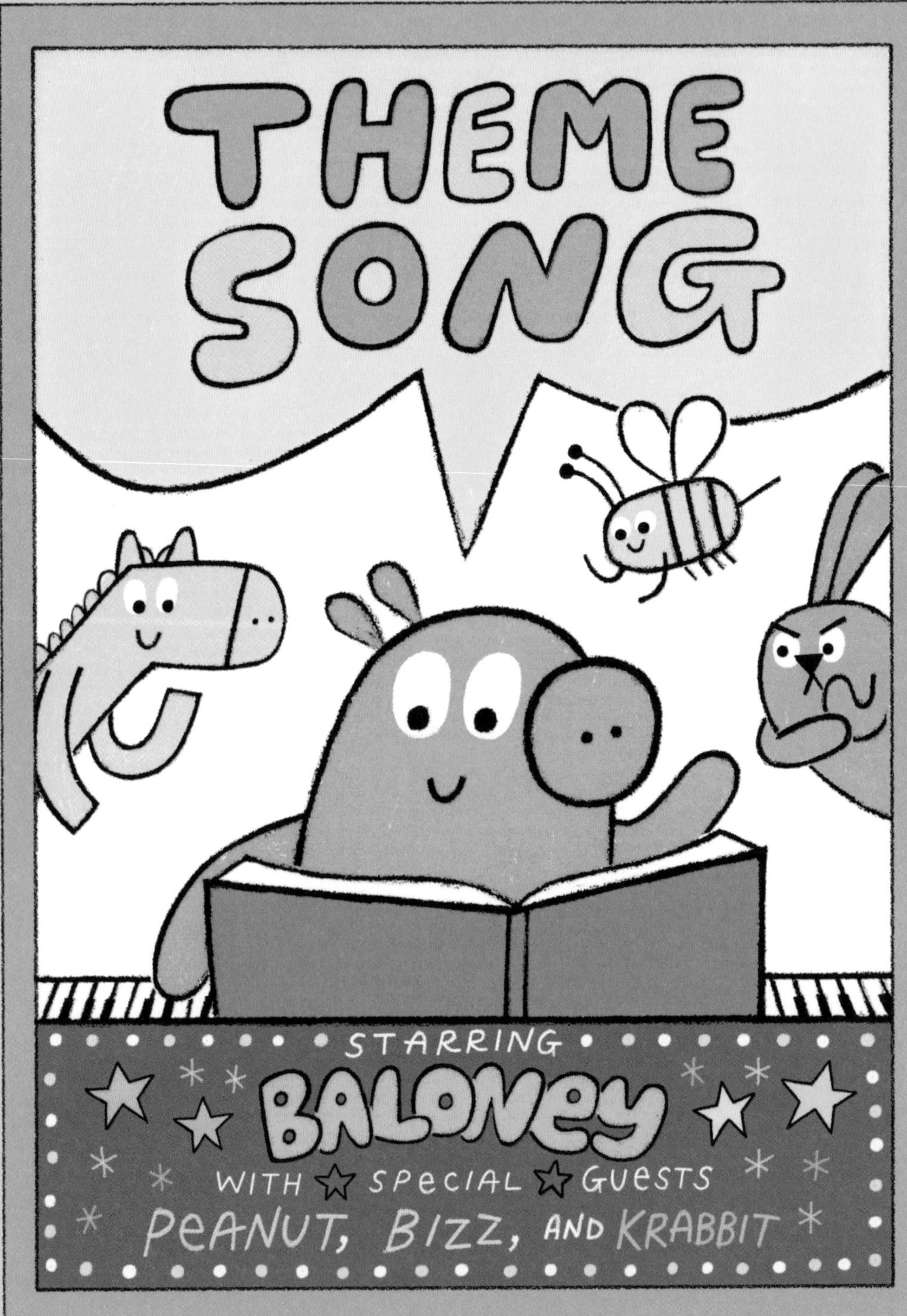
THEME SONG
STARRING
BALONEY
WITH SPECIAL GUESTS
PEANUT, BIZZ, AND KRABBIT

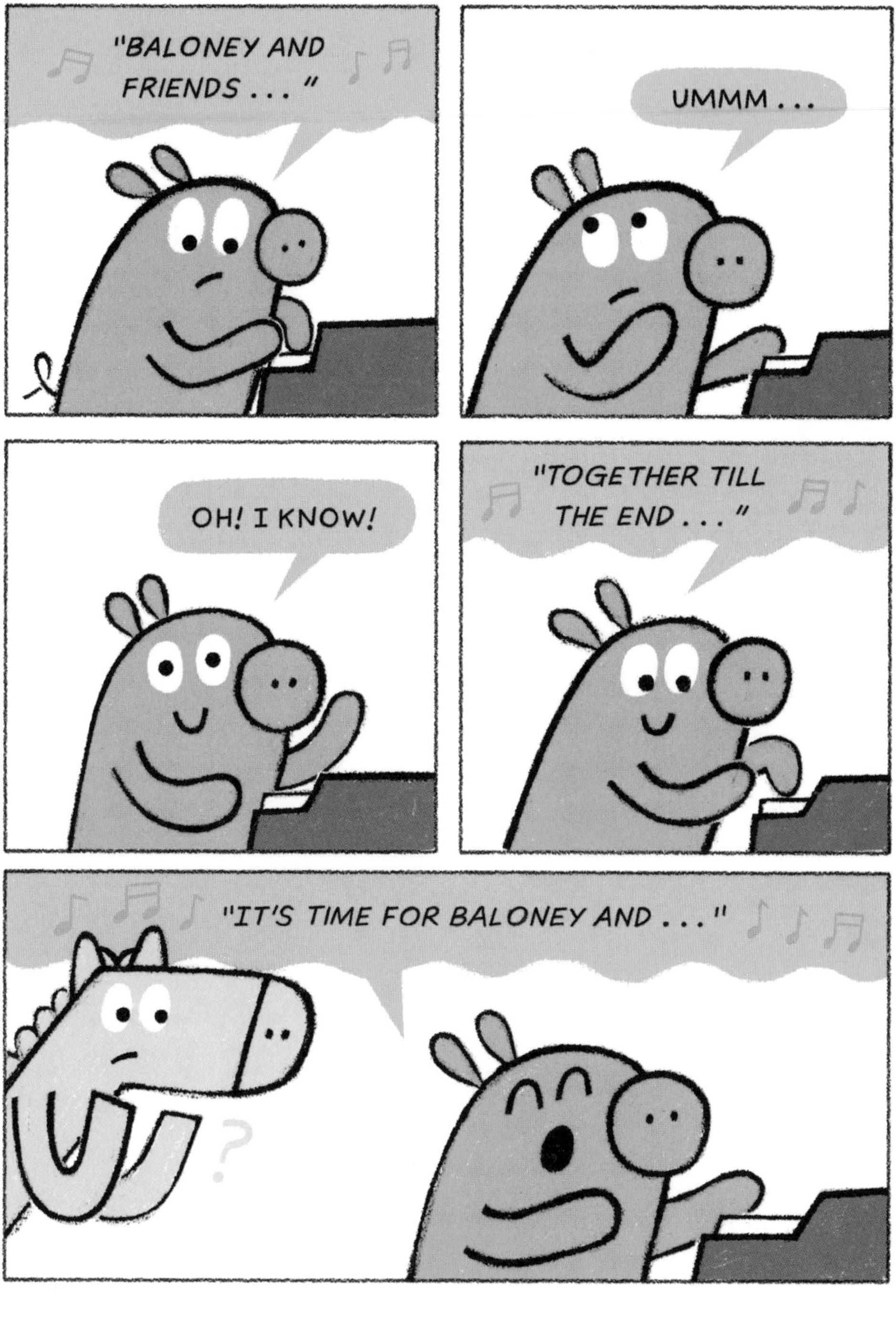

"BALONEY AND FRIENDS . . . "
UMMM . . .
OH! I KNOW!
"TOGETHER TILL THE END . . . "
"IT'S TIME FOR BALONEY AND . . . "
?

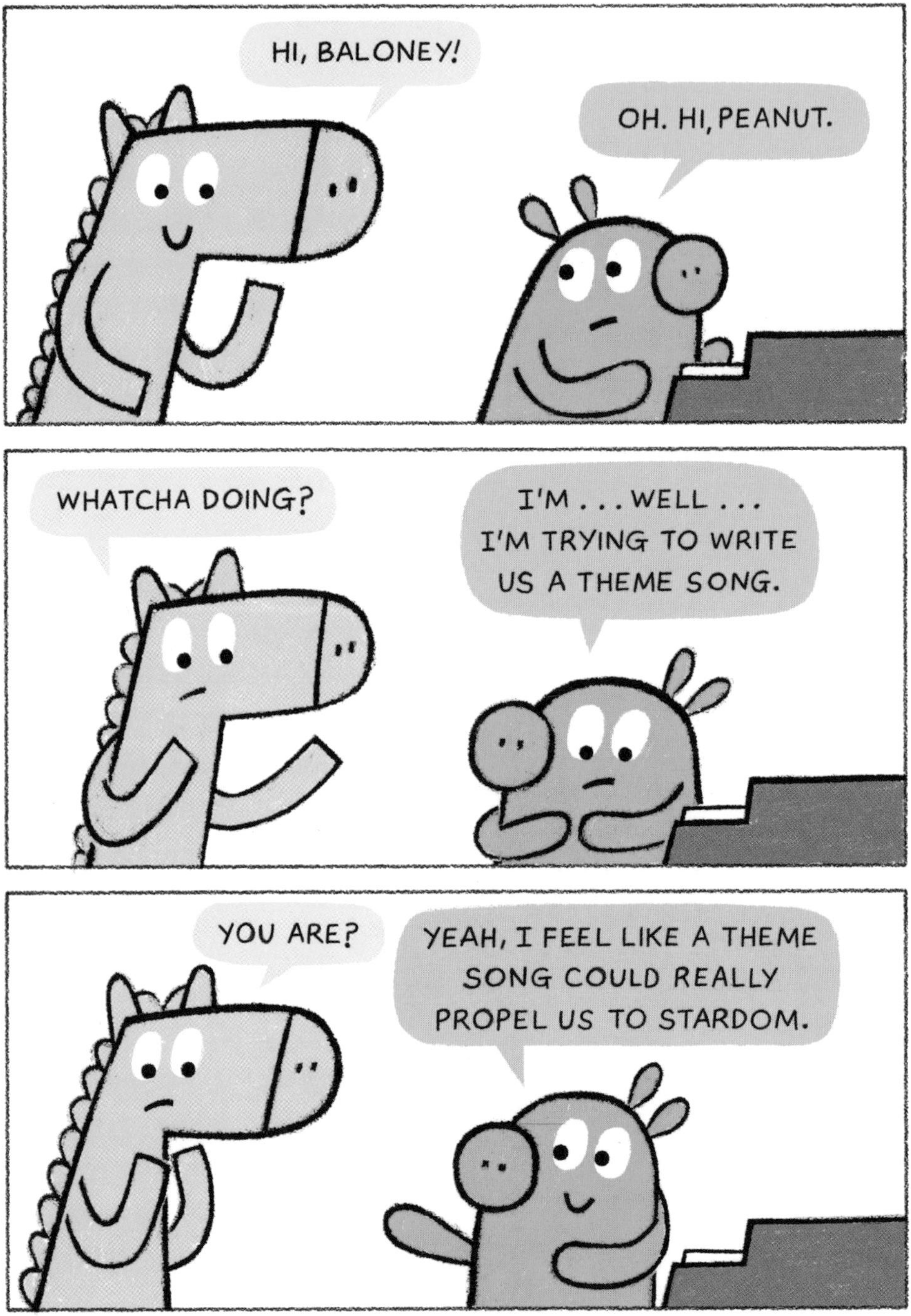
HI, BALONEY!
OH. HI, PEANUT.
WHATCHA DOING?
I'M . . . WELL . . . I'M TRYING TO WRITE US A THEME SONG.
YOU ARE?
YEAH, I FEEL LIKE A THEME SONG COULD REALLY PROPEL US TO STARDOM.

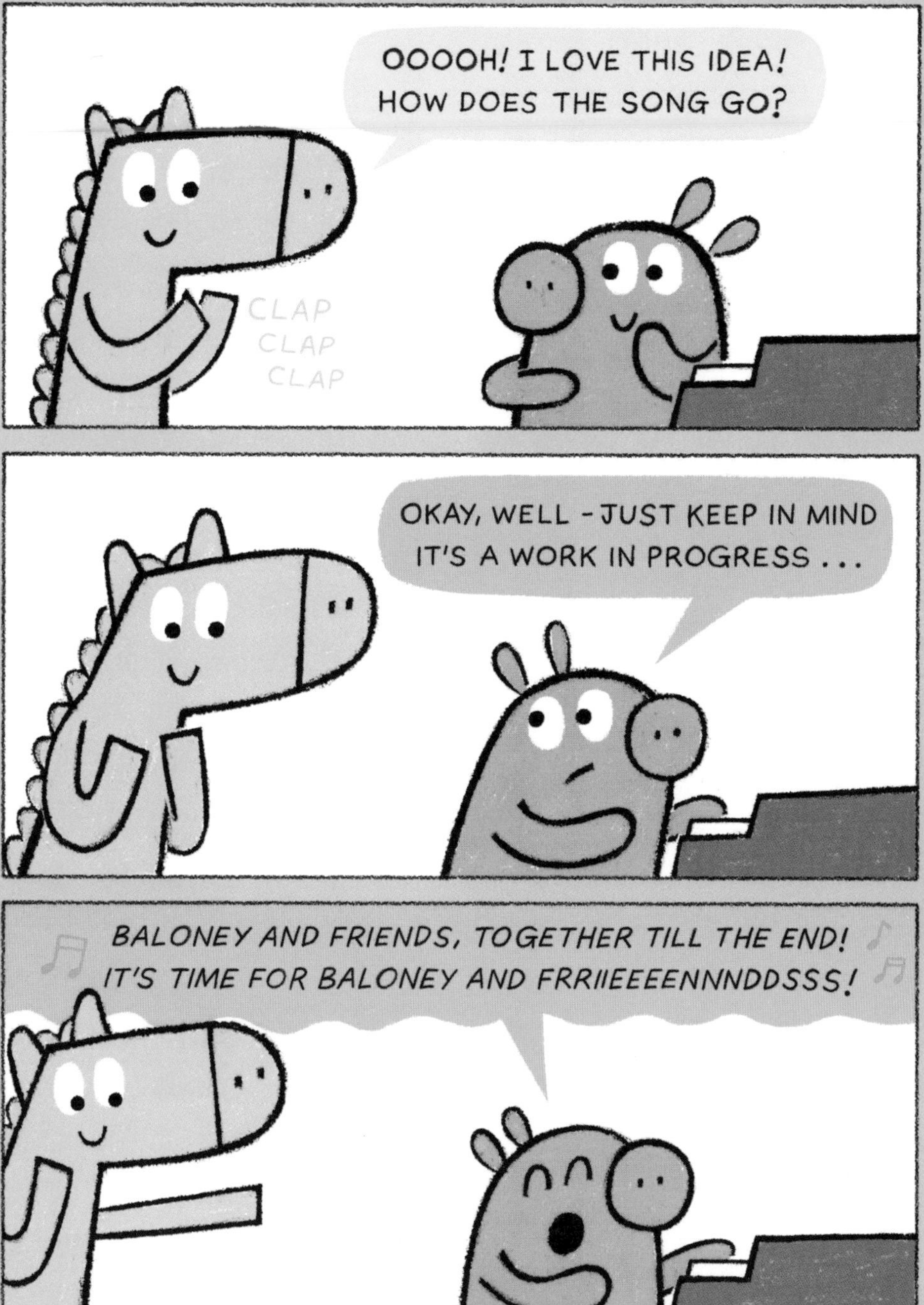
OOOOH! I LOVE THIS IDEA! HOW DOES THE SONG GO?
CLAP CLAP CLAP
OKAY, WELL - JUST KEEP IN MIND IT'S A WORK IN PROGRESS . . .
BALONEY AND FRIENDS, TOGETHER TILL THE END! IT'S TIME FOR BALONEY AND FRRIIEEEEENNNDDSSS!

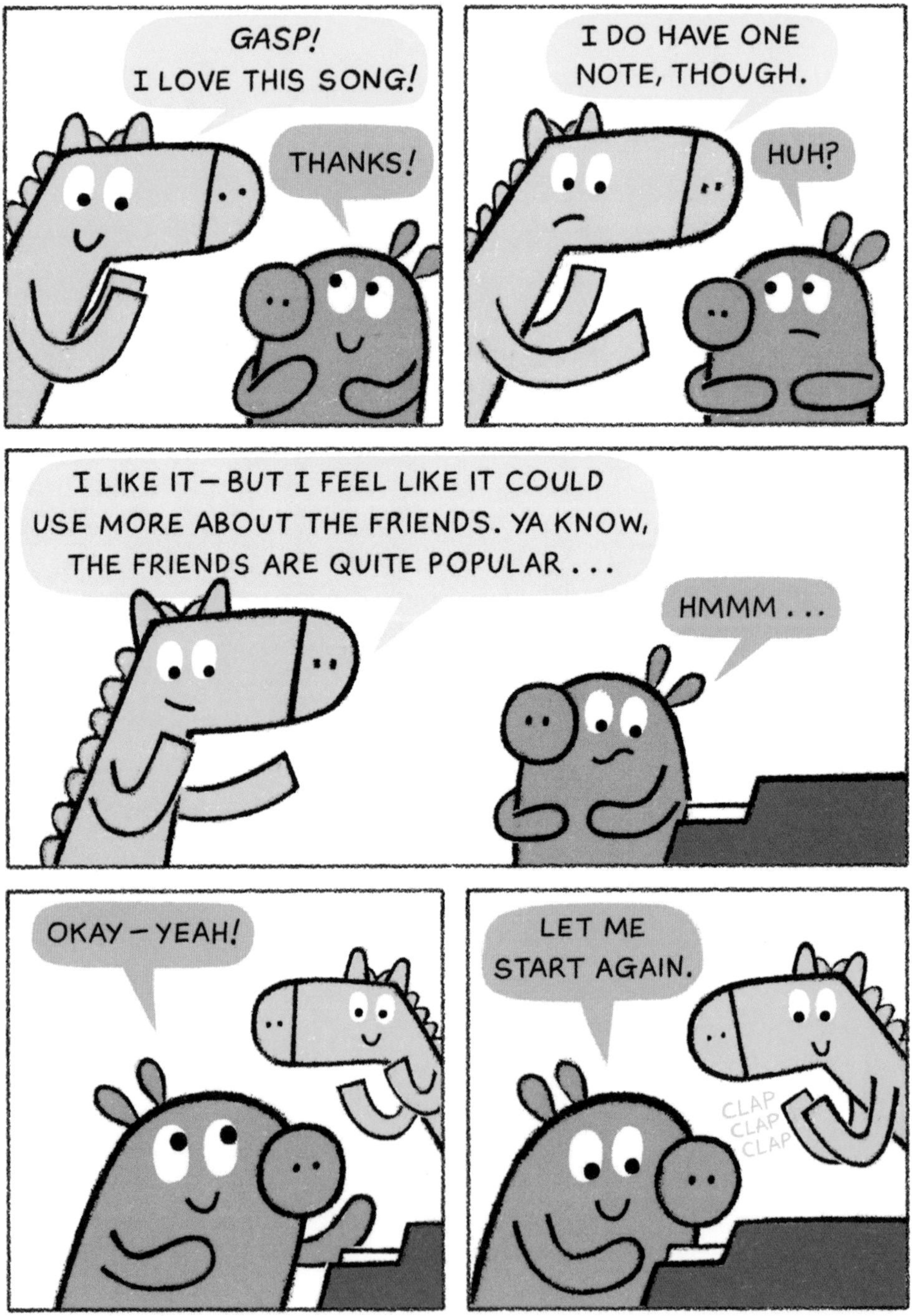
GASP!
I LOVE THIS SONG!
THANKS!
I DO HAVE ONE NOTE, THOUGH.
HUH?
I LIKE IT—BUT I FEEL LIKE IT COULD USE MORE ABOUT THE FRIENDS. YA KNOW, THE FRIENDS ARE QUITE POPULAR . . .
HMMM . . .
OKAY—YEAH!
LET ME START AGAIN.
CLAP
CLAP
CLAP

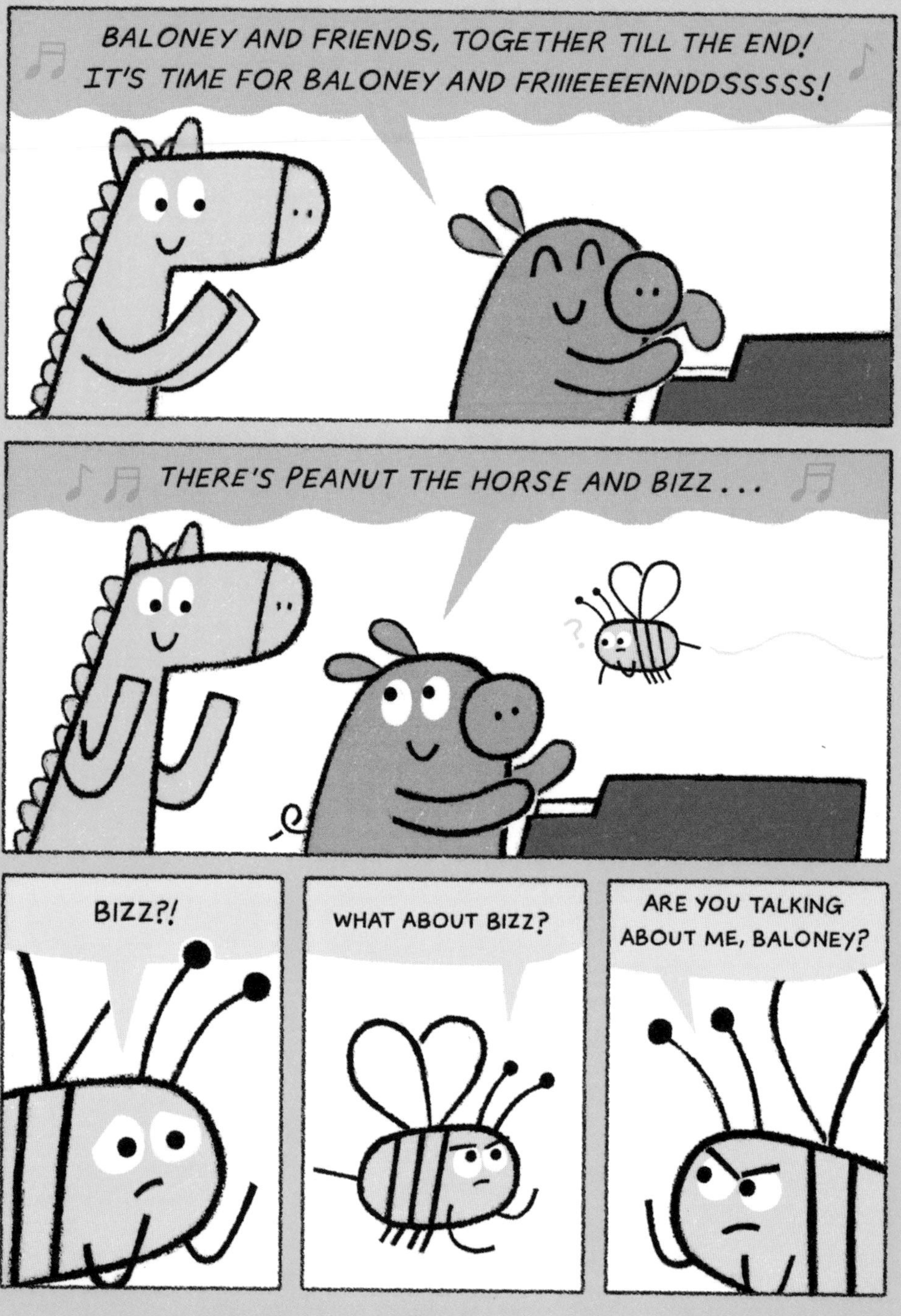
BALONEY AND FRIENDS, TOGETHER TILL THE END! IT'S TIME FOR BALONEY AND FRIIIEEEEENNDDSSSSS!
THERE'S PEANUT THE HORSE AND BIZZ . . .
BIZZ?!
WHAT ABOUT BIZZ?
ARE YOU TALKING ABOUT ME, BALONEY?

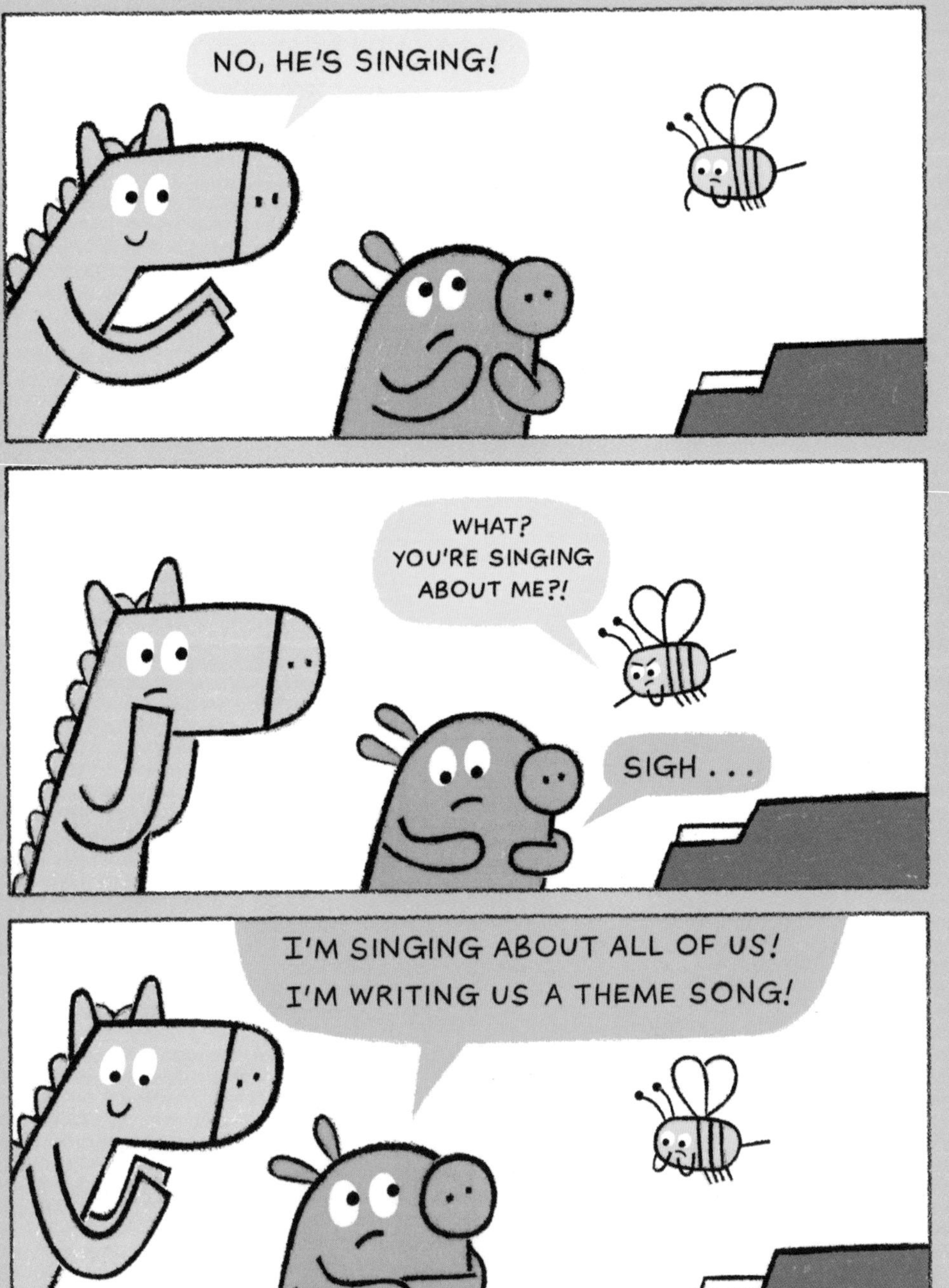
NO, HE'S SINGING!
WHAT? YOU'RE SINGING ABOUT ME?!
SIGH . . .
I'M SINGING ABOUT ALL OF US! I'M WRITING US A THEME SONG!

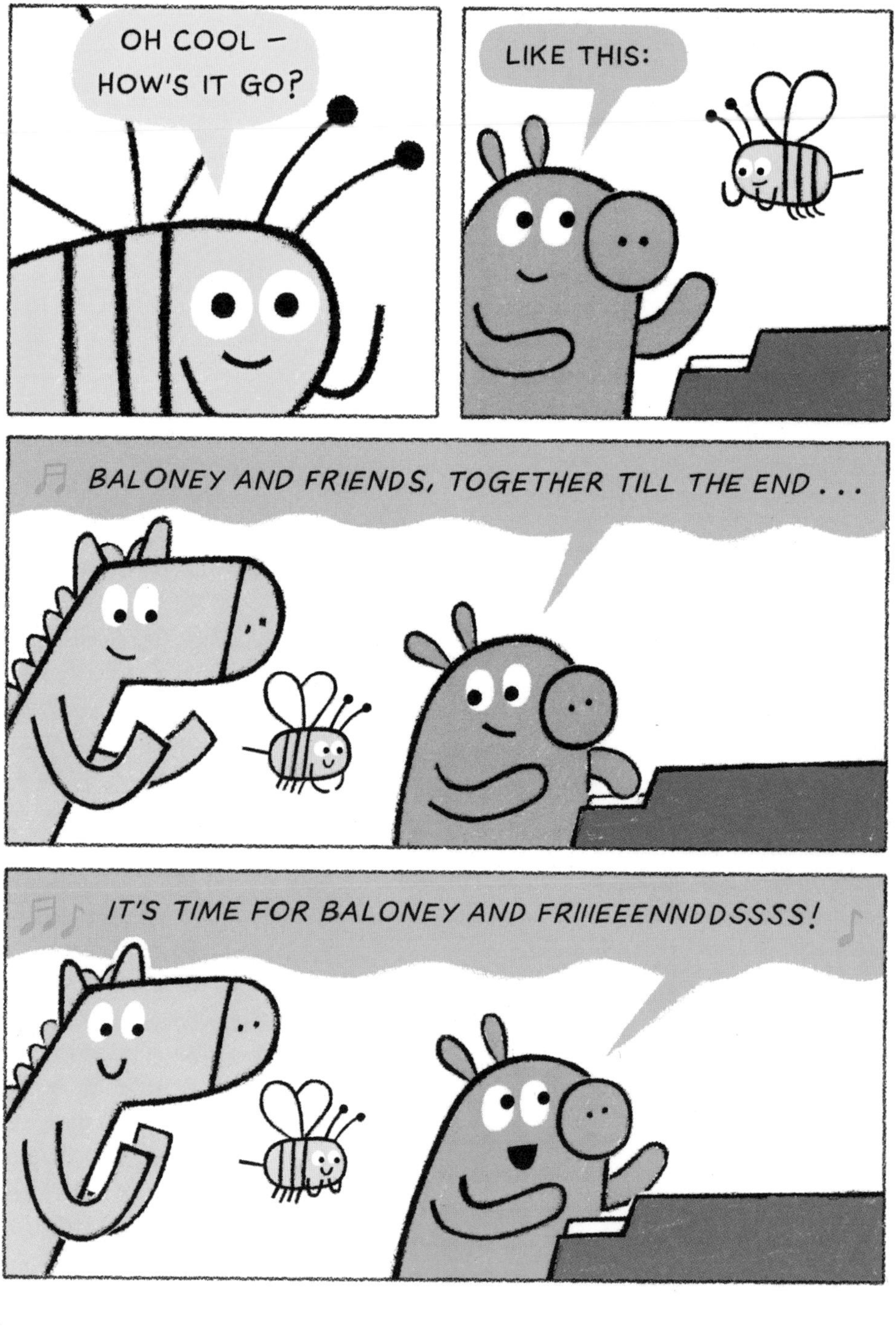
OH COOL — HOW'S IT GO?
LIKE THIS:
BALONEY AND FRIENDS, TOGETHER TILL THE END . . .
IT'S TIME FOR BALONEY AND FRIIIEEENNDDSSSS!

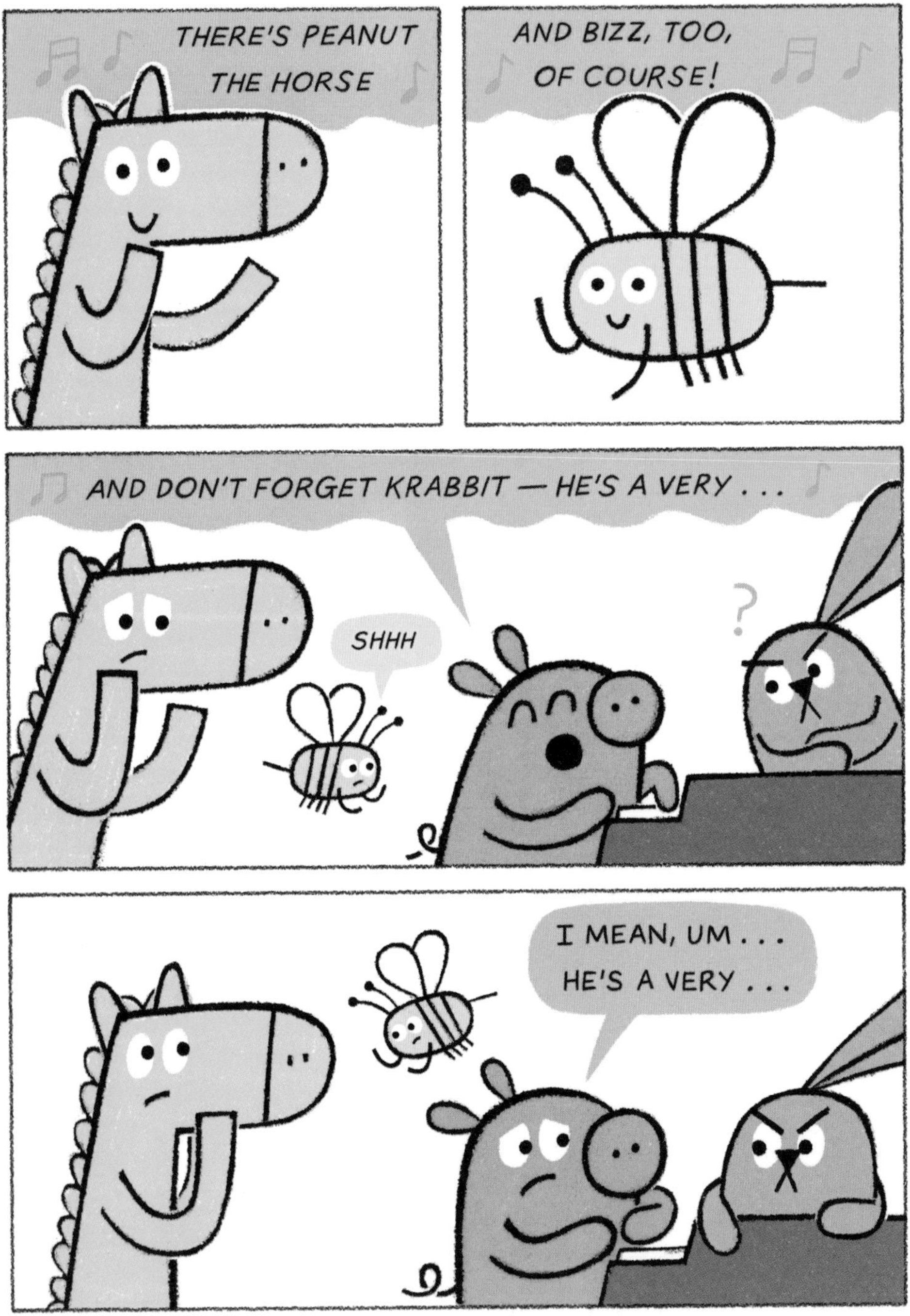
THERE'S PEANUT THE HORSE
AND BIZZ, TOO, OF COURSE!
AND DON'T FORGET KRABBIT — HE'S A VERY . . .
SHHH
?
I MEAN, UM . . . HE'S A VERY . . .

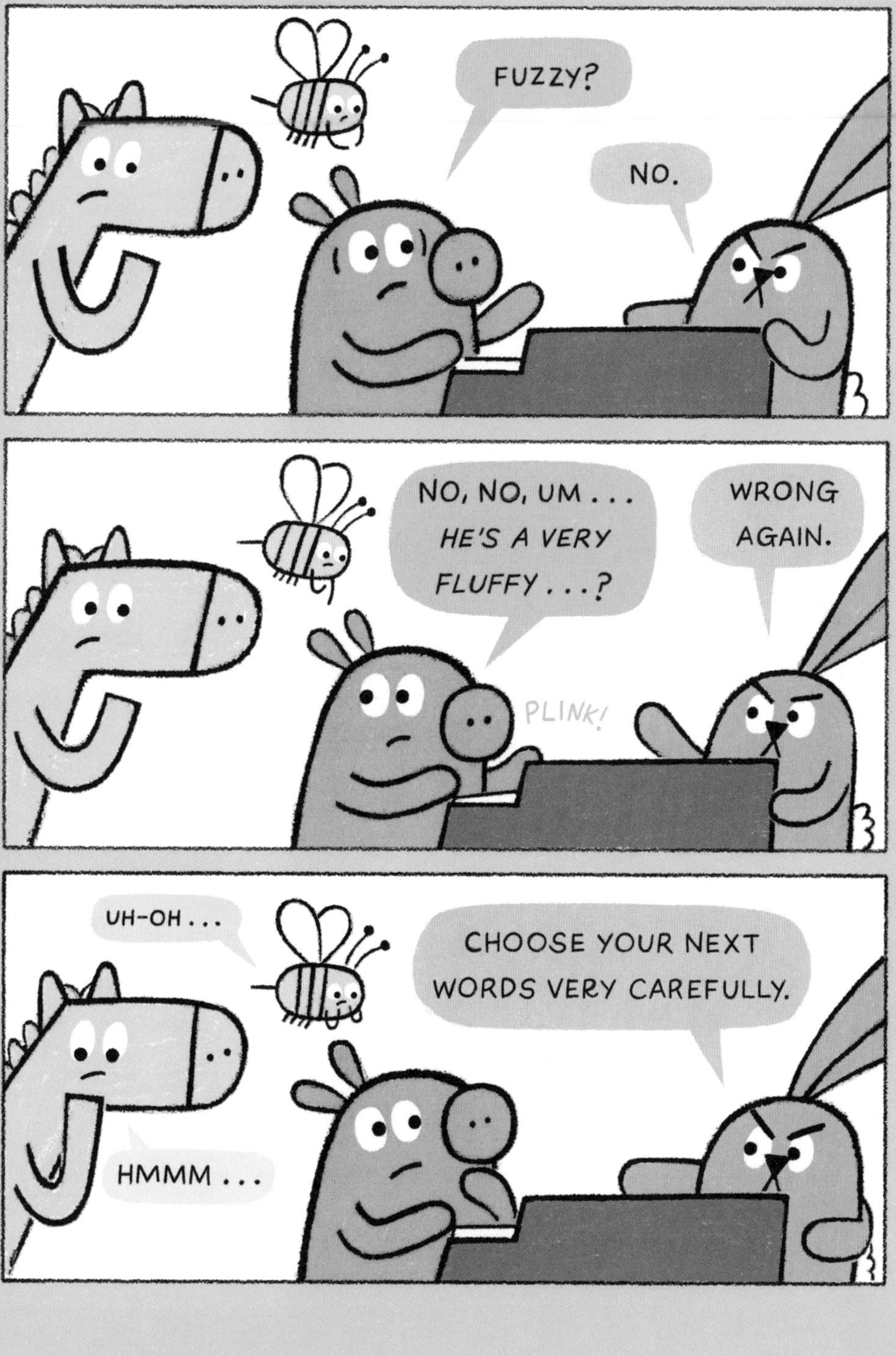
FUZZY?
NO.
NO, NO, UM . . .
HE'S A VERY FLUFFY . . .?
WRONG AGAIN.
PLINK!
UH-OH . . .
CHOOSE YOUR NEXT WORDS VERY CAREFULLY.
HMMM . . .

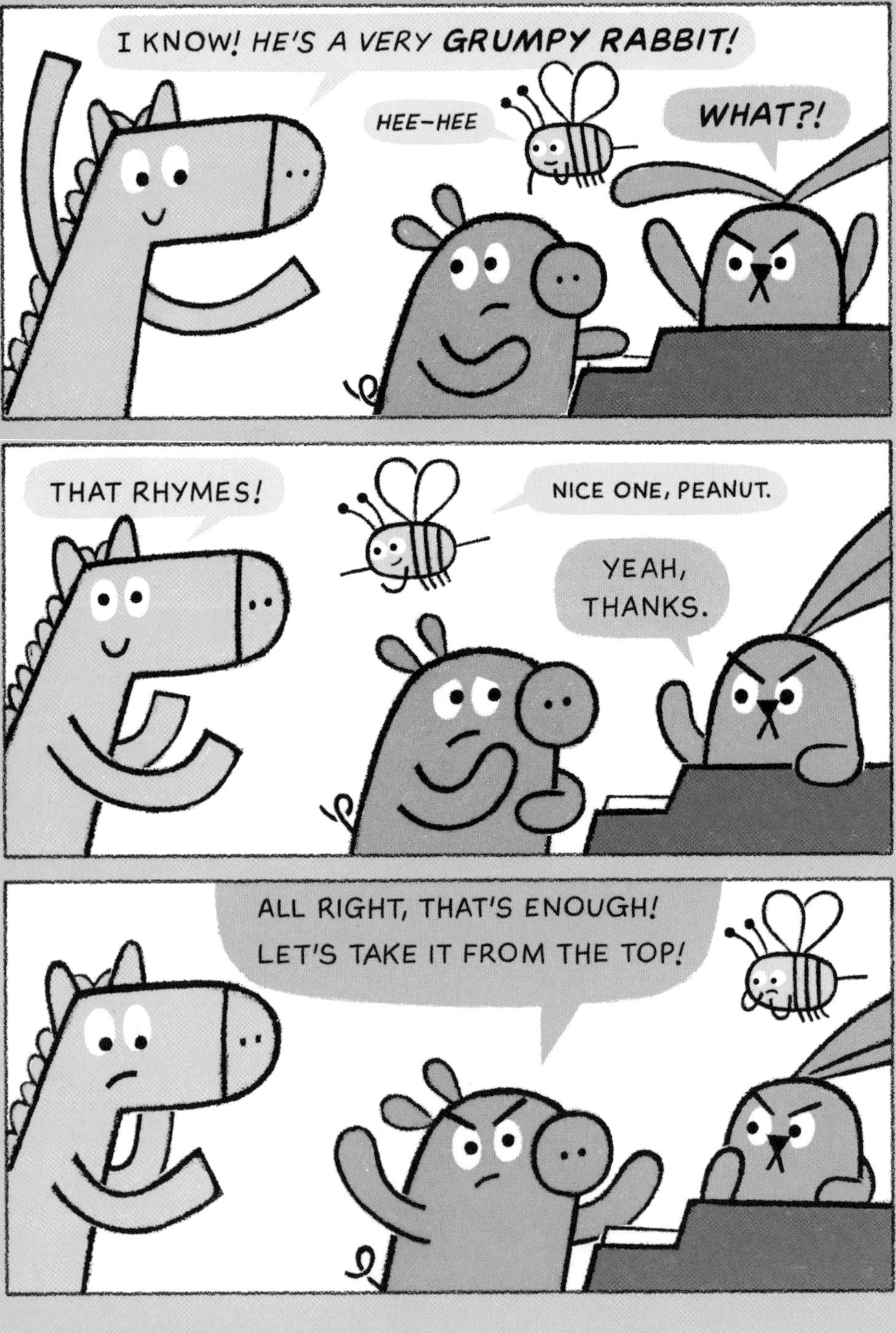
I KNOW! *HE'S A VERY* ***GRUMPY RABBIT!***
HEE-HEE
WHAT?!
THAT RHYMES!
NICE ONE, PEANUT.
YEAH, THANKS.
ALL RIGHT, THAT'S ENOUGH! LET'S TAKE IT FROM THE TOP!

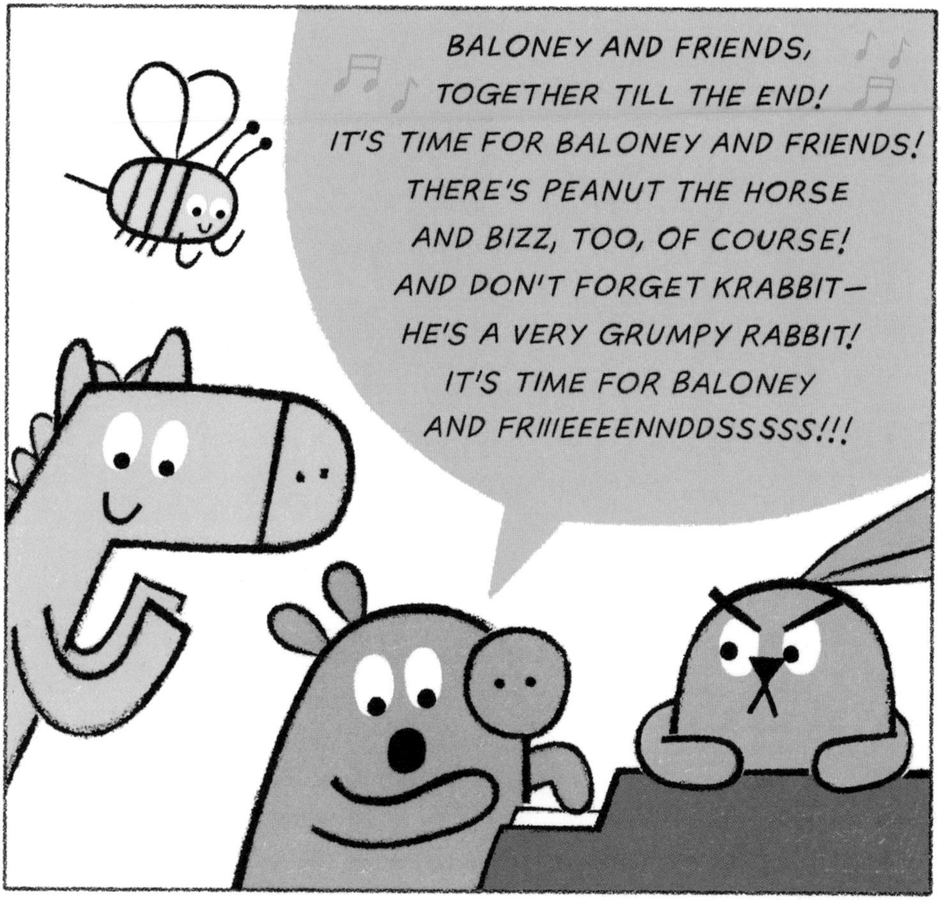
BALONEY AND FRIENDS,
TOGETHER TILL THE END!
IT'S TIME FOR BALONEY AND FRIENDS!
THERE'S PEANUT THE HORSE
AND BIZZ, TOO, OF COURSE!
AND DON'T FORGET KRABBIT—
HE'S A VERY GRUMPY RABBIT!
IT'S TIME FOR BALONEY
AND FRIIIEEEENNDDSSSSS!!!

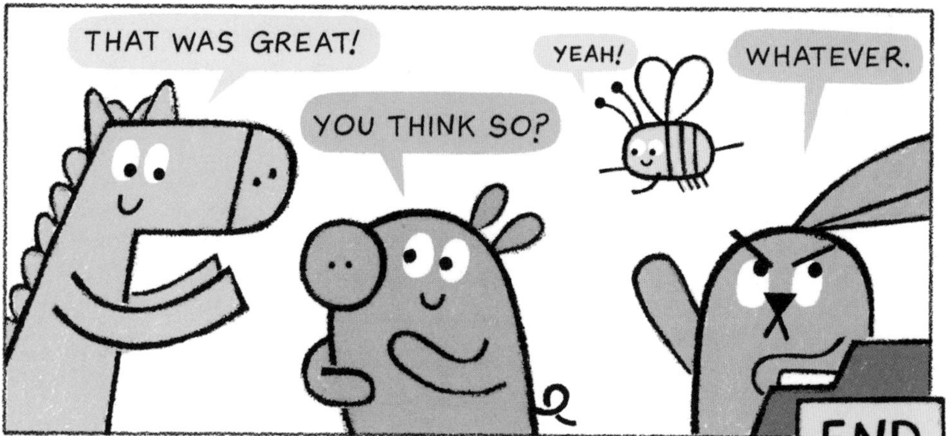
THAT WAS GREAT!
YOU THINK SO?
YEAH!
WHATEVER.
END

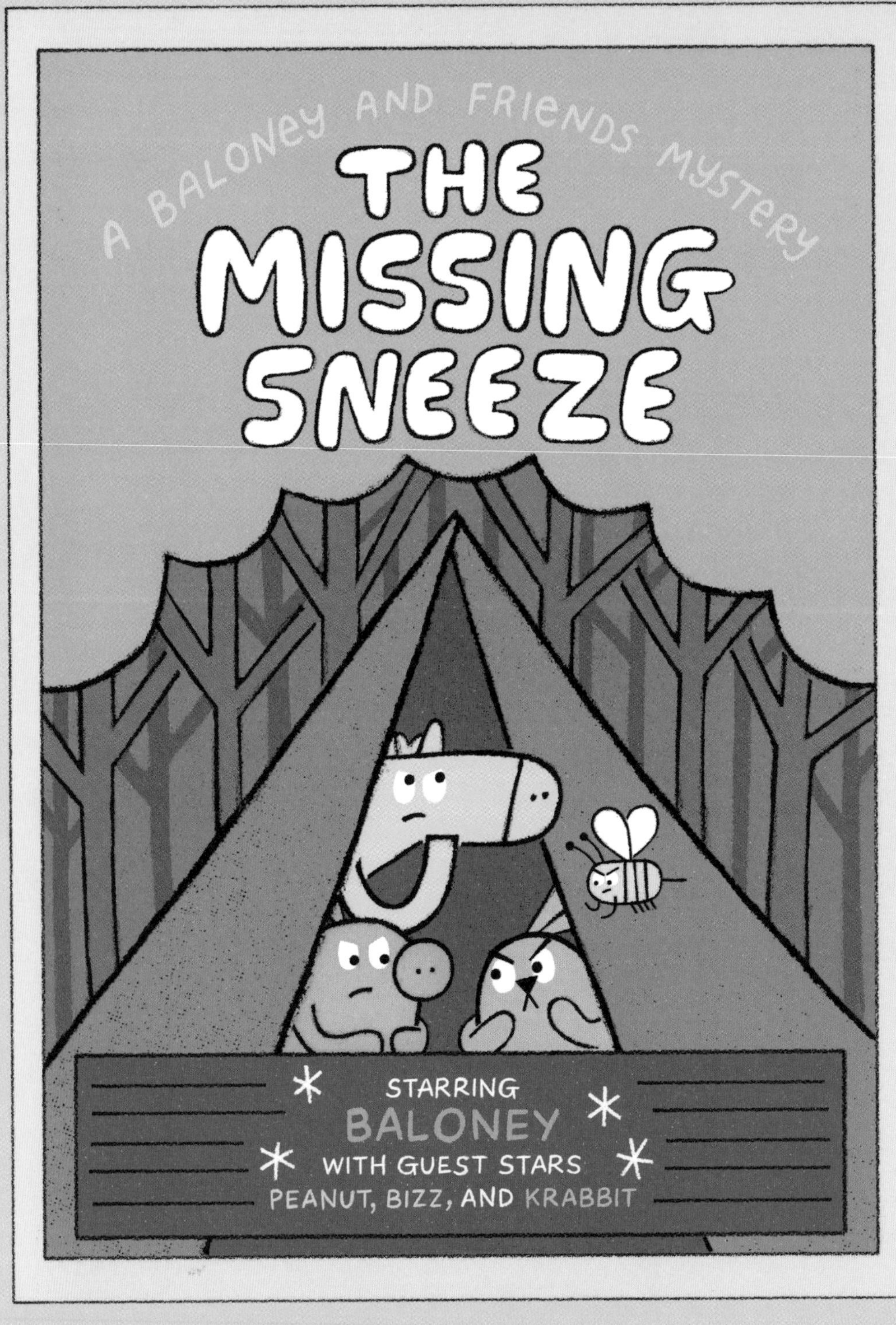
A BALONEY AND FRIENDS MYSTERY
THE MISSING SNEEZE
STARRING
BALONEY
WITH GUEST STARS
PEANUT, BIZZ, AND KRABBIT

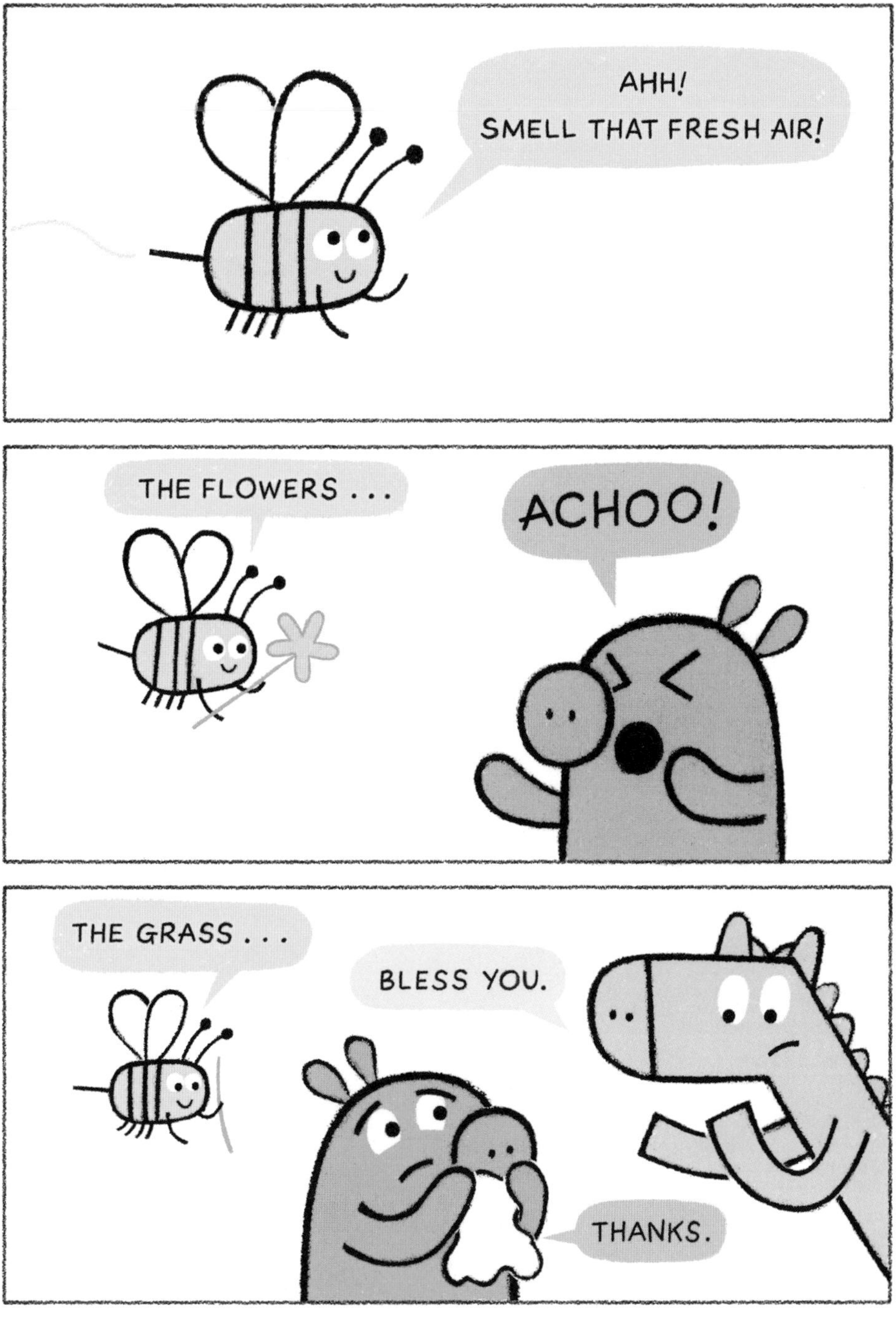
AHH!
SMELL THAT FRESH AIR!
THE FLOWERS . . .
ACHOO!
THE GRASS . . .
BLESS YOU.
THANKS.

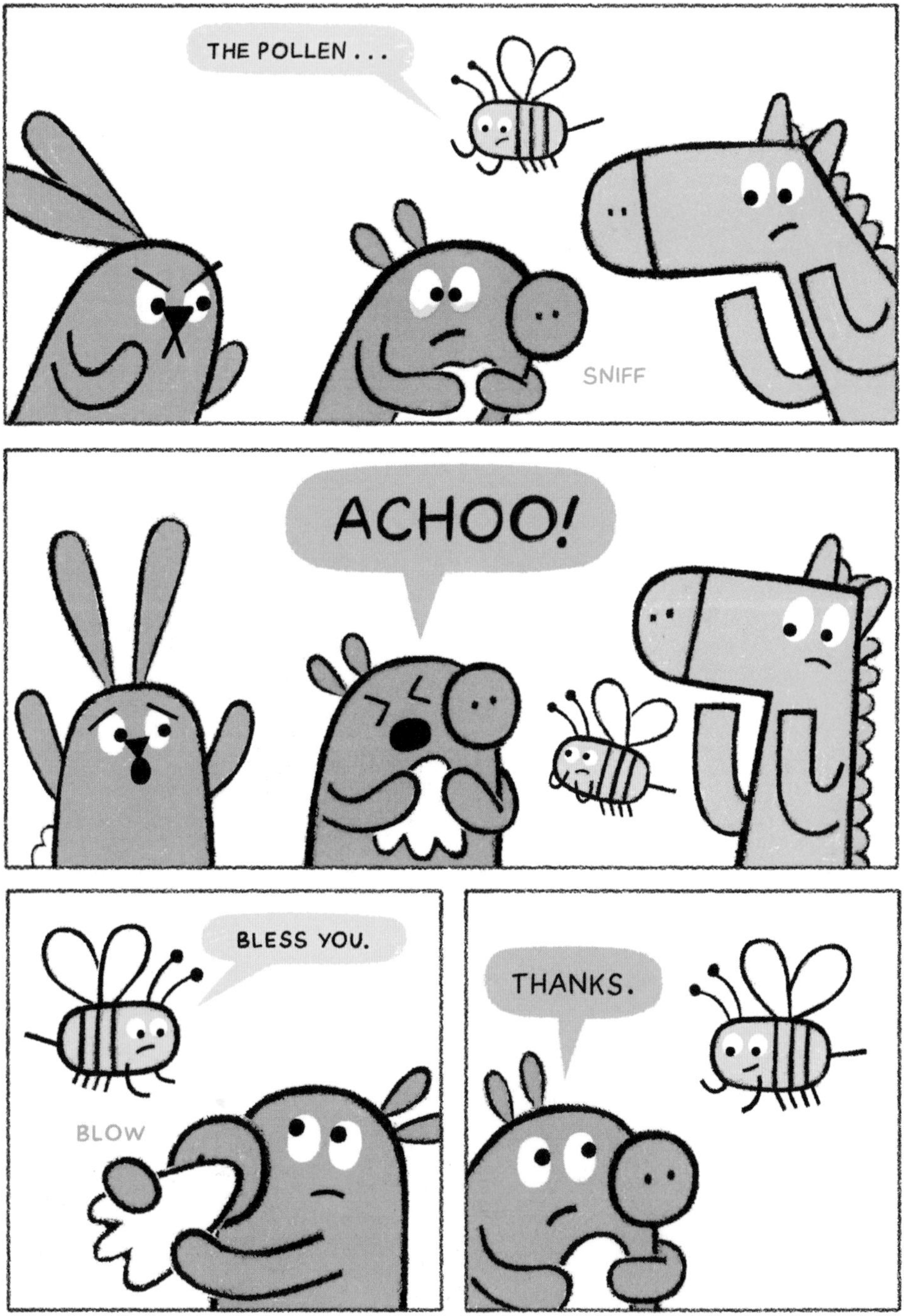
THE POLLEN . . .
SNIFF
ACHOO!
BLESS YOU.
BLOW
THANKS.

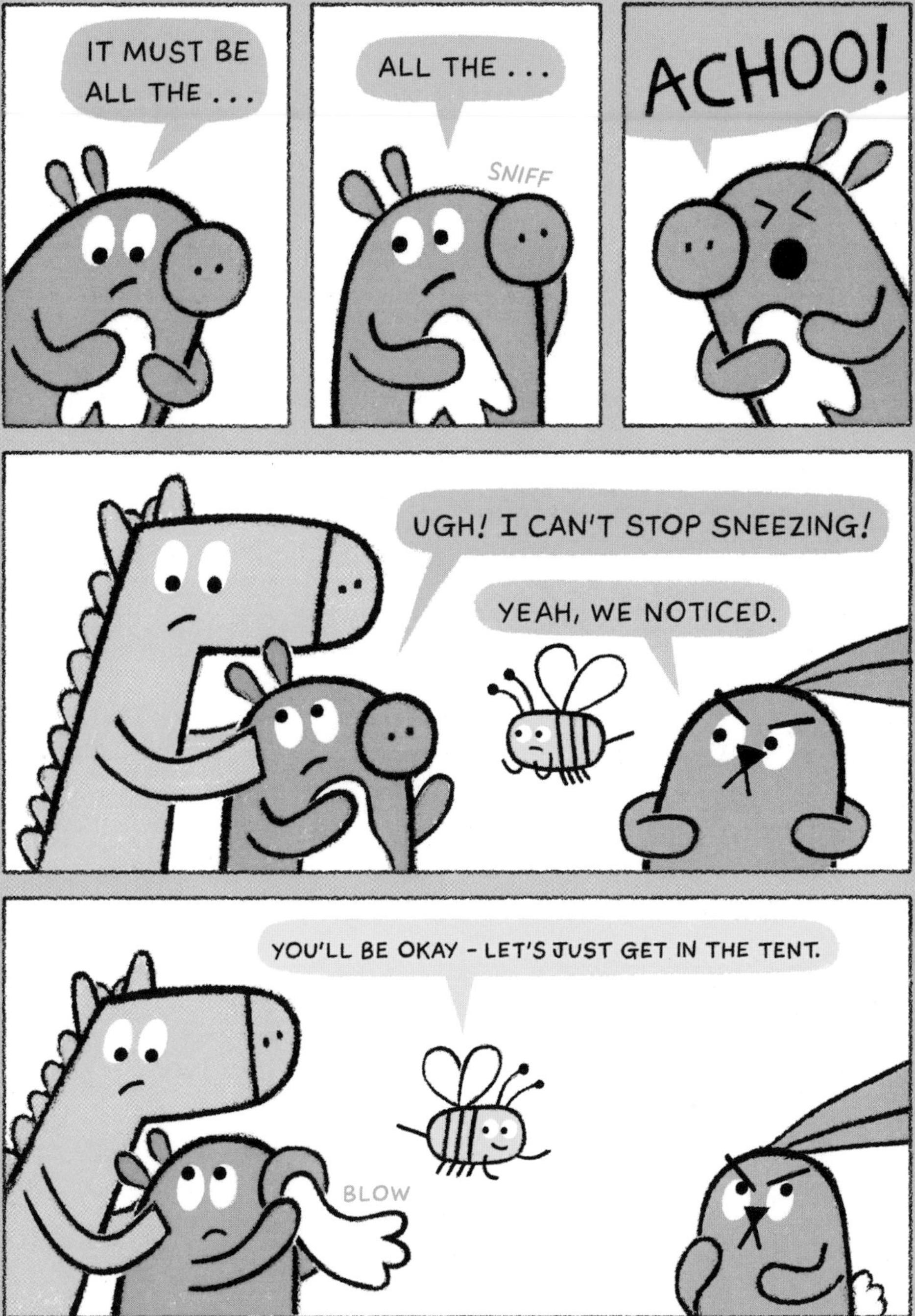
IT MUST BE ALL THE . . .
ALL THE . . .
SNIFF
ACHOO!
UGH! I CAN'T STOP SNEEZING!
YEAH, WE NOTICED.
YOU'LL BE OKAY - LET'S JUST GET IN THE TENT.
BLOW

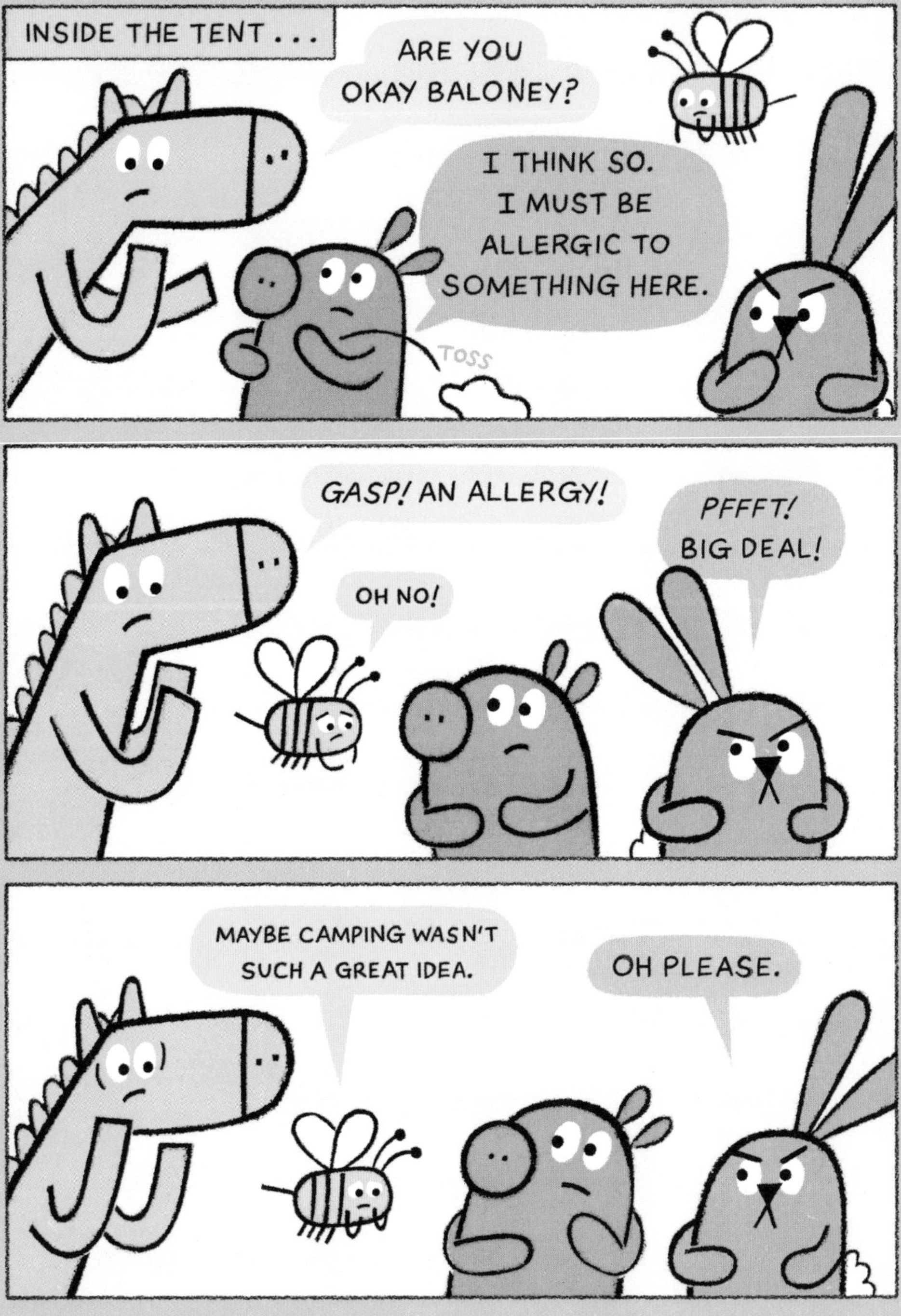
INSIDE THE TENT . . .
ARE YOU OKAY BALONEY?
I THINK SO. I MUST BE ALLERGIC TO SOMETHING HERE.
TOSS
GASP! AN ALLERGY!
PFFFT! BIG DEAL!
OH NO!
MAYBE CAMPING WASN'T SUCH A GREAT IDEA.
OH PLEASE.

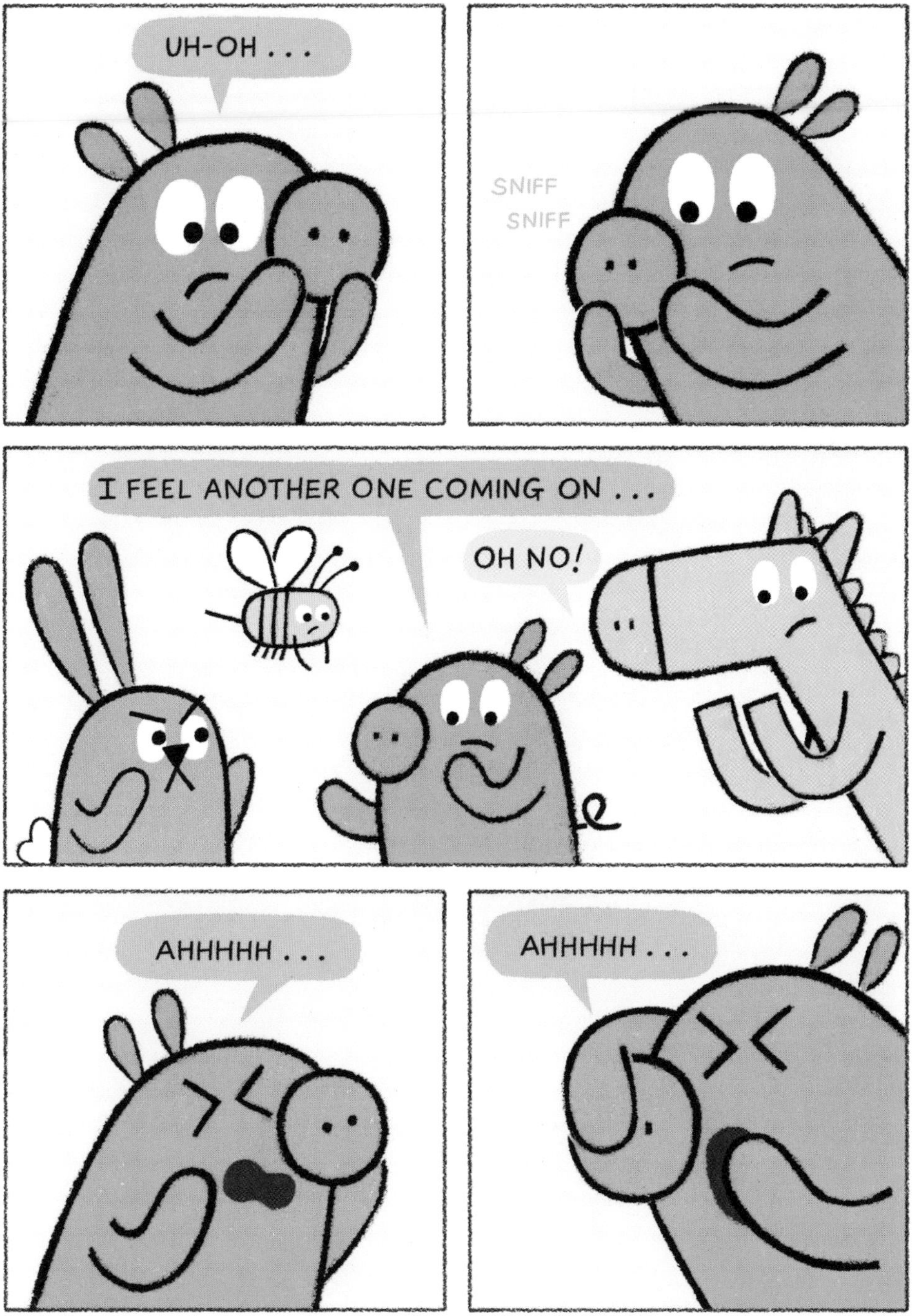
UH-OH . . .
SNIFF
SNIFF
I FEEL ANOTHER ONE COMING ON . . .
OH NO!
AHHHHH . . .
AHHHHH . . .

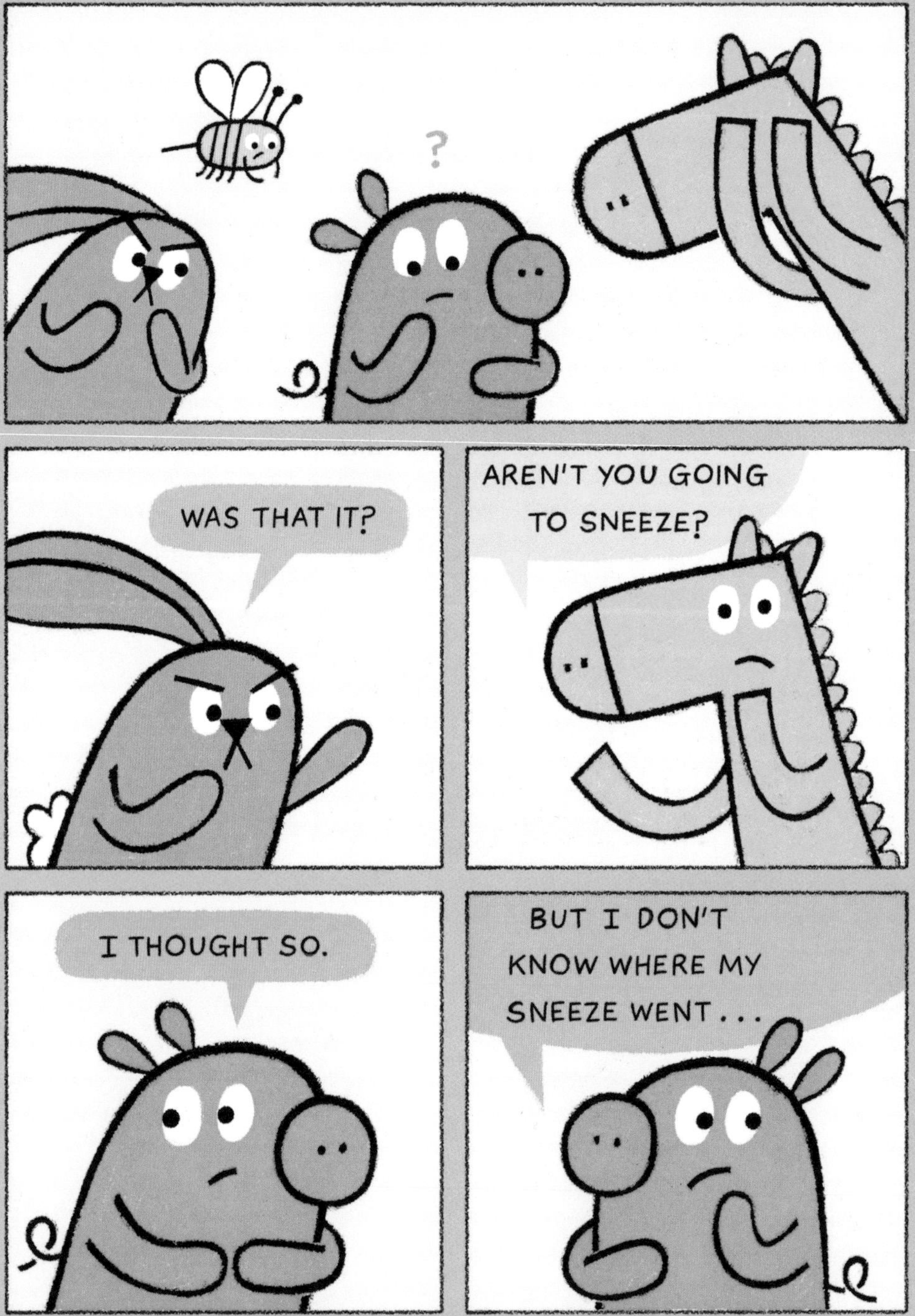
?
WAS THAT IT?
AREN'T YOU GOING TO SNEEZE?
I THOUGHT SO.
BUT I DON'T KNOW WHERE MY SNEEZE WENT . . .

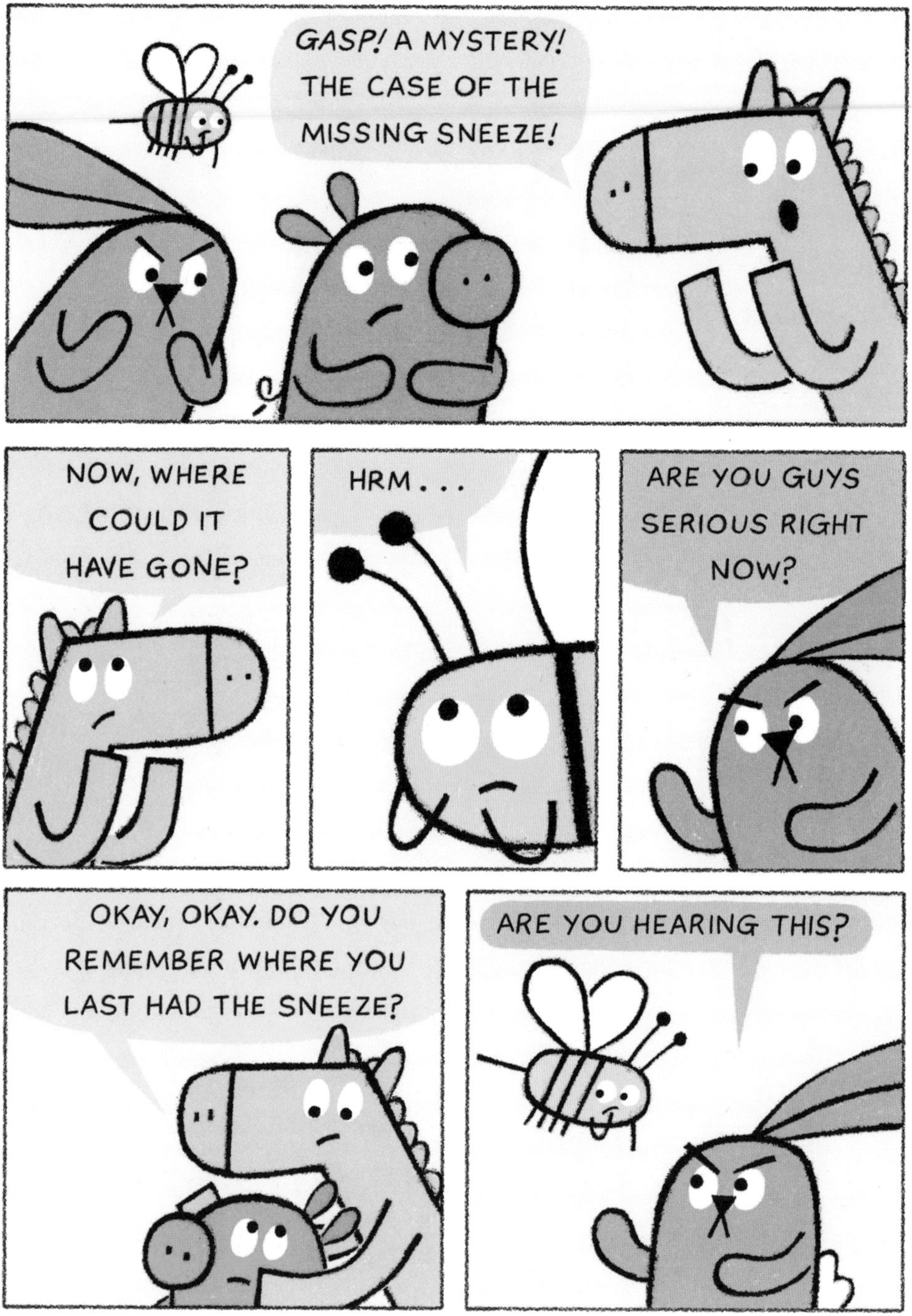

GASP! A MYSTERY! THE CASE OF THE MISSING SNEEZE!
NOW, WHERE COULD IT HAVE GONE?
HRM . . .
ARE YOU GUYS SERIOUS RIGHT NOW?
OKAY, OKAY. DO YOU REMEMBER WHERE YOU LAST HAD THE SNEEZE?
ARE YOU HEARING THIS?

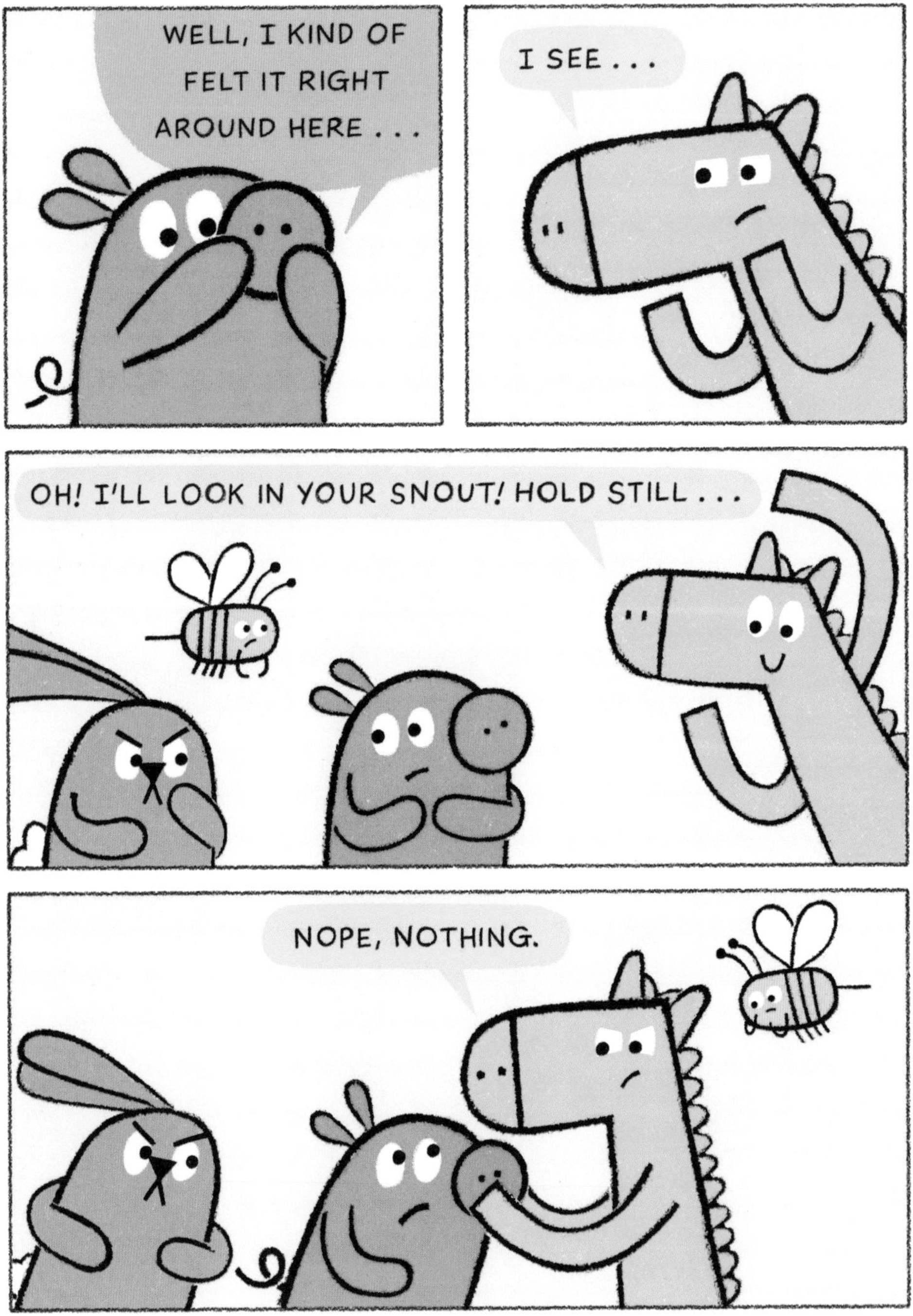
WELL, I KIND OF FELT IT RIGHT AROUND HERE . . .
I SEE . . .
OH! I'LL LOOK IN YOUR SNOUT! HOLD STILL . . .
NOPE, NOTHING.

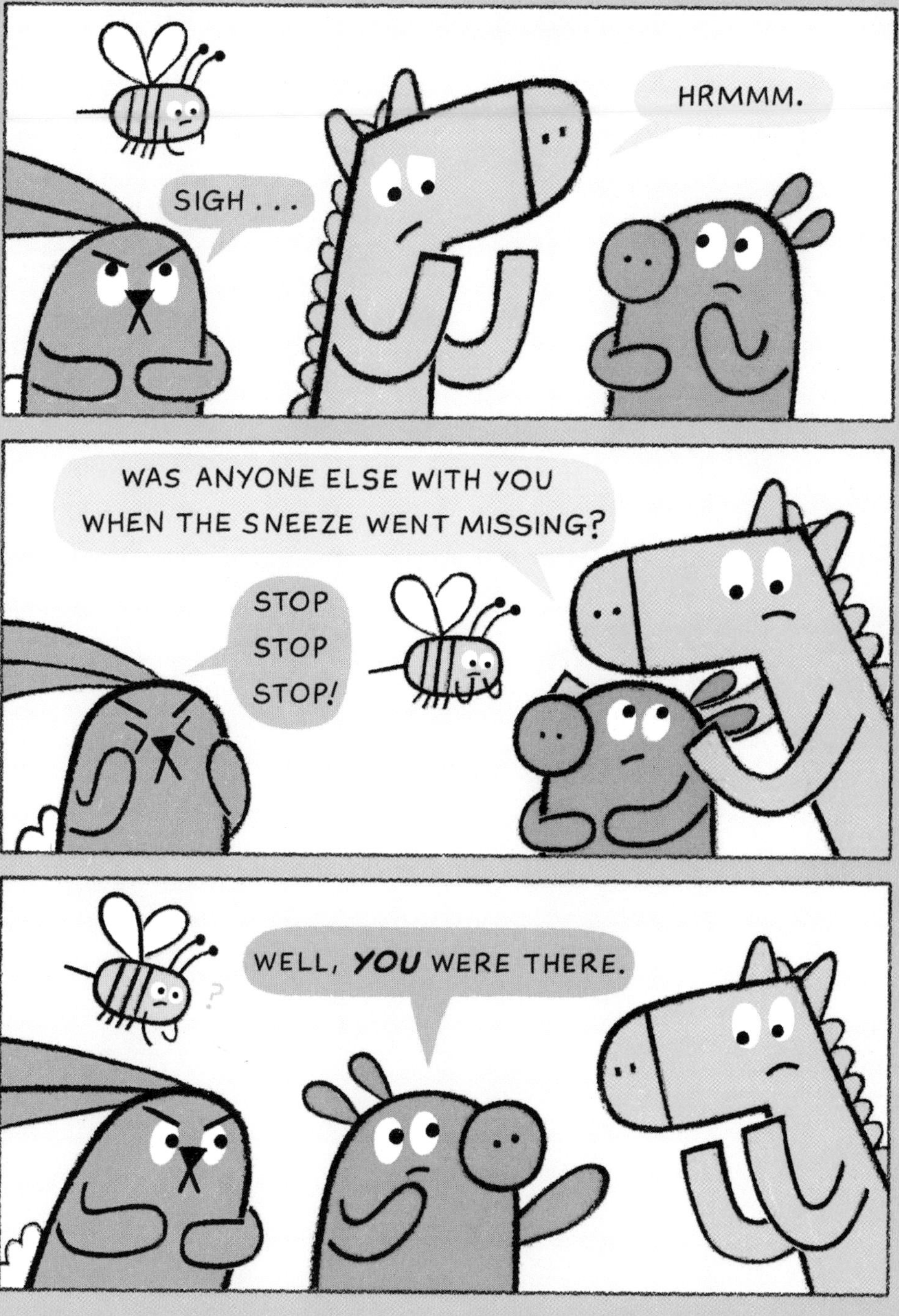
HRMMM.
SIGH . . .
WAS ANYONE ELSE WITH YOU WHEN THE SNEEZE WENT MISSING?
STOP STOP STOP!
WELL, ***YOU*** WERE THERE.

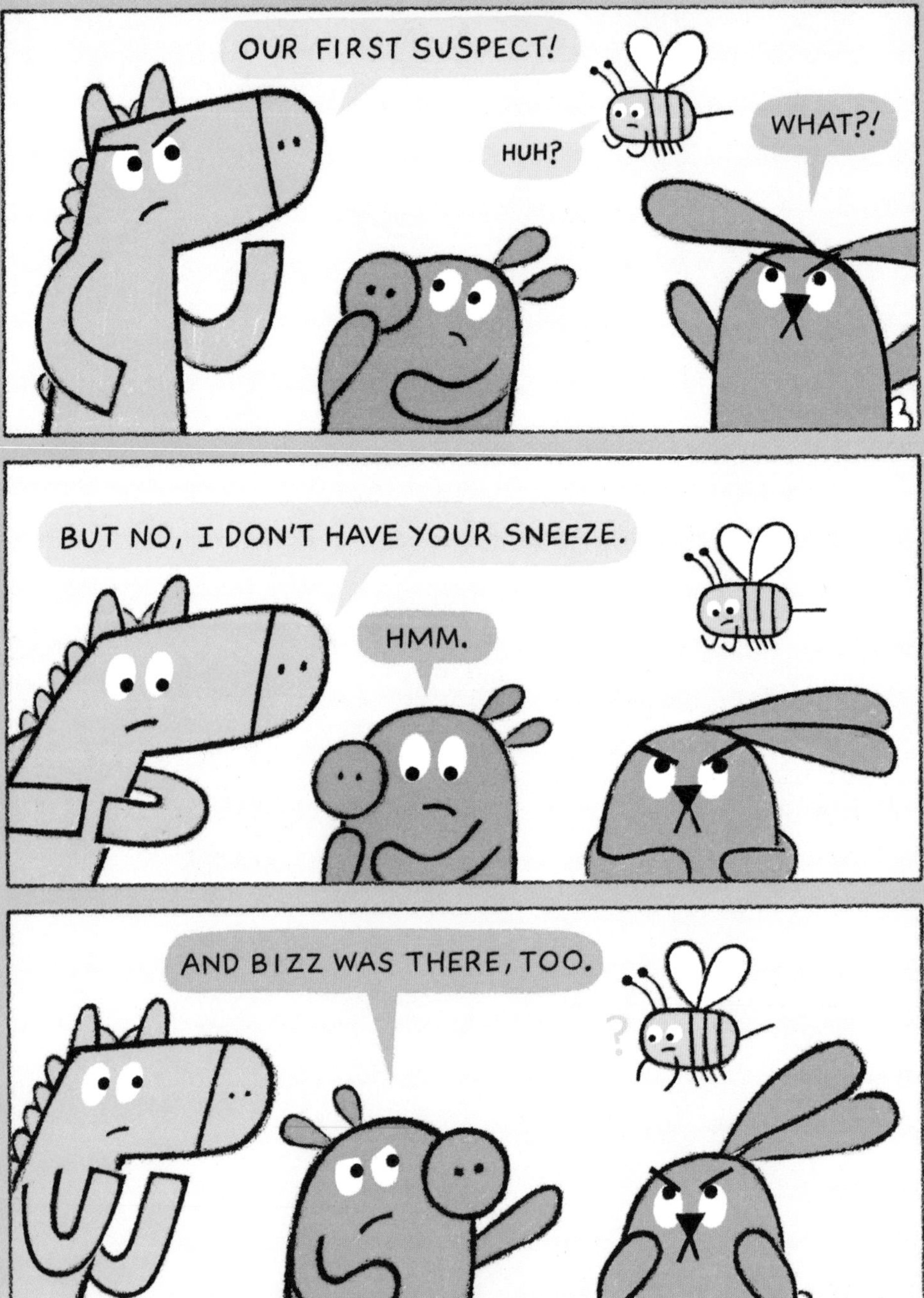
OUR FIRST SUSPECT!
HUH?
WHAT?!
BUT NO, I DON'T HAVE YOUR SNEEZE.
HMM.
AND BIZZ WAS THERE, TOO.

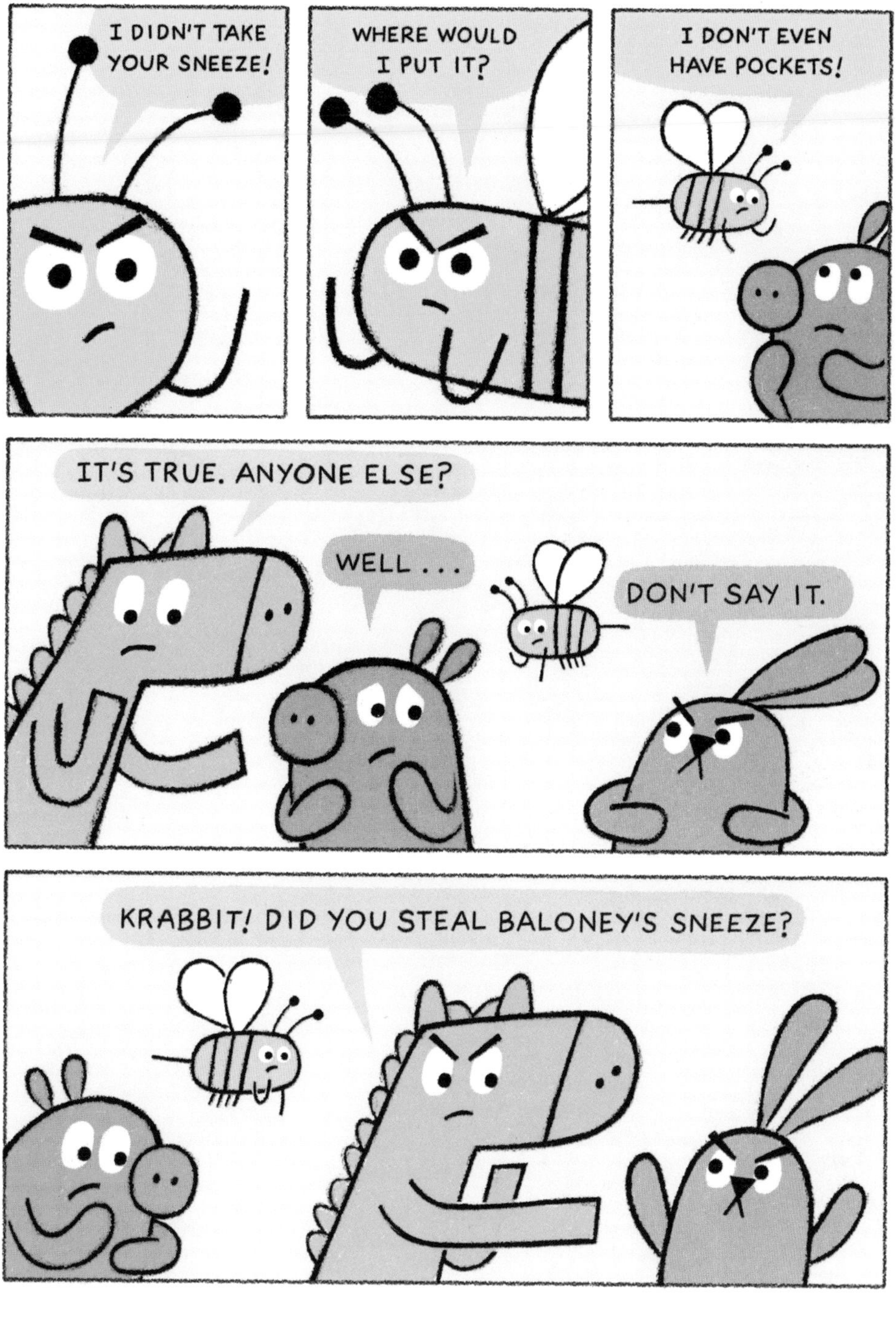
I DIDN'T TAKE YOUR SNEEZE!
WHERE WOULD I PUT IT?
I DON'T EVEN HAVE POCKETS!
IT'S TRUE. ANYONE ELSE?
WELL . . .
DON'T SAY IT.
KRABBIT! DID YOU STEAL BALONEY'S SNEEZE?

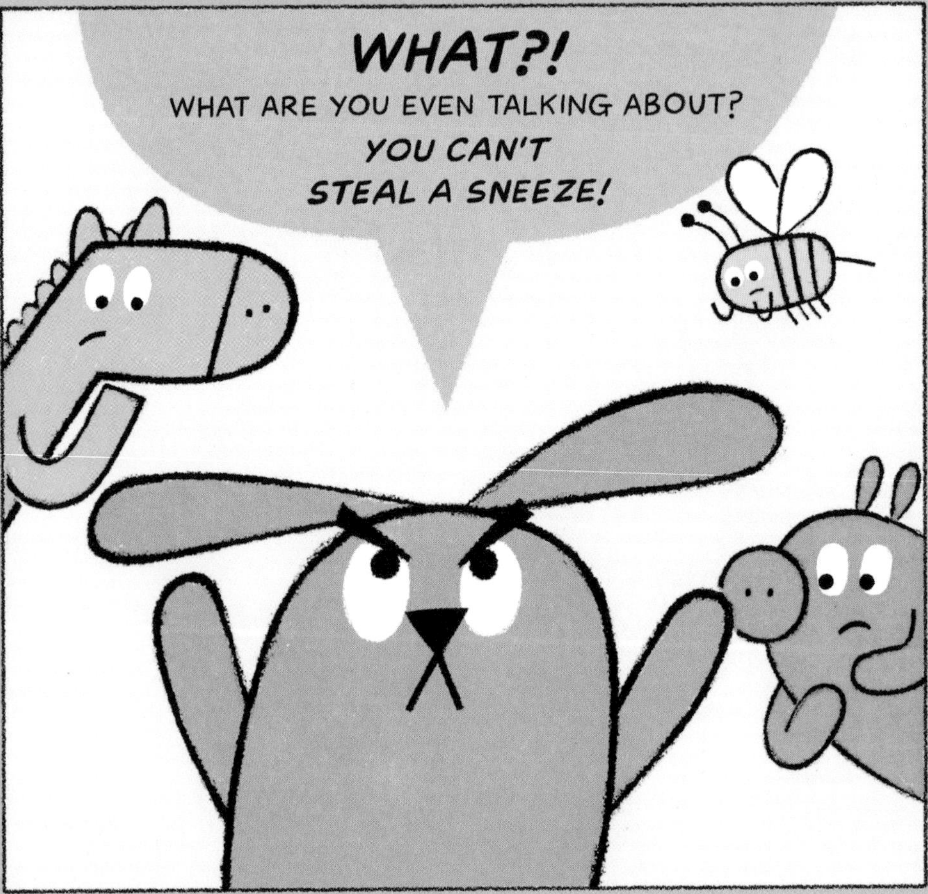
WHAT?!
WHAT ARE YOU EVEN TALKING ABOUT?
YOU CAN'T STEAL A SNEEZE!

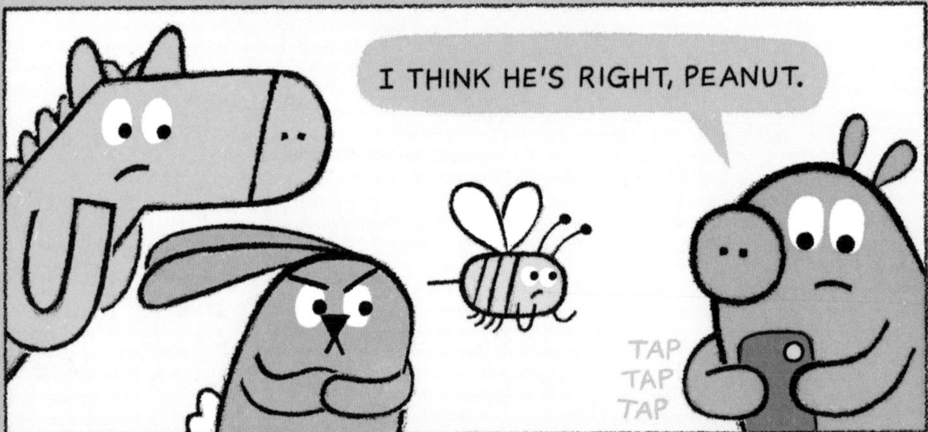
I THINK HE'S RIGHT, PEANUT.
TAP TAP TAP

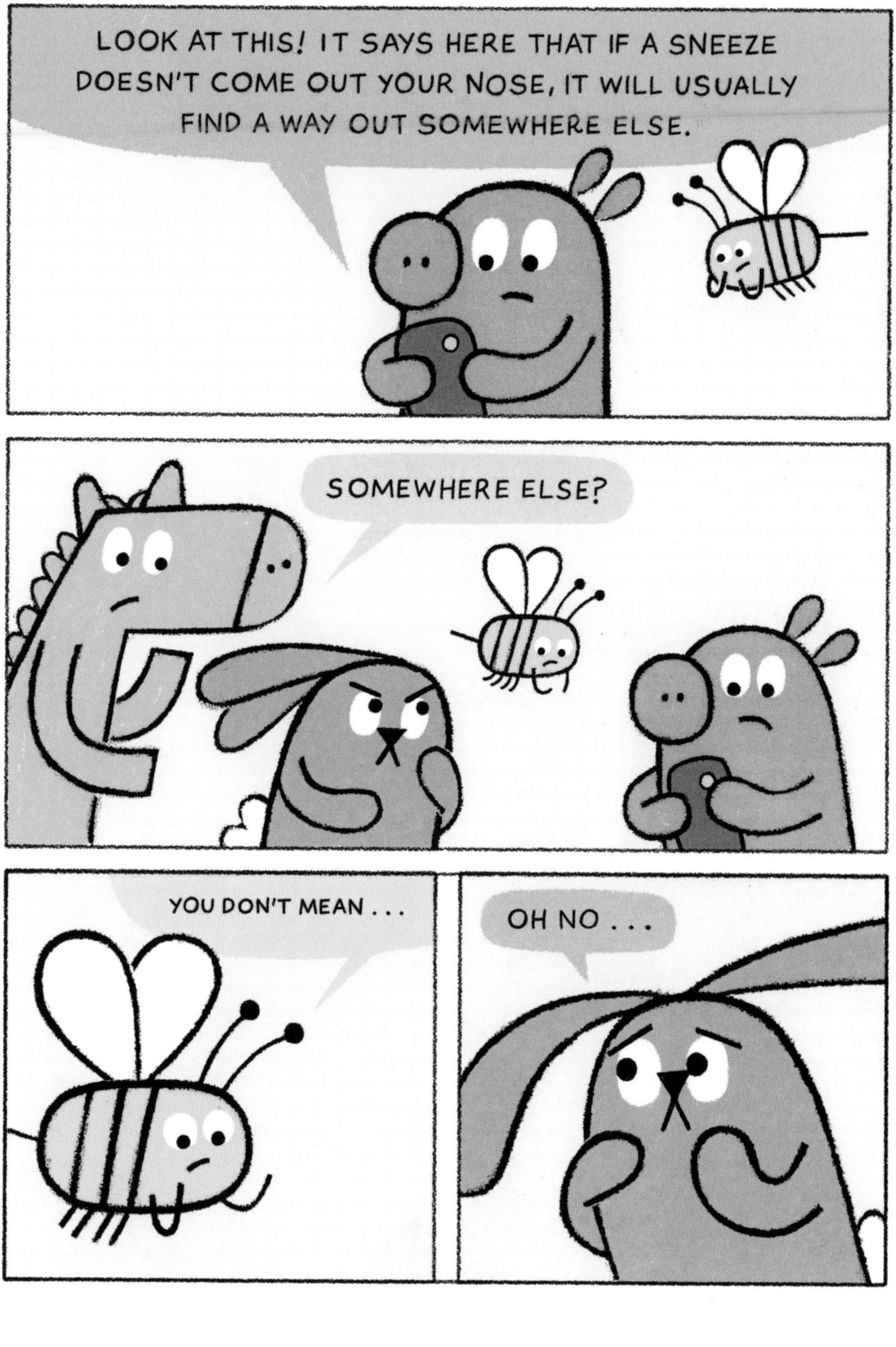
LOOK AT THIS! IT SAYS HERE THAT IF A SNEEZE DOESN'T COME OUT YOUR NOSE, IT WILL USUALLY FIND A WAY OUT SOMEWHERE ELSE.
SOMEWHERE ELSE?
YOU DON'T MEAN . . .
OH NO . . .

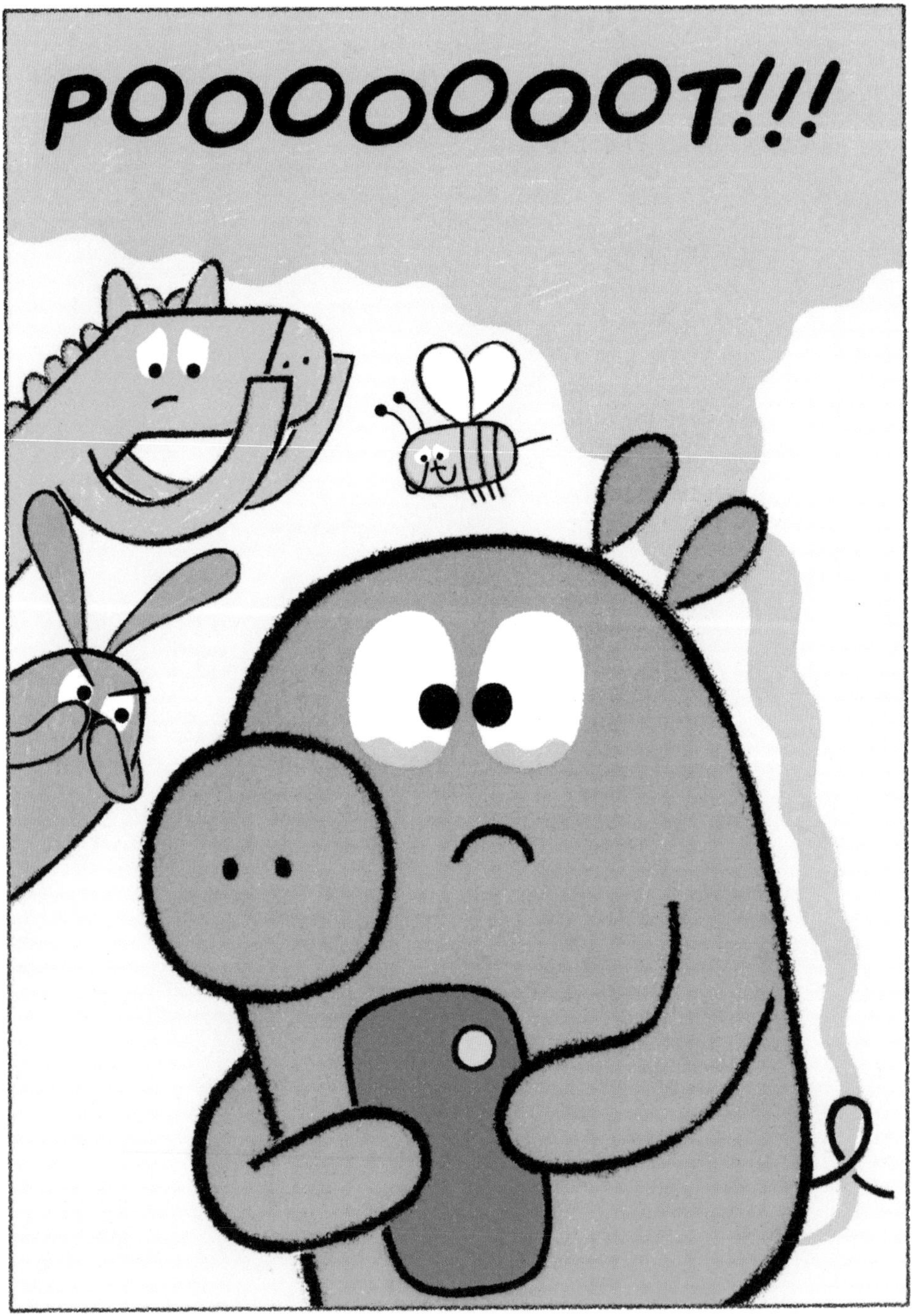
POOOOOOOT!!!

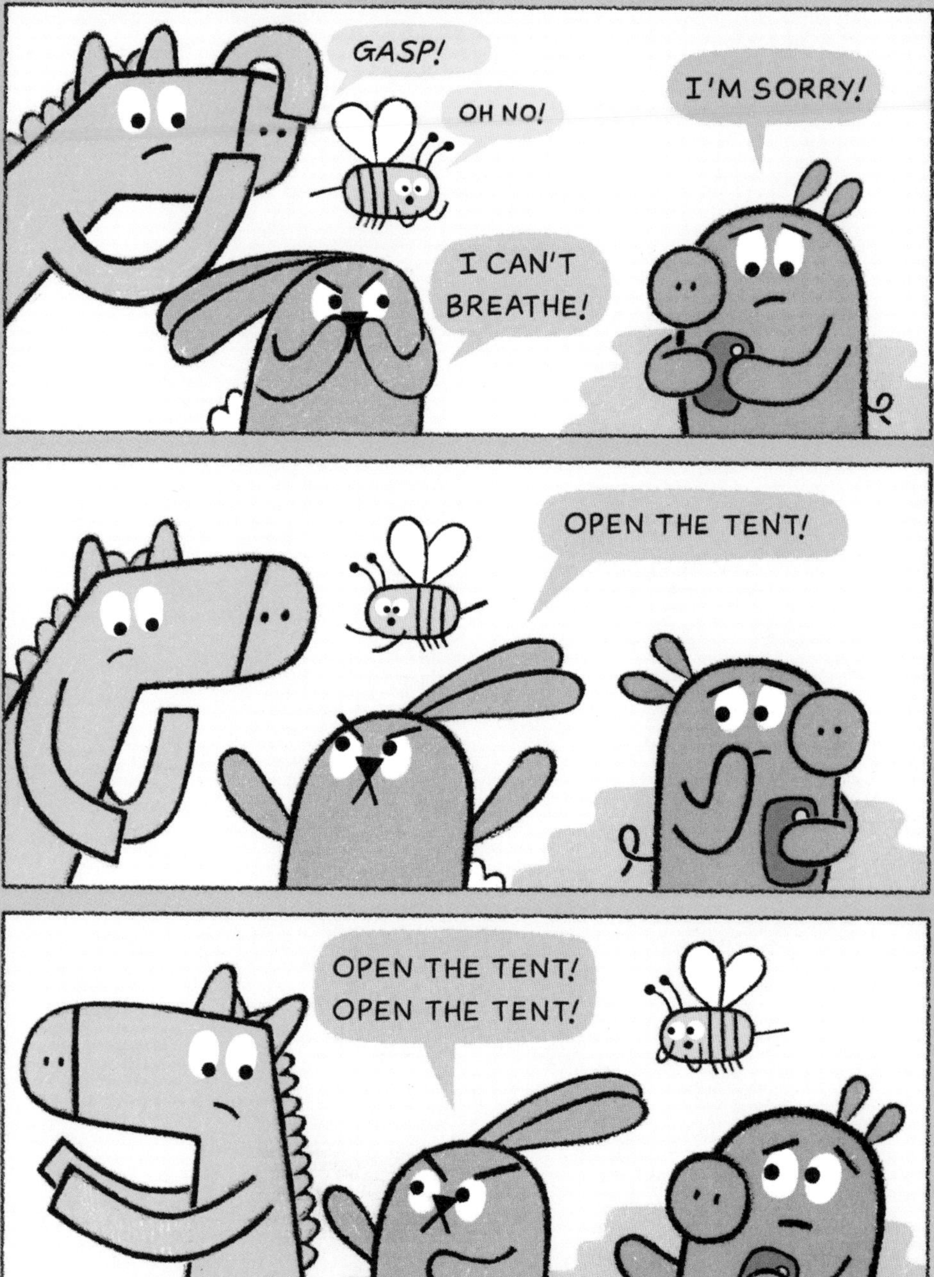
GASP!
OH NO!
I'M SORRY!
I CAN'T BREATHE!
OPEN THE TENT!
OPEN THE TENT! OPEN THE TENT!

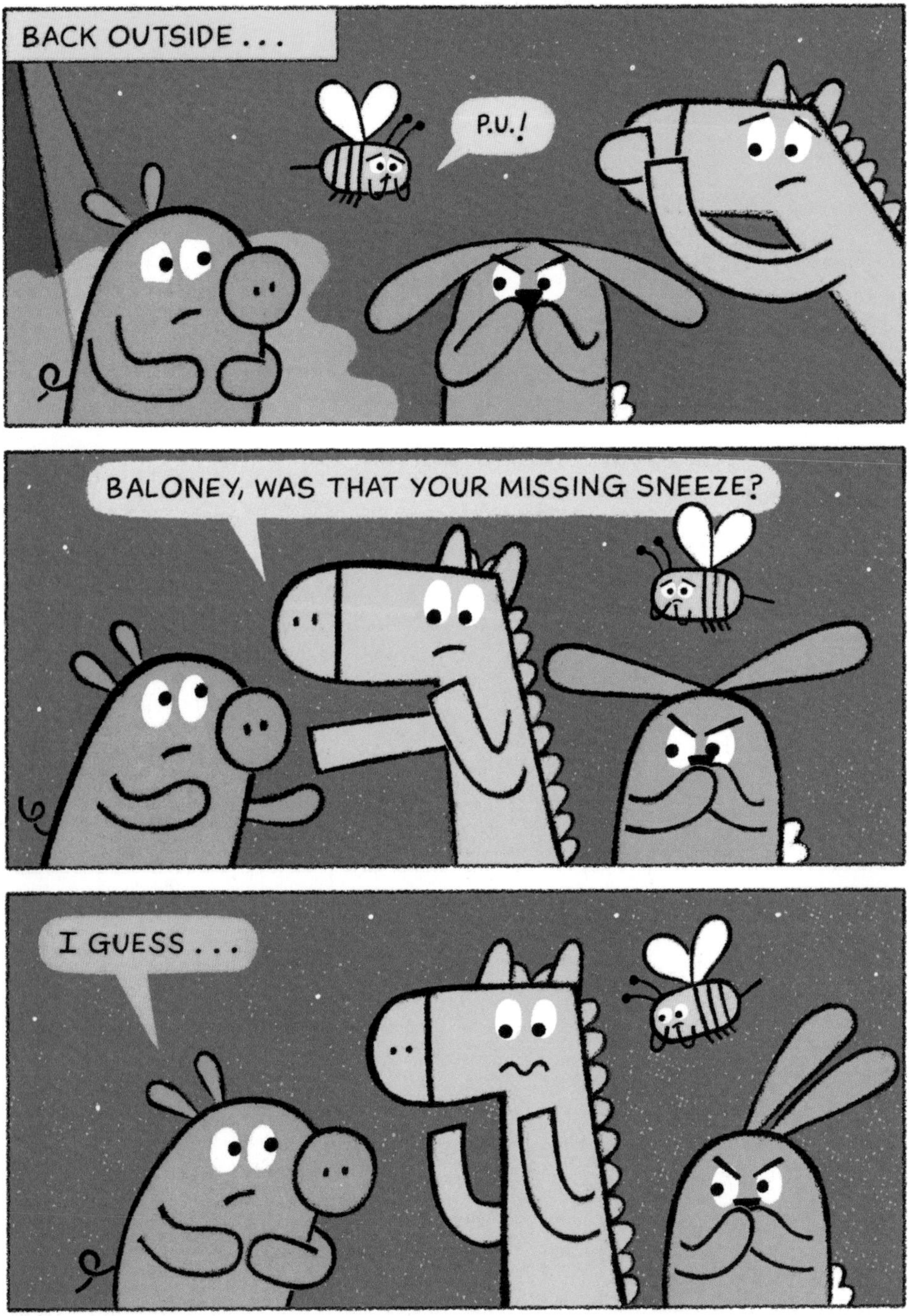
BACK OUTSIDE . . .
P.U.!
BALONEY, WAS THAT YOUR MISSING SNEEZE?
I GUESS . . .

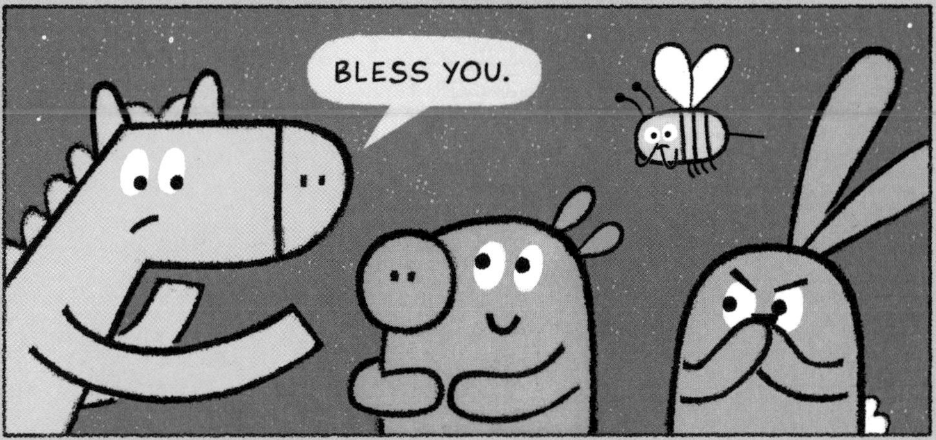
BLESS YOU.

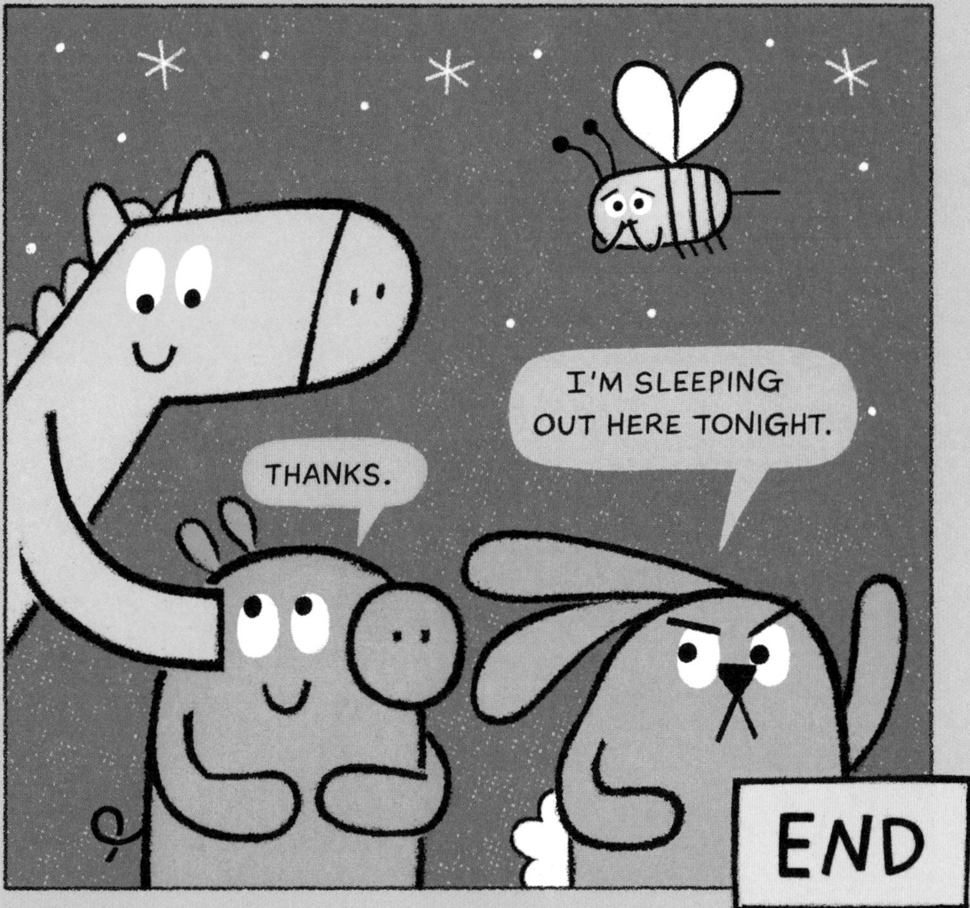
I'M SLEEPING
OUT HERE TONIGHT.
THANKS.
END

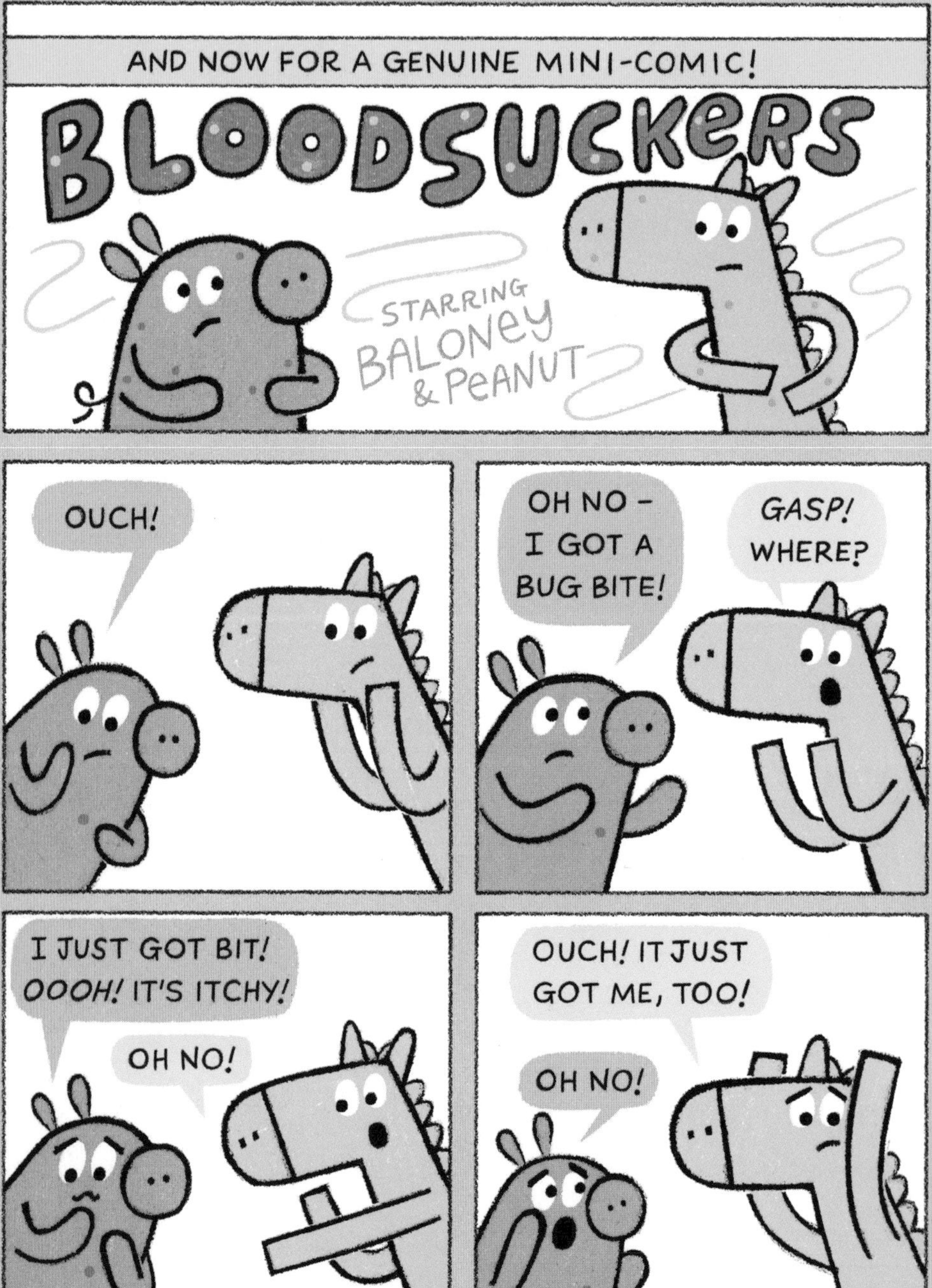
AND NOW FOR A GENUINE MINI-COMIC!
BLOODSUCKERS
STARRING BALONEY & PEANUT
OUCH!
OH NO – I GOT A BUG BITE!
GASP! WHERE?
I JUST GOT BIT! OOOH! IT'S ITCHY!
OH NO!
OUCH! IT JUST GOT ME, TOO!
OH NO!

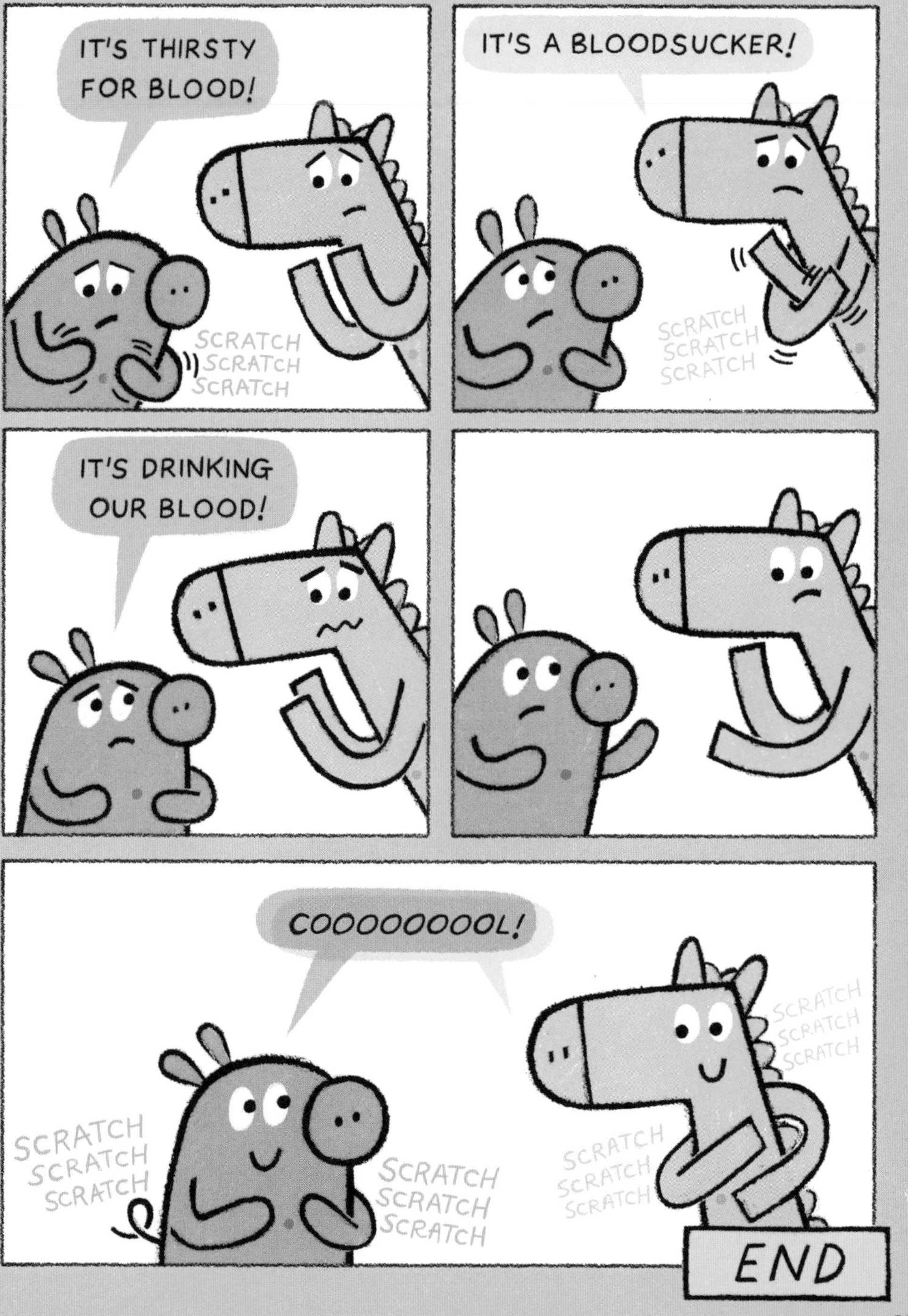
IT'S THIRSTY FOR BLOOD!
SCRATCH SCRATCH SCRATCH
IT'S A BLOODSUCKER!
SCRATCH SCRATCH SCRATCH
IT'S DRINKING OUR BLOOD!
COOOOOOOOL!
SCRATCH SCRATCH SCRATCH
SCRATCH SCRATCH SCRATCH
SCRATCH SCRATCH SCRATCH
SCRATCH SCRATCH SCRATCH
END

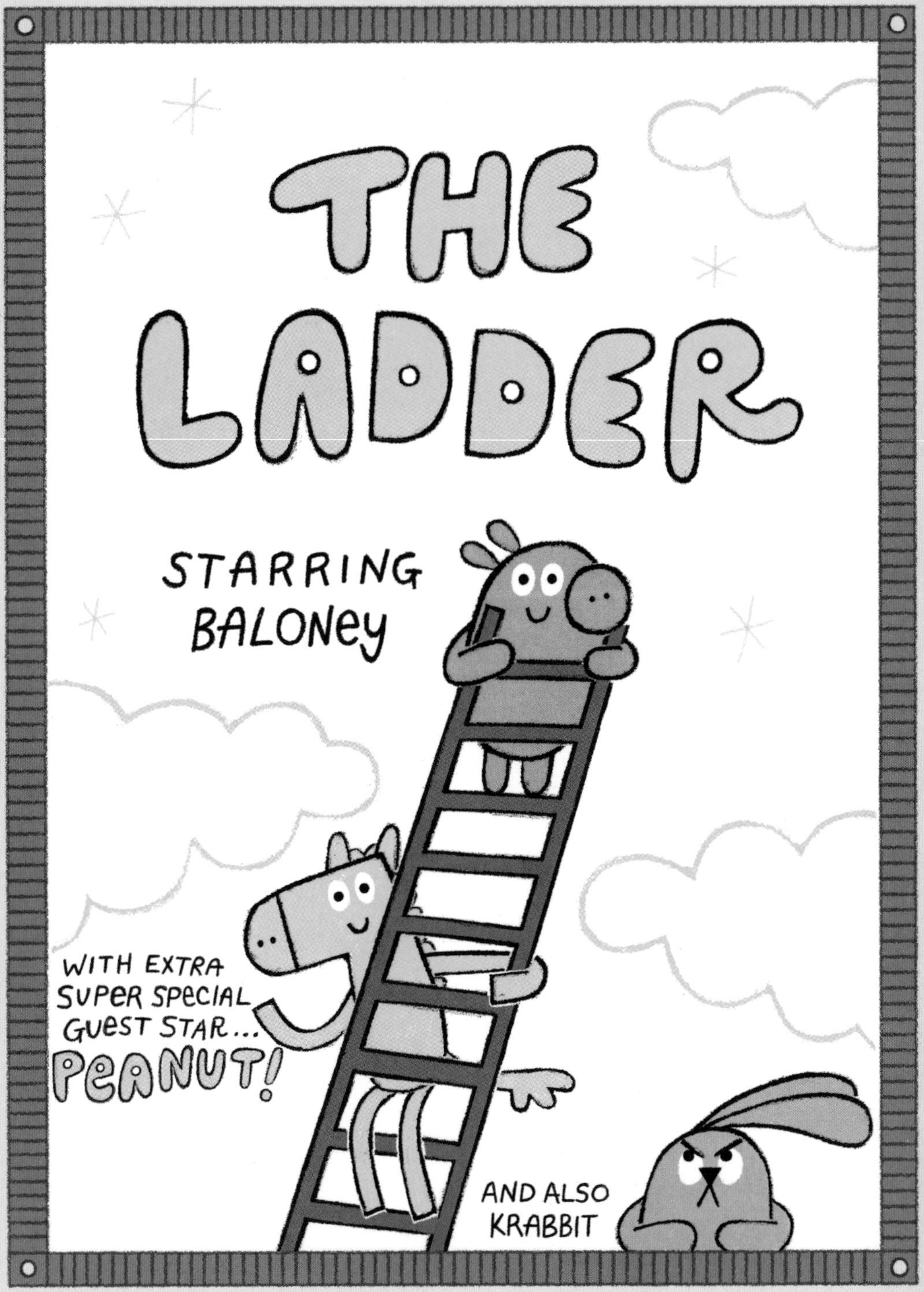
THE LADDER
STARRING
BALONEY
WITH EXTRA
SUPER SPECIAL
GUEST STAR...
PEANUT!
AND ALSO
KRABBIT

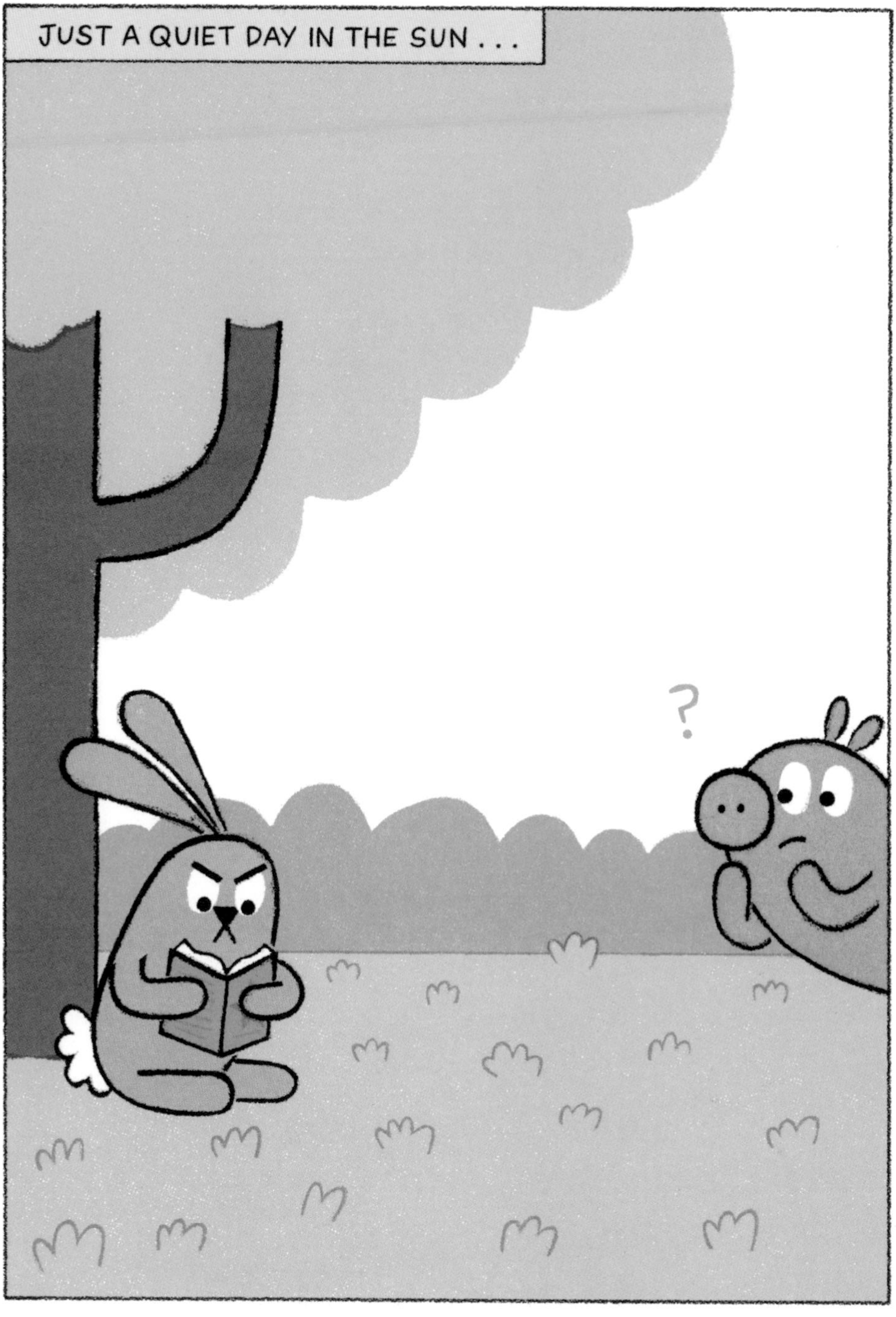
JUST A QUIET DAY IN THE SUN . . .
?

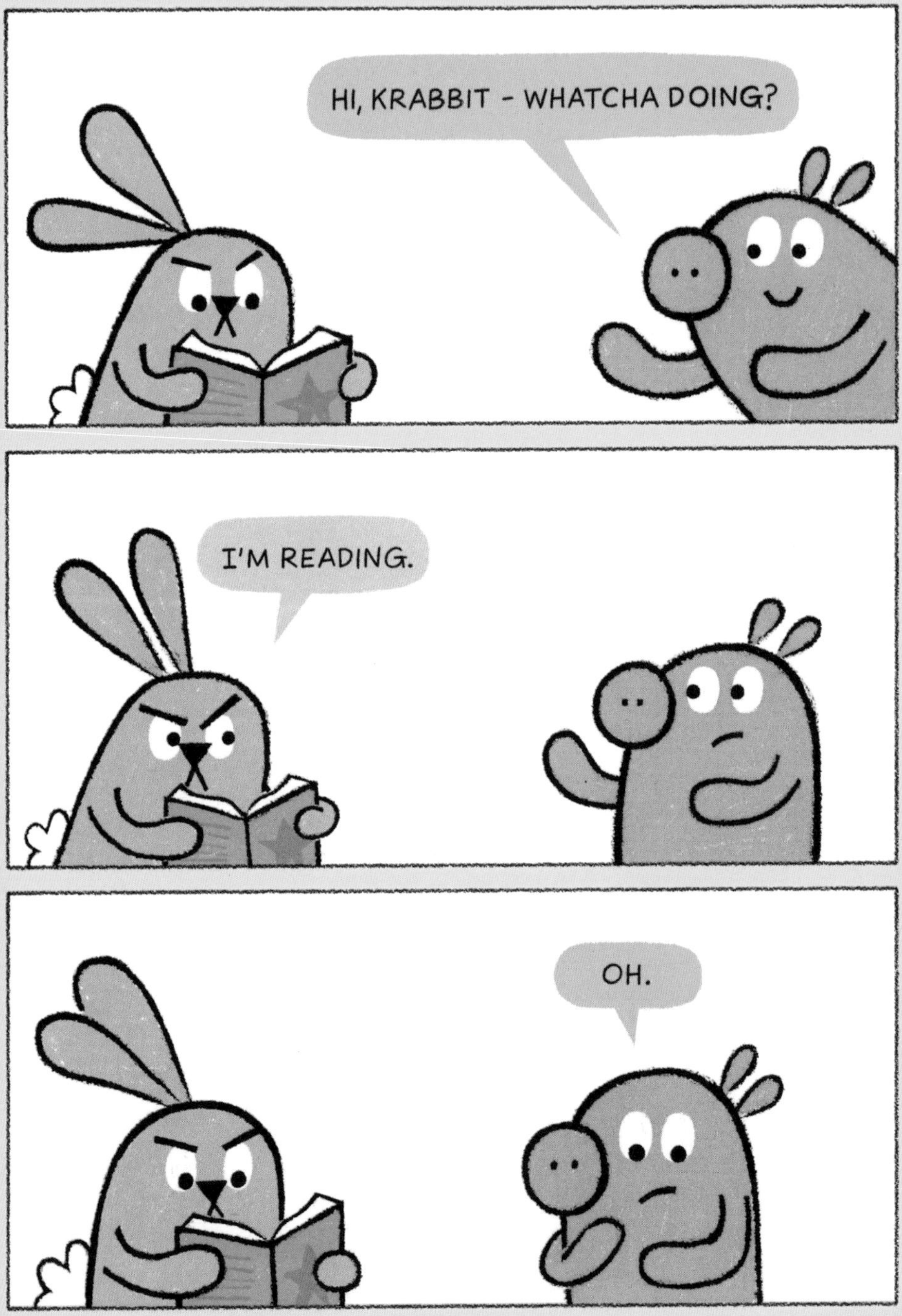
HI, KRABBIT - WHATCHA DOING?
I'M READING.
OH.

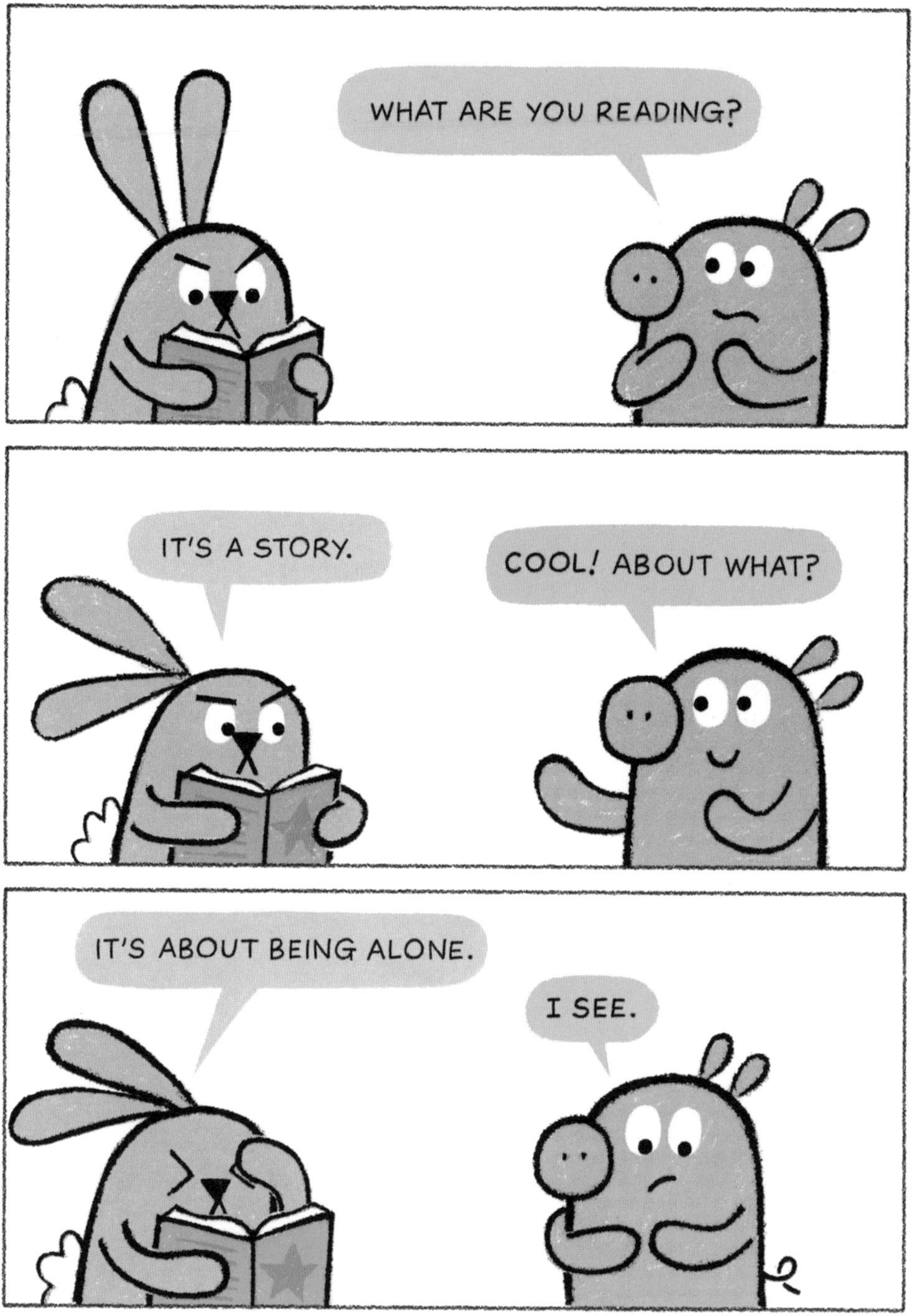
WHAT ARE YOU READING?
IT'S A STORY.
COOL! ABOUT WHAT?
IT'S ABOUT BEING ALONE.
I SEE.

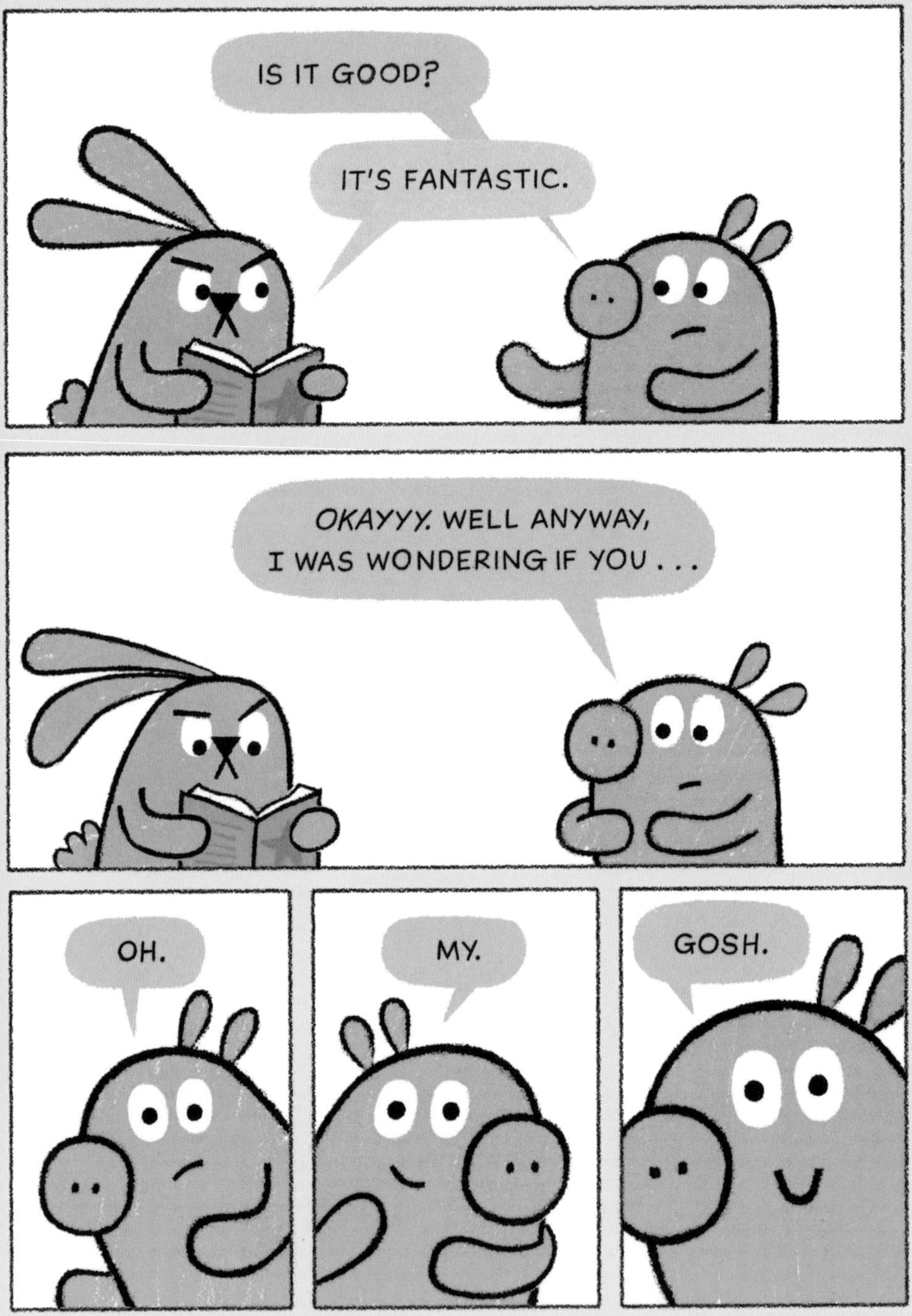
IS IT GOOD?
IT'S FANTASTIC.
OKAYYY. WELL ANYWAY, I WAS WONDERING IF YOU . . .
OH.
MY.
GOSH.

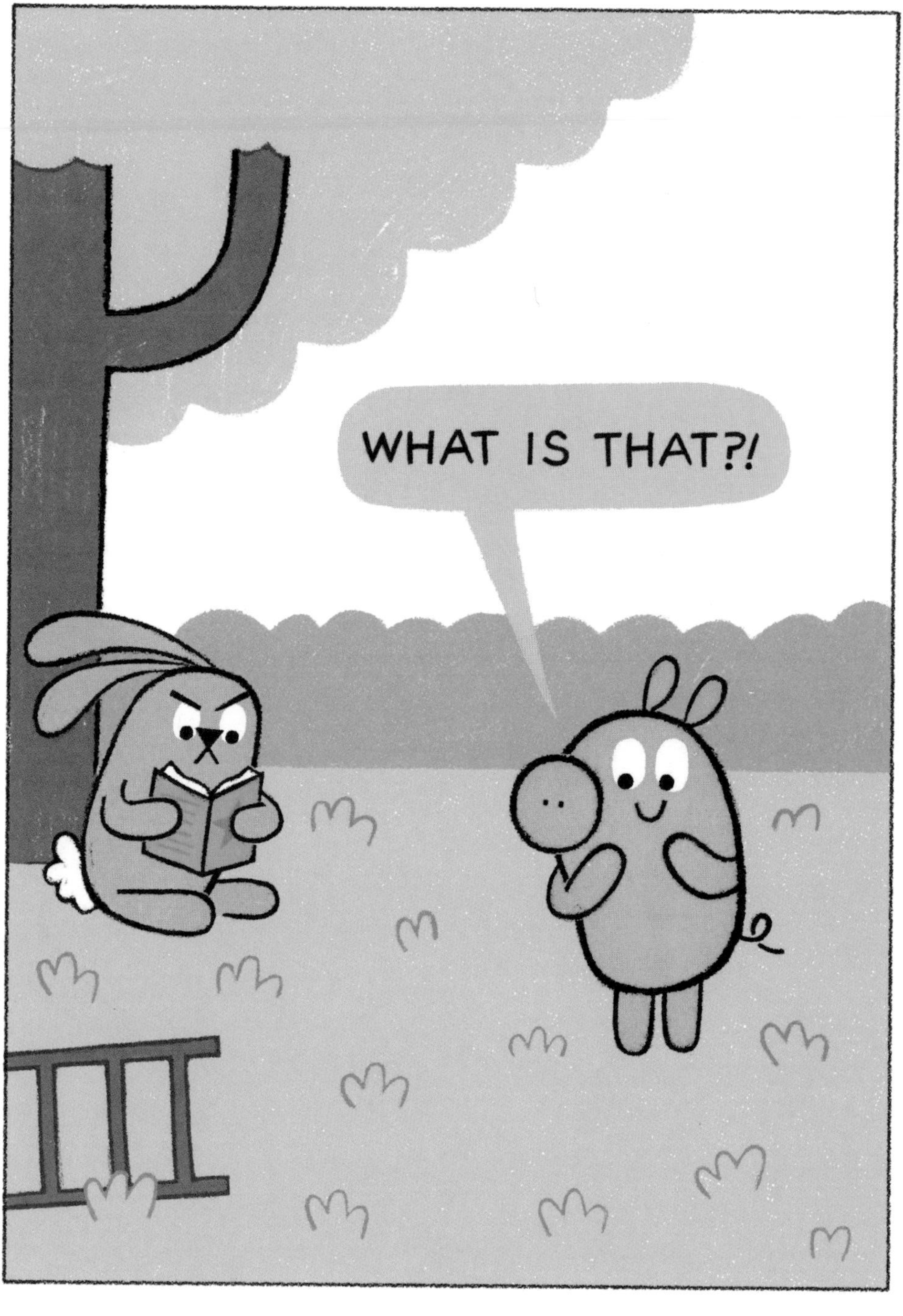
WHAT IS THAT?!

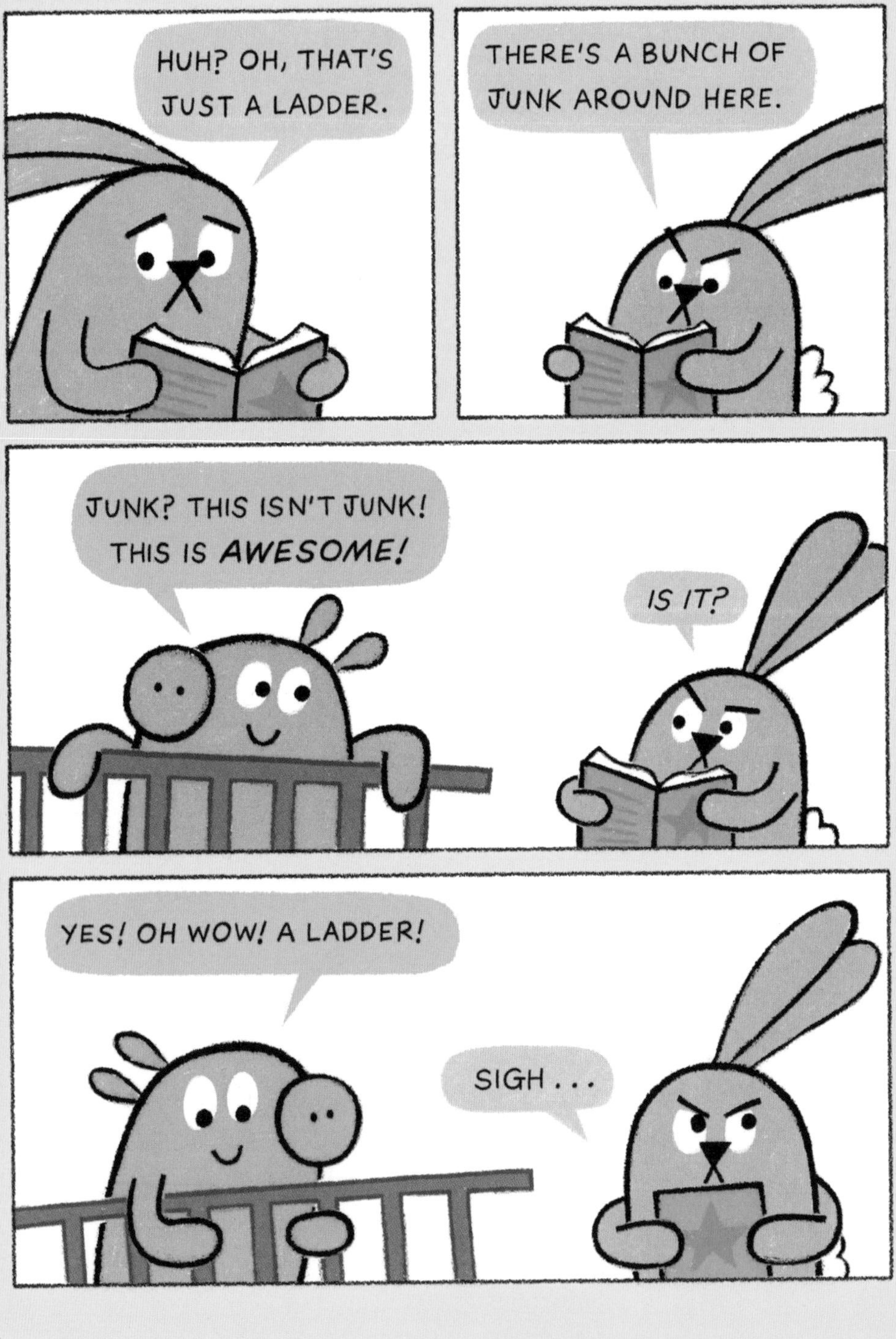
HUH? OH, THAT'S JUST A LADDER.
THERE'S A BUNCH OF JUNK AROUND HERE.
JUNK? THIS ISN'T JUNK! THIS IS *AWESOME!*
IS IT?
YES! OH WOW! A LADDER!
SIGH . . .

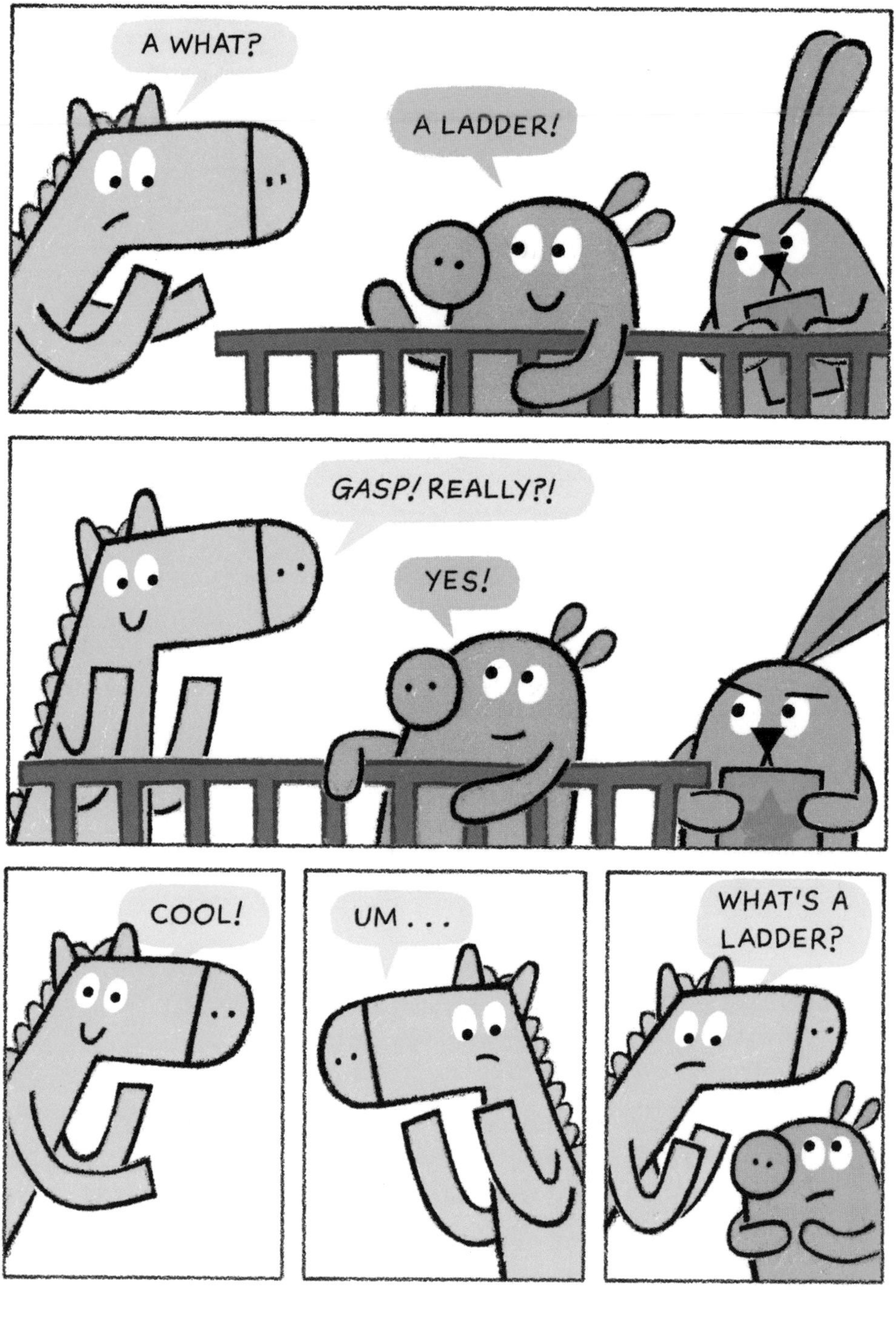
A WHAT?
A LADDER!
GASP! REALLY?!
YES!
COOL!
UM . . .
WHAT'S A LADDER?

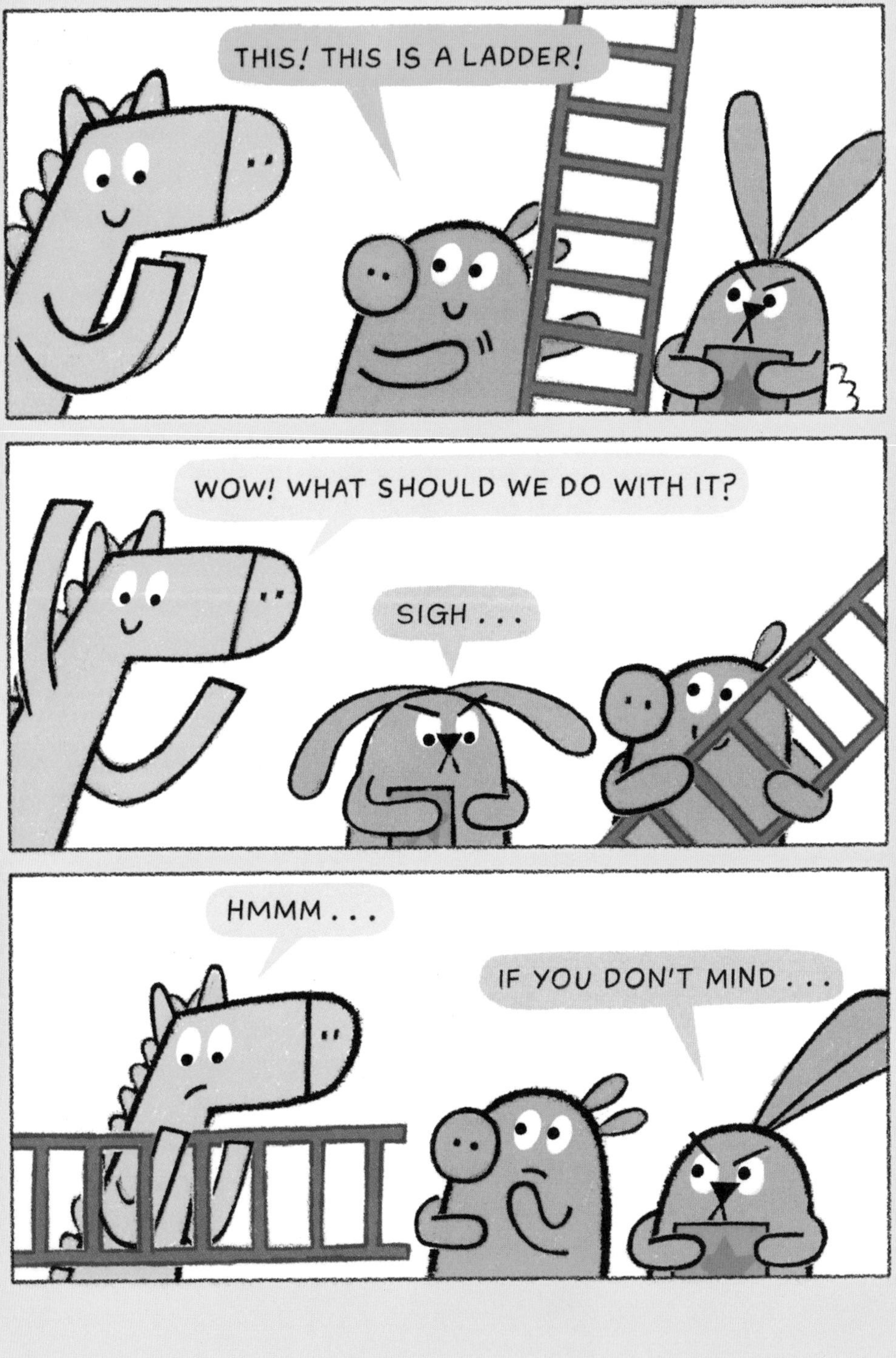
THIS! THIS IS A LADDER!
WOW! WHAT SHOULD WE DO WITH IT?
SIGH . . .
HMMM . . .
IF YOU DON'T MIND . . .

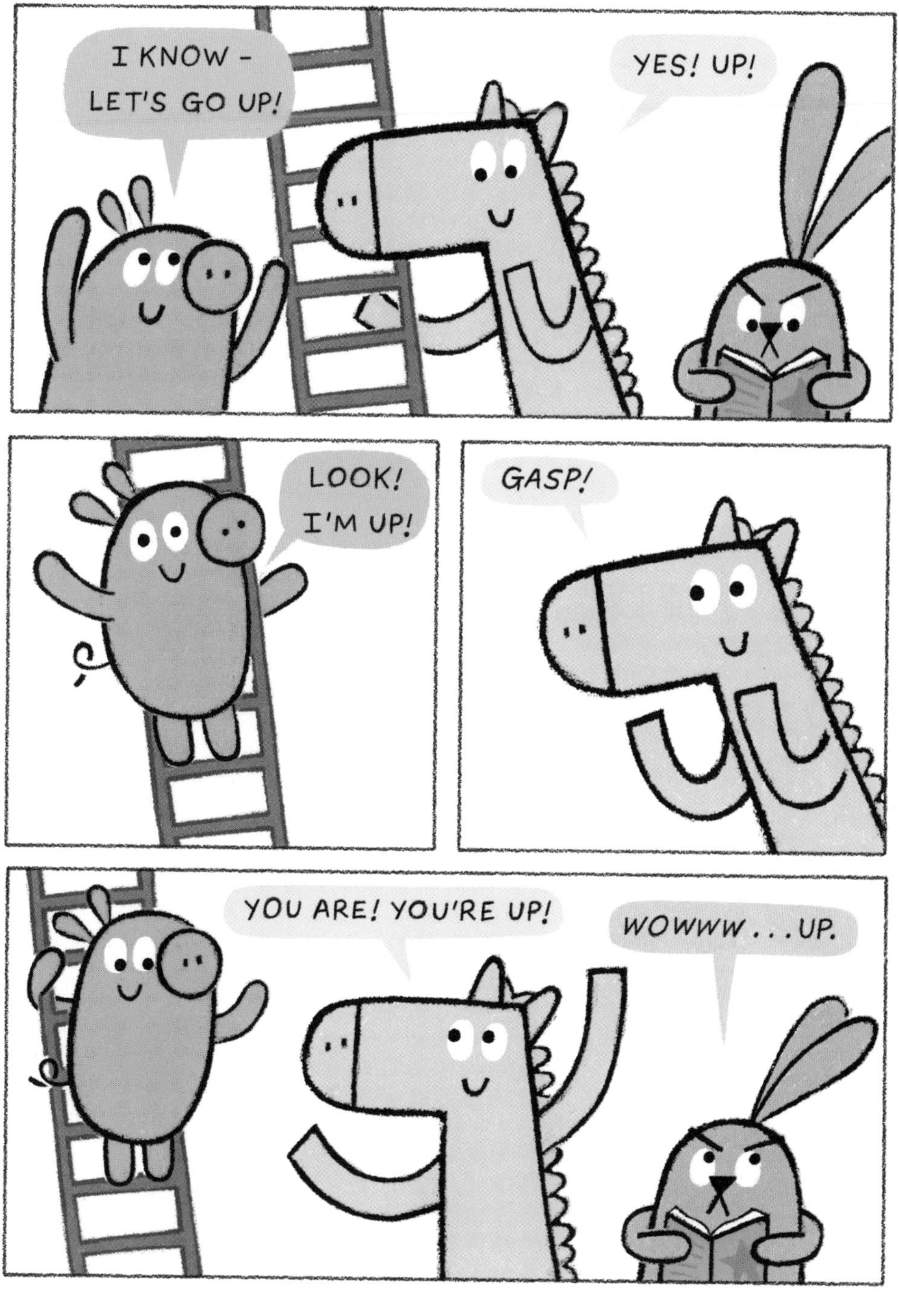
I KNOW - LET'S GO UP!
YES! UP!
LOOK! I'M UP!
GASP!
YOU ARE! YOU'RE UP!
WOWWW . . . UP.

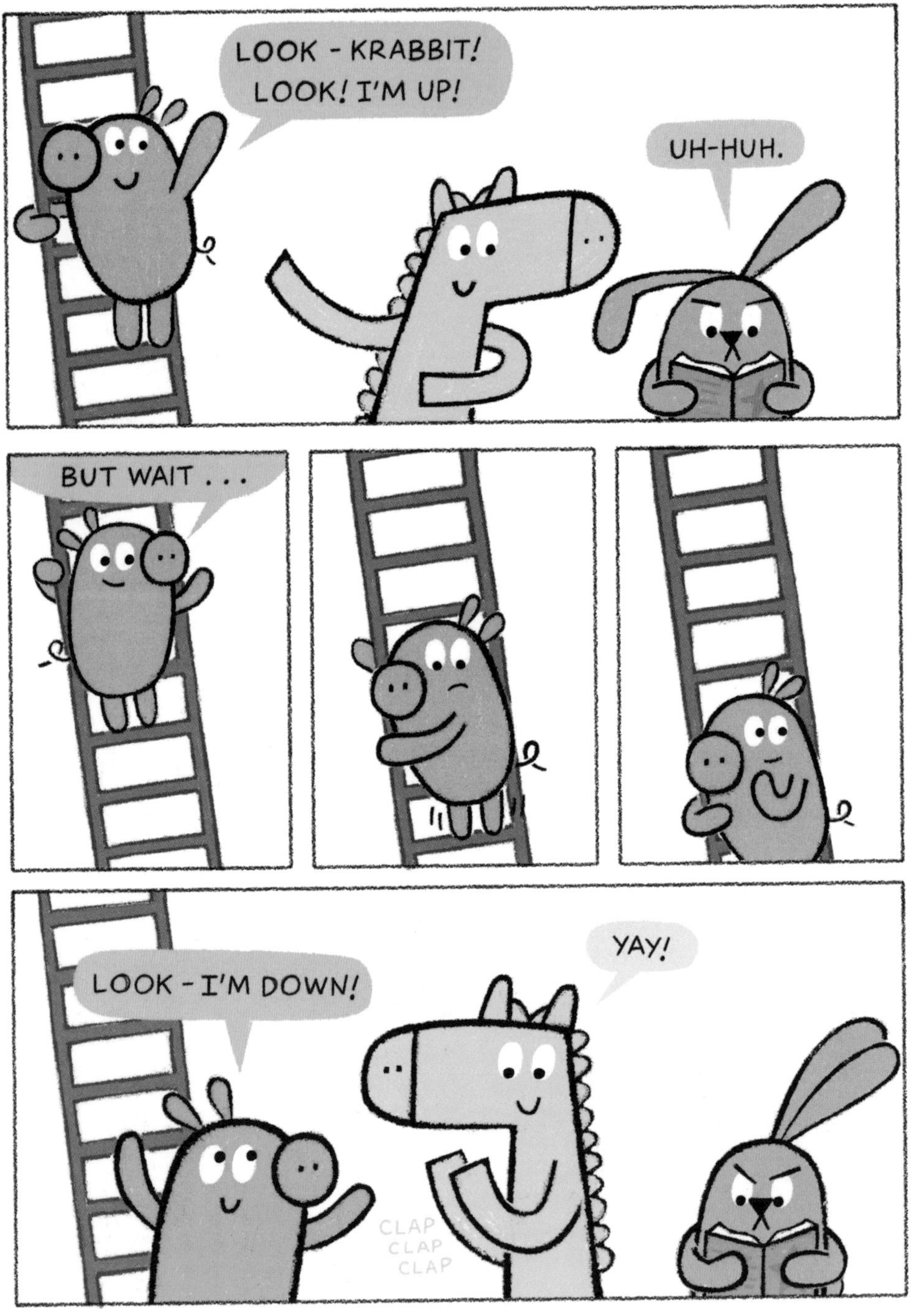

LOOK - KRABBIT!
LOOK! I'M UP!
UH-HUH.
BUT WAIT . . .
LOOK - I'M DOWN!
YAY!
CLAP
CLAP
CLAP

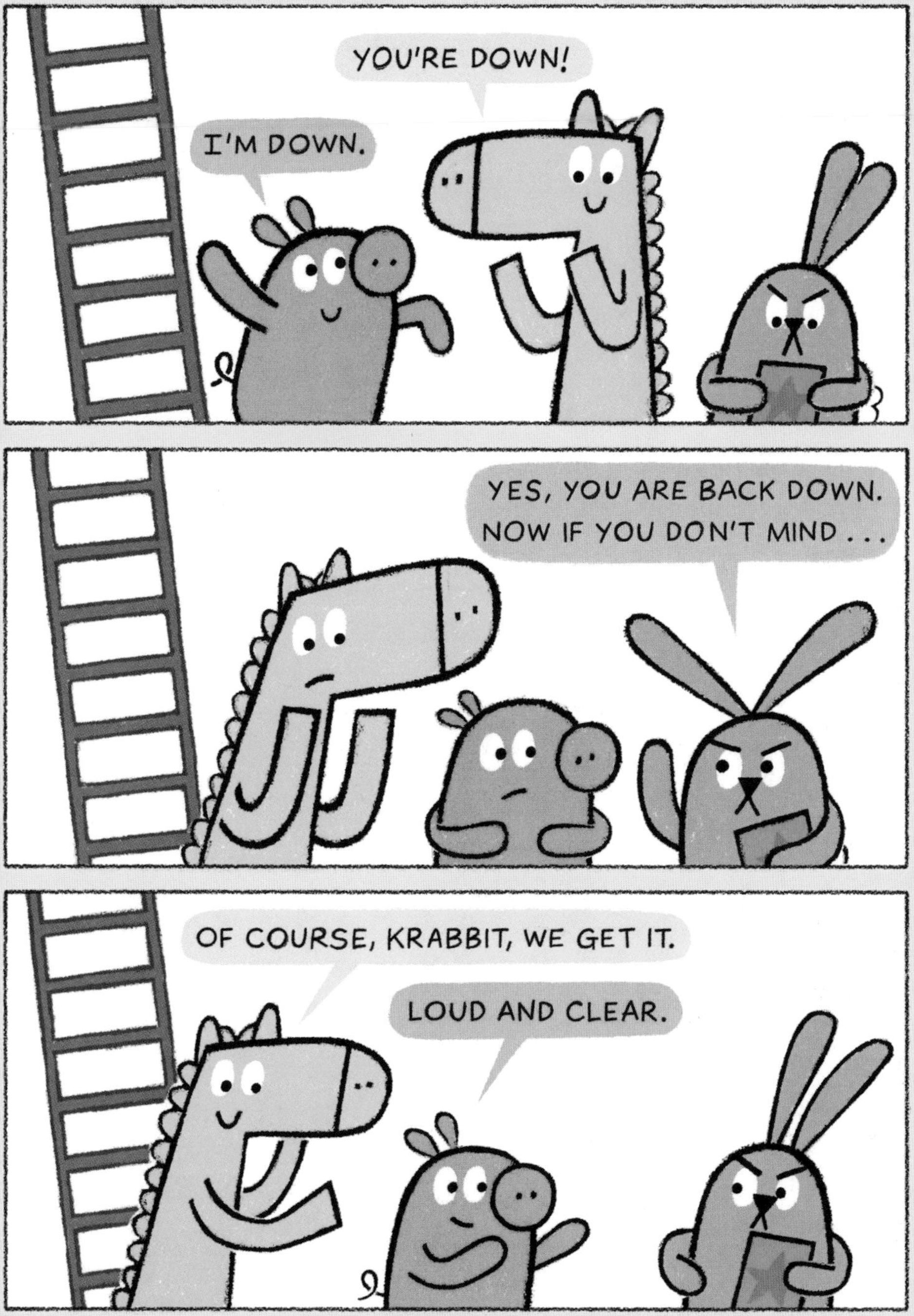
I'M DOWN.
YOU'RE DOWN!
YES, YOU ARE BACK DOWN. NOW IF YOU DON'T MIND . . .
OF COURSE, KRABBIT, WE GET IT.
LOUD AND CLEAR.

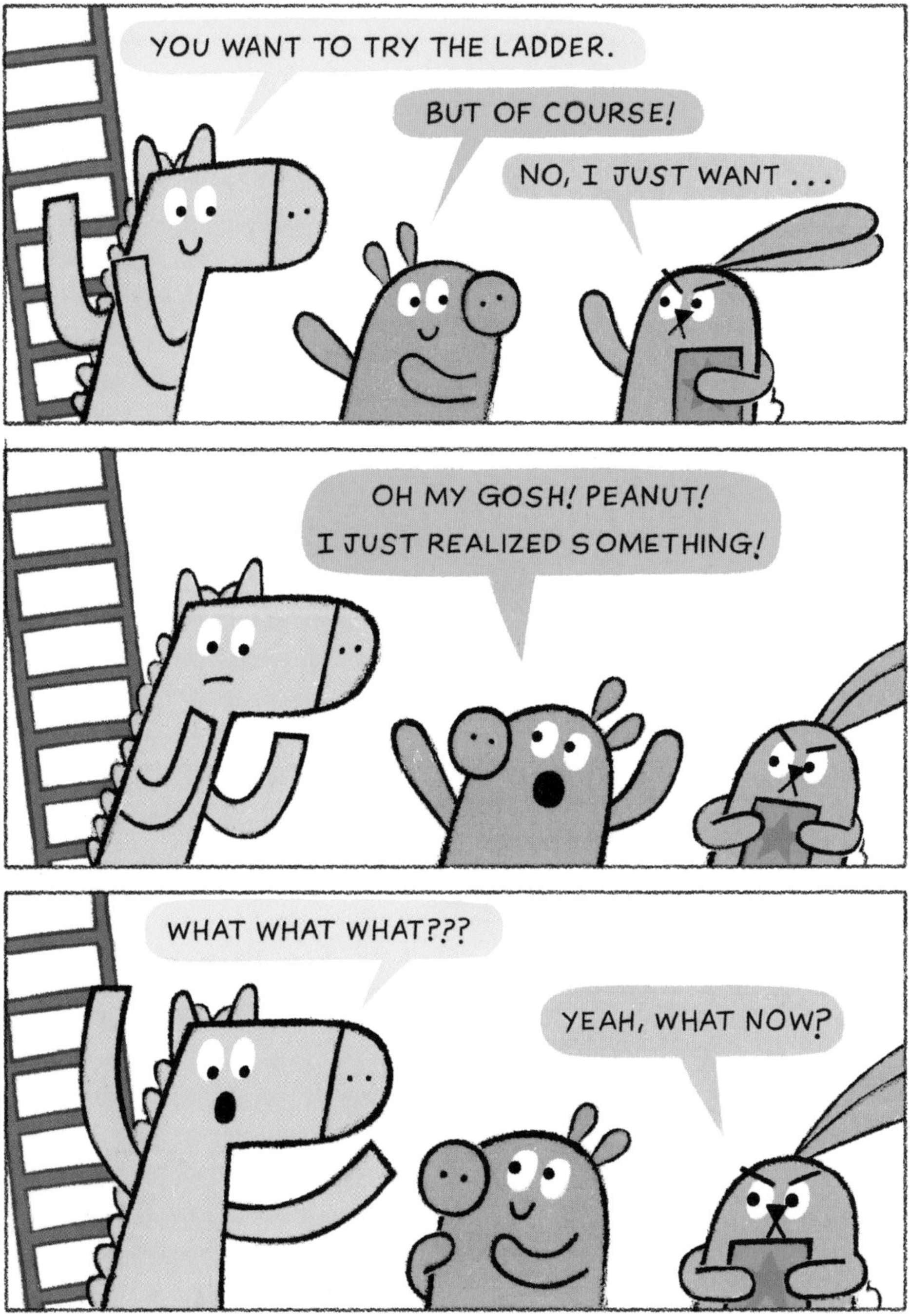
YOU WANT TO TRY THE LADDER.
BUT OF COURSE!
NO, I JUST WANT . . .
OH MY GOSH! PEANUT!
I JUST REALIZED SOMETHING!
WHAT WHAT WHAT???
YEAH, WHAT NOW?

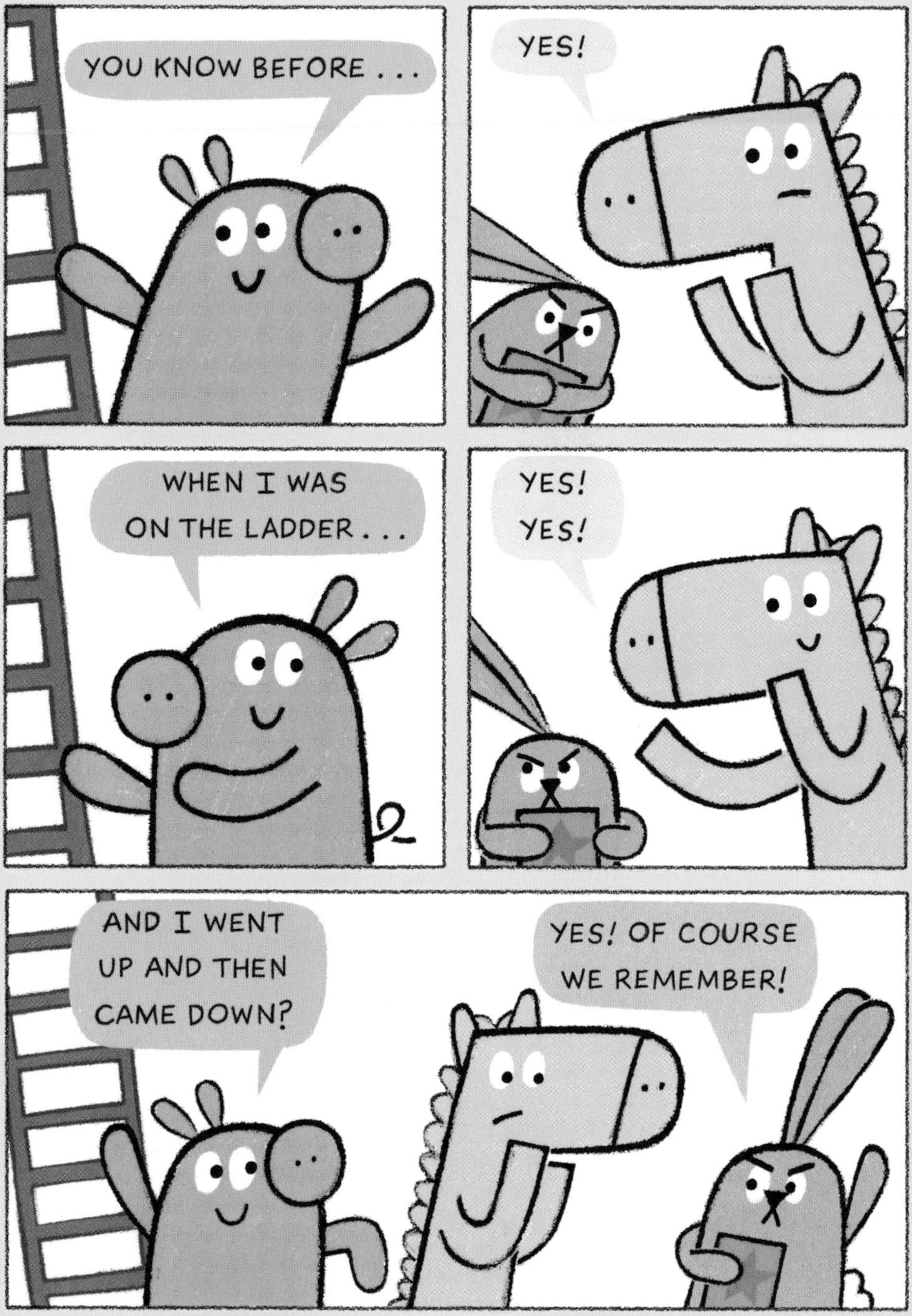
YOU KNOW BEFORE . . .
YES!
WHEN I WAS ON THE LADDER . . .
YES! YES!
AND I WENT UP AND THEN CAME DOWN?
YES! OF COURSE WE REMEMBER!

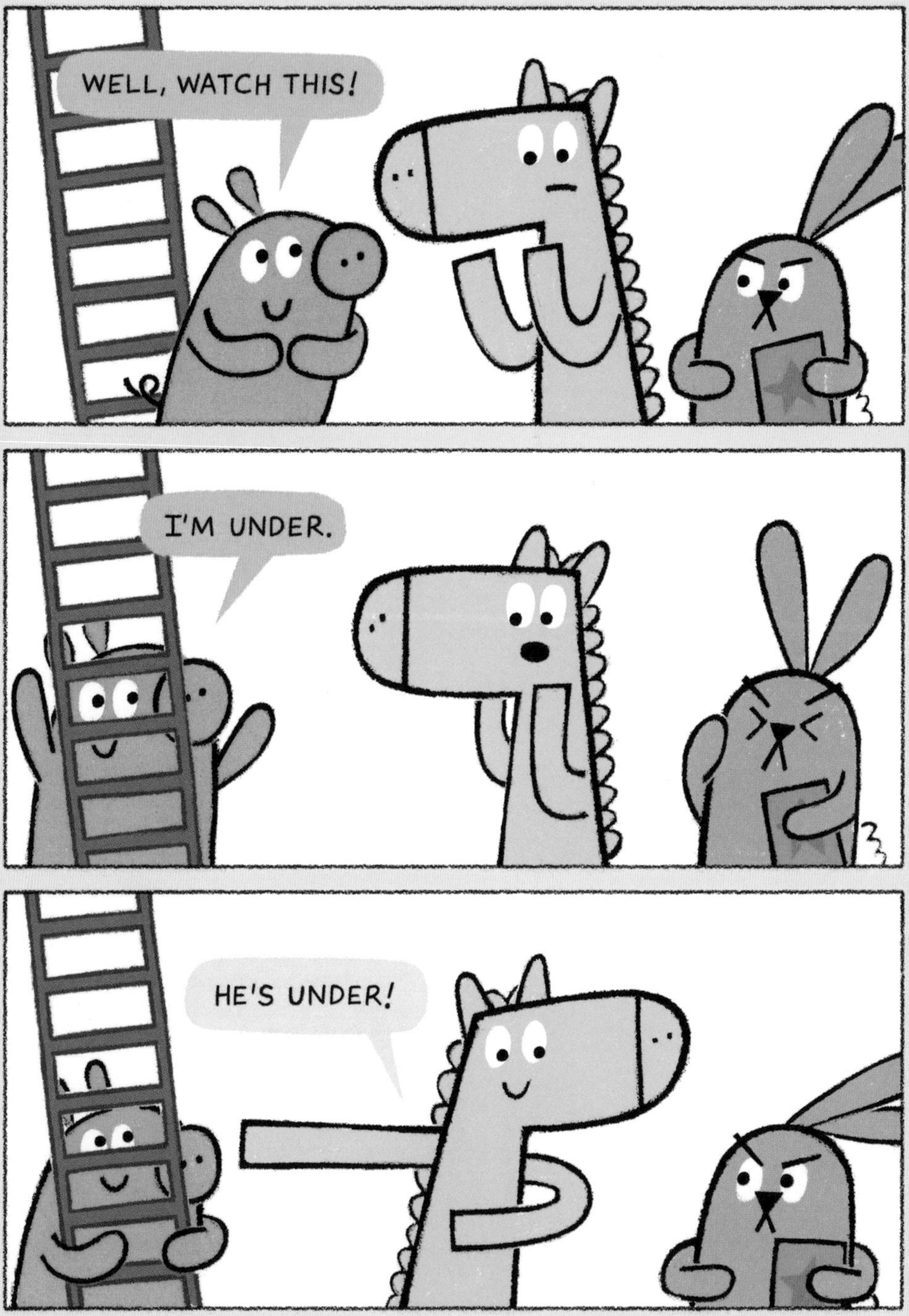
WELL, WATCH THIS!
I'M UNDER.
HE'S UNDER!

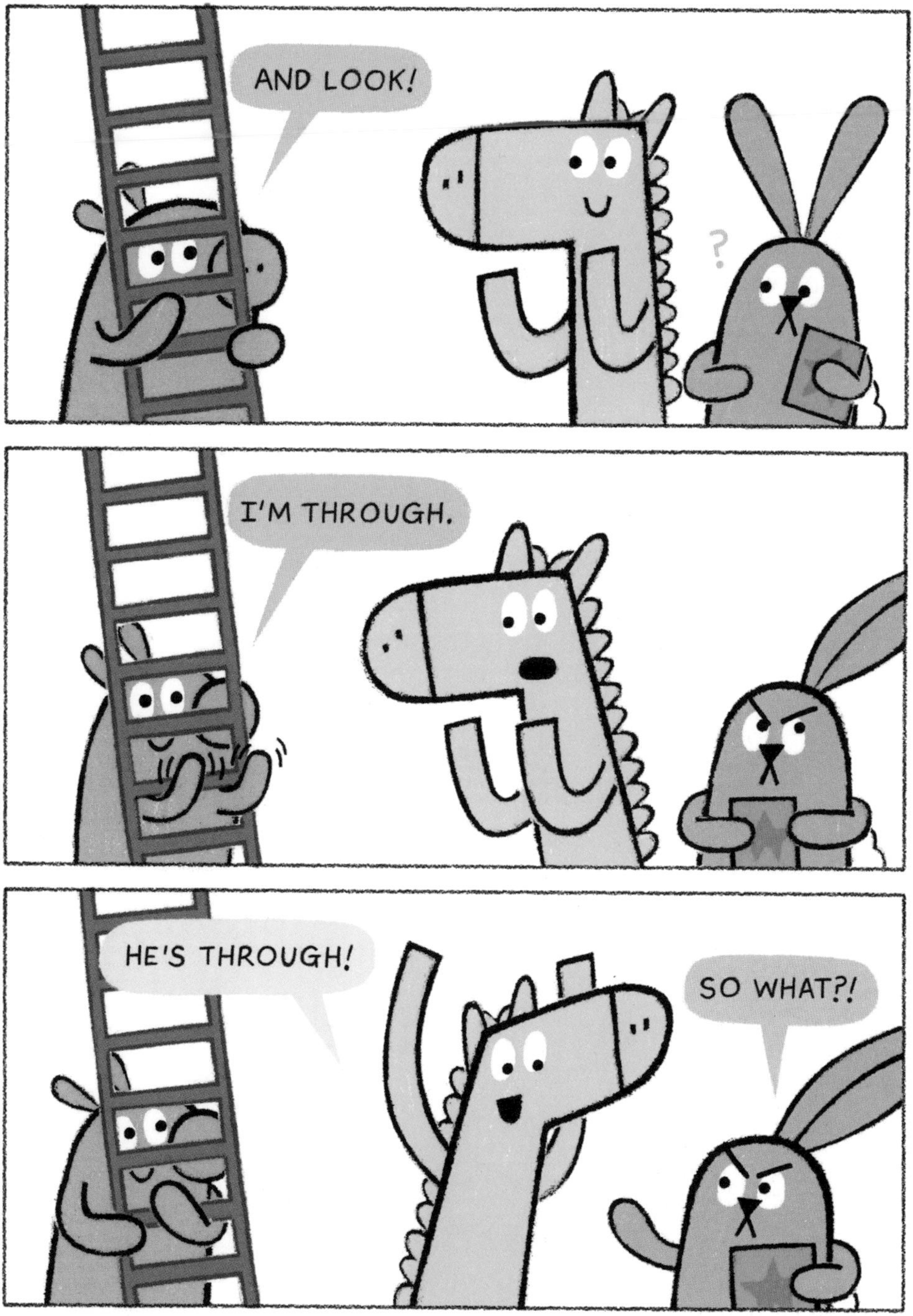
AND LOOK!
?
I'M THROUGH.
HE'S THROUGH!
SO WHAT?!

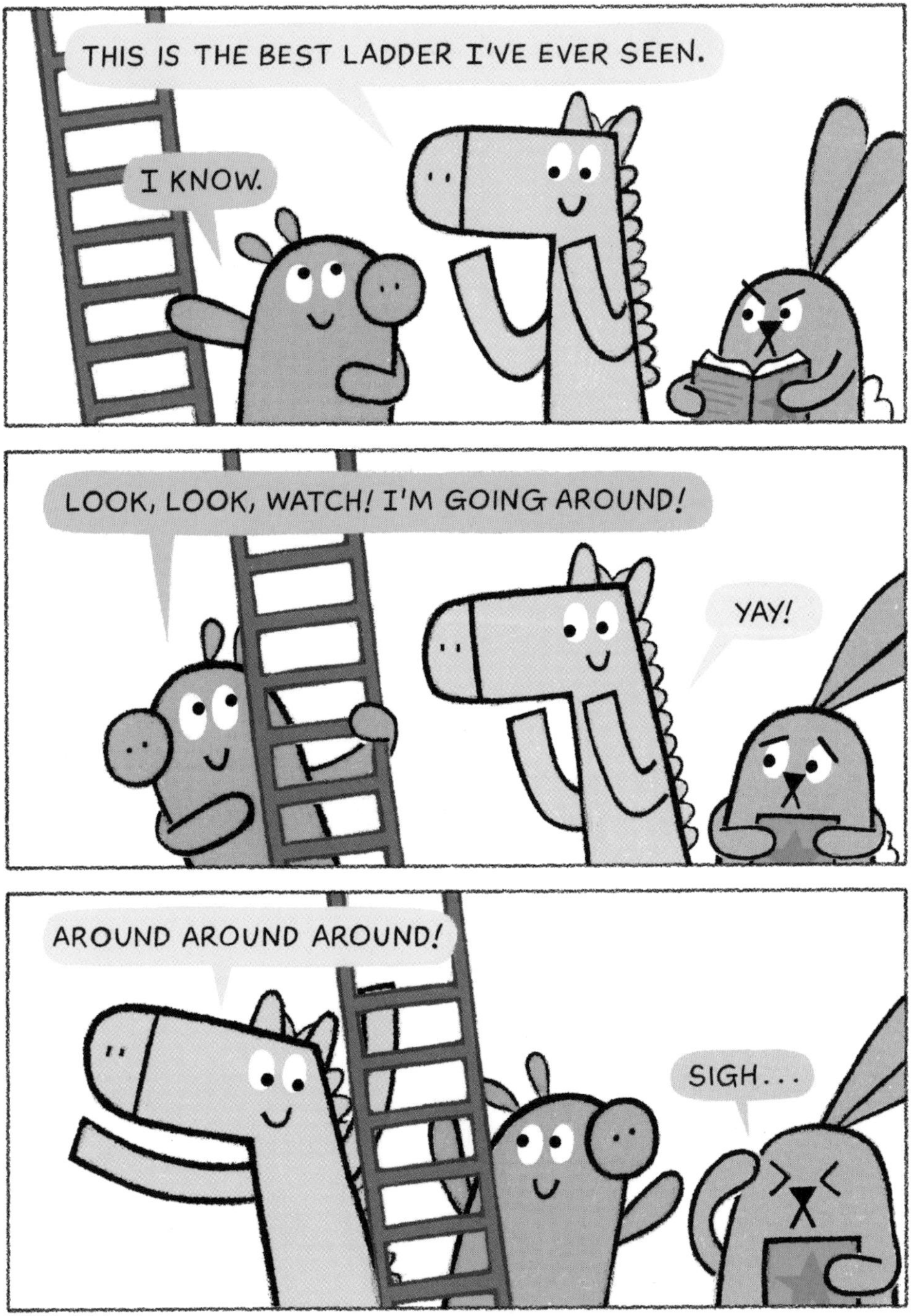
THIS IS THE BEST LADDER I'VE EVER SEEN.
I KNOW.
LOOK, LOOK, WATCH! I'M GOING AROUND!
YAY!
AROUND AROUND AROUND!
SIGH...

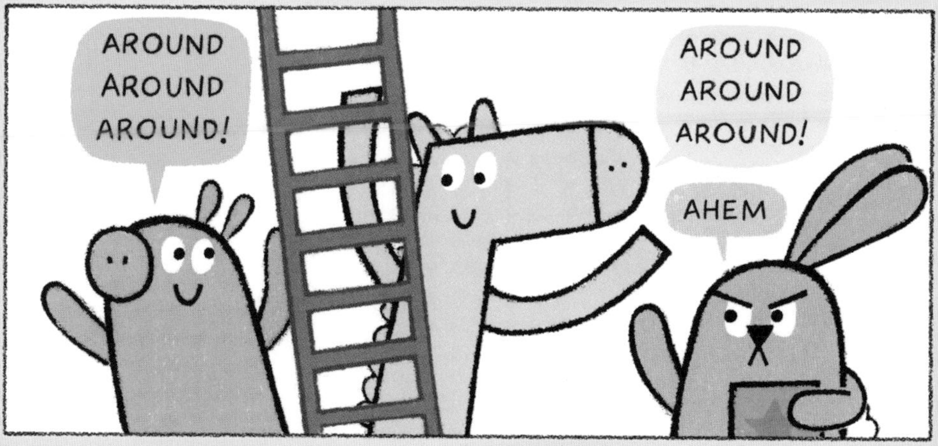
AROUND AROUND AROUND!
AROUND AROUND AROUND!
AHEM
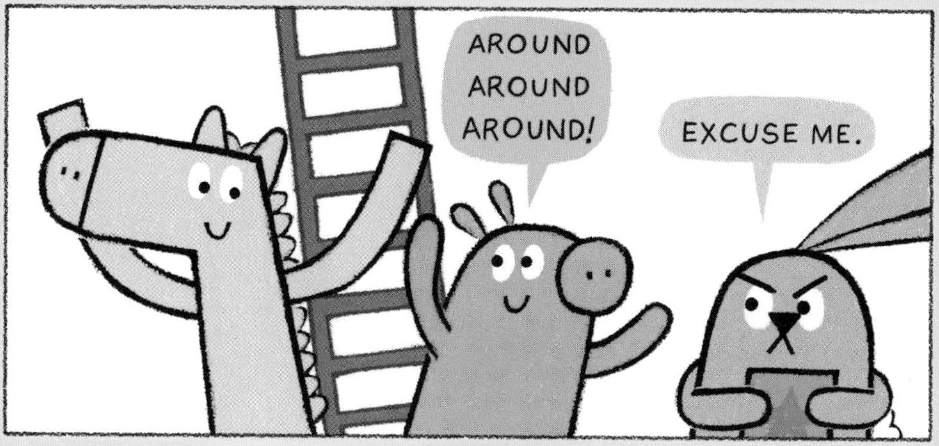
AROUND AROUND AROUND!
EXCUSE ME.
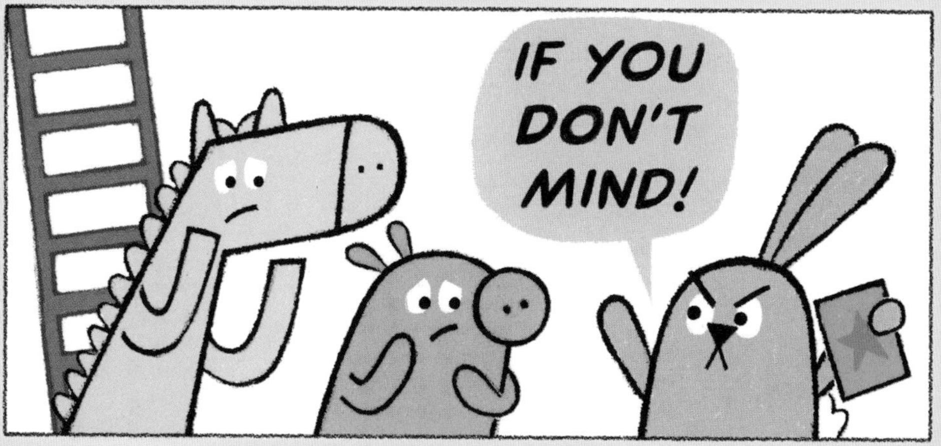
IF YOU DON'T MIND!

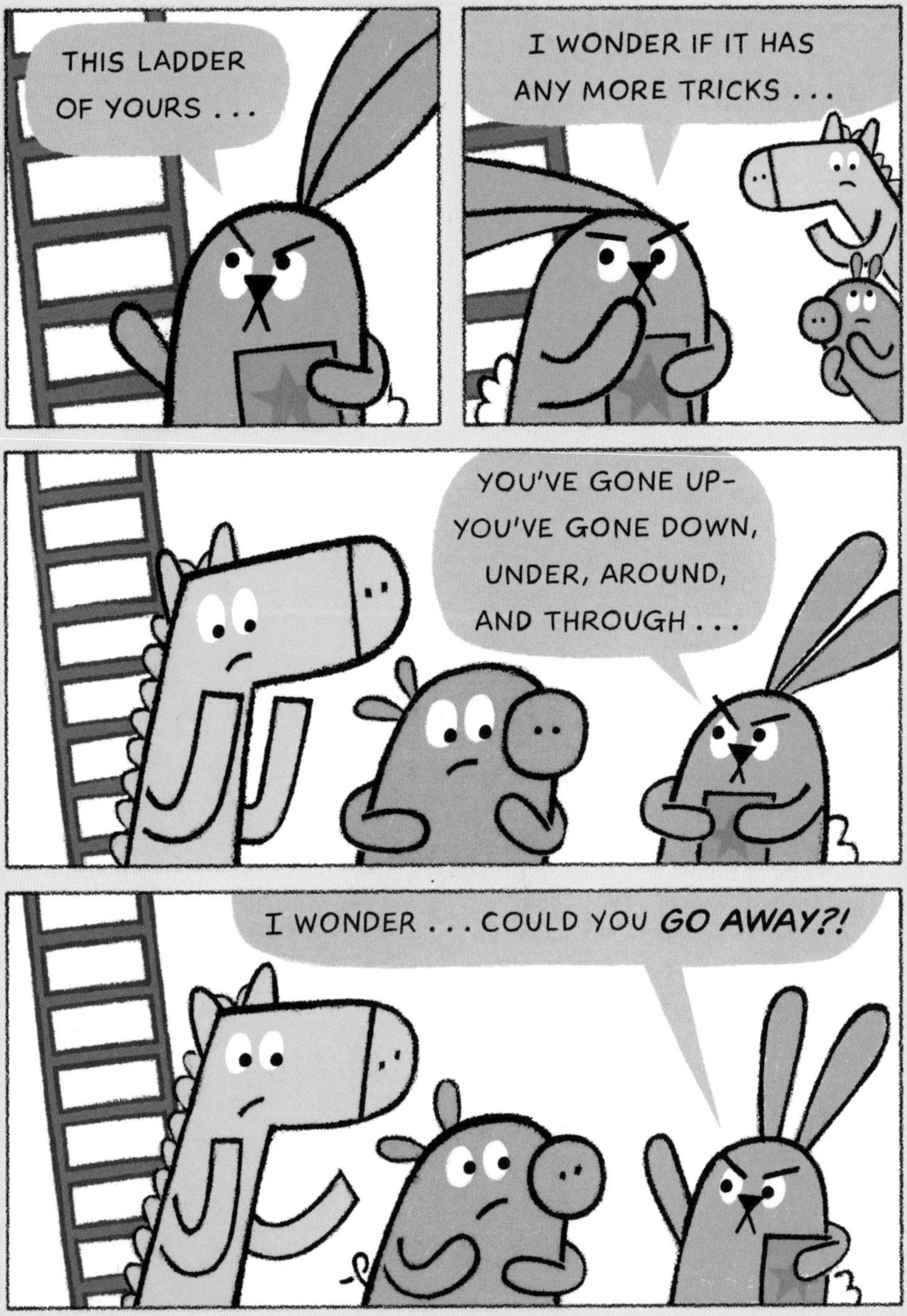
THIS LADDER OF YOURS . . .
I WONDER IF IT HAS ANY MORE TRICKS . . .
YOU'VE GONE UP- YOU'VE GONE DOWN, UNDER, AROUND, AND THROUGH . . .
I WONDER . . . COULD YOU ***GO AWAY?!***

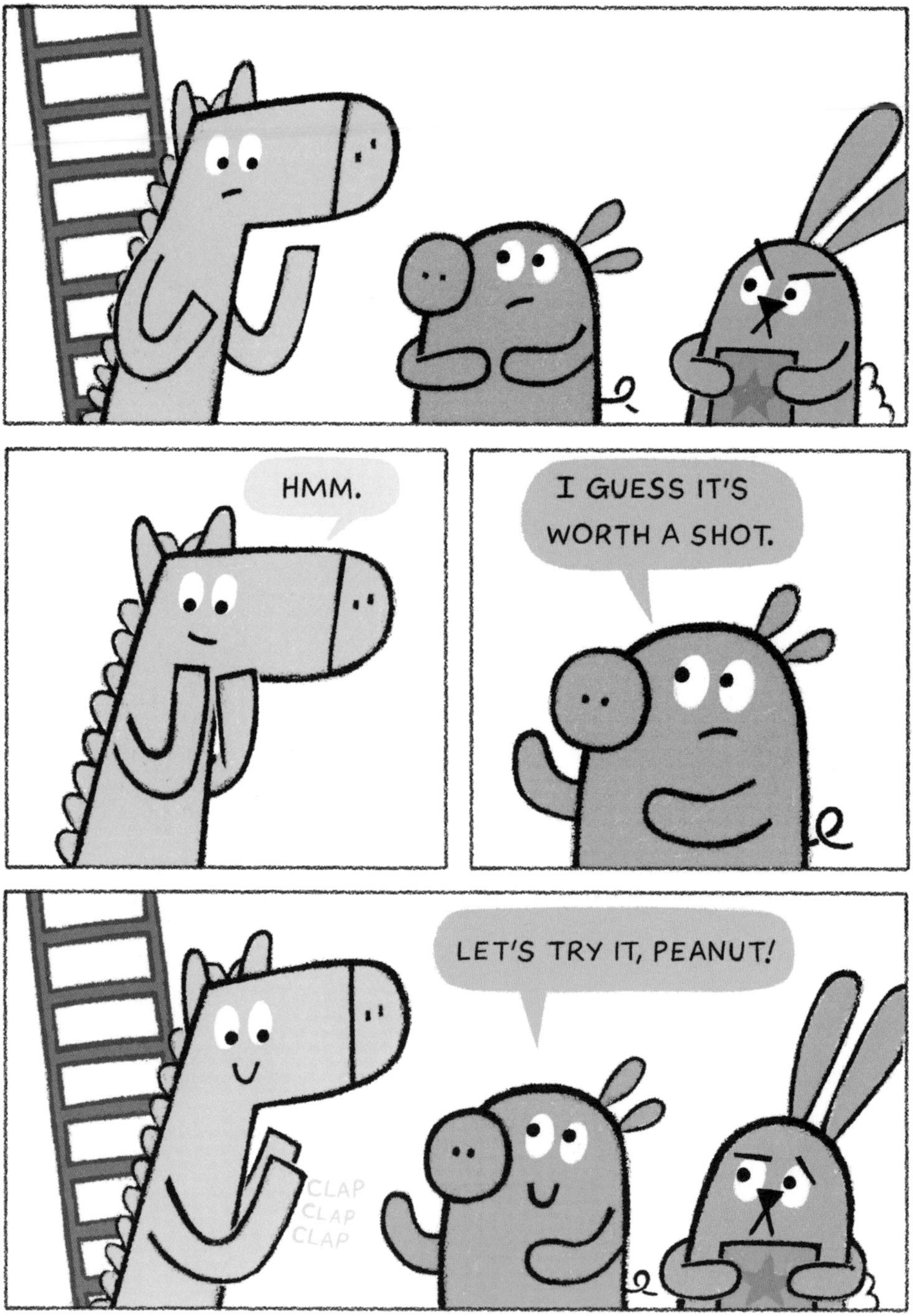
HMM.
I GUESS IT'S WORTH A SHOT.
LET'S TRY IT, PEANUT!
CLAP
CLAP
CLAP

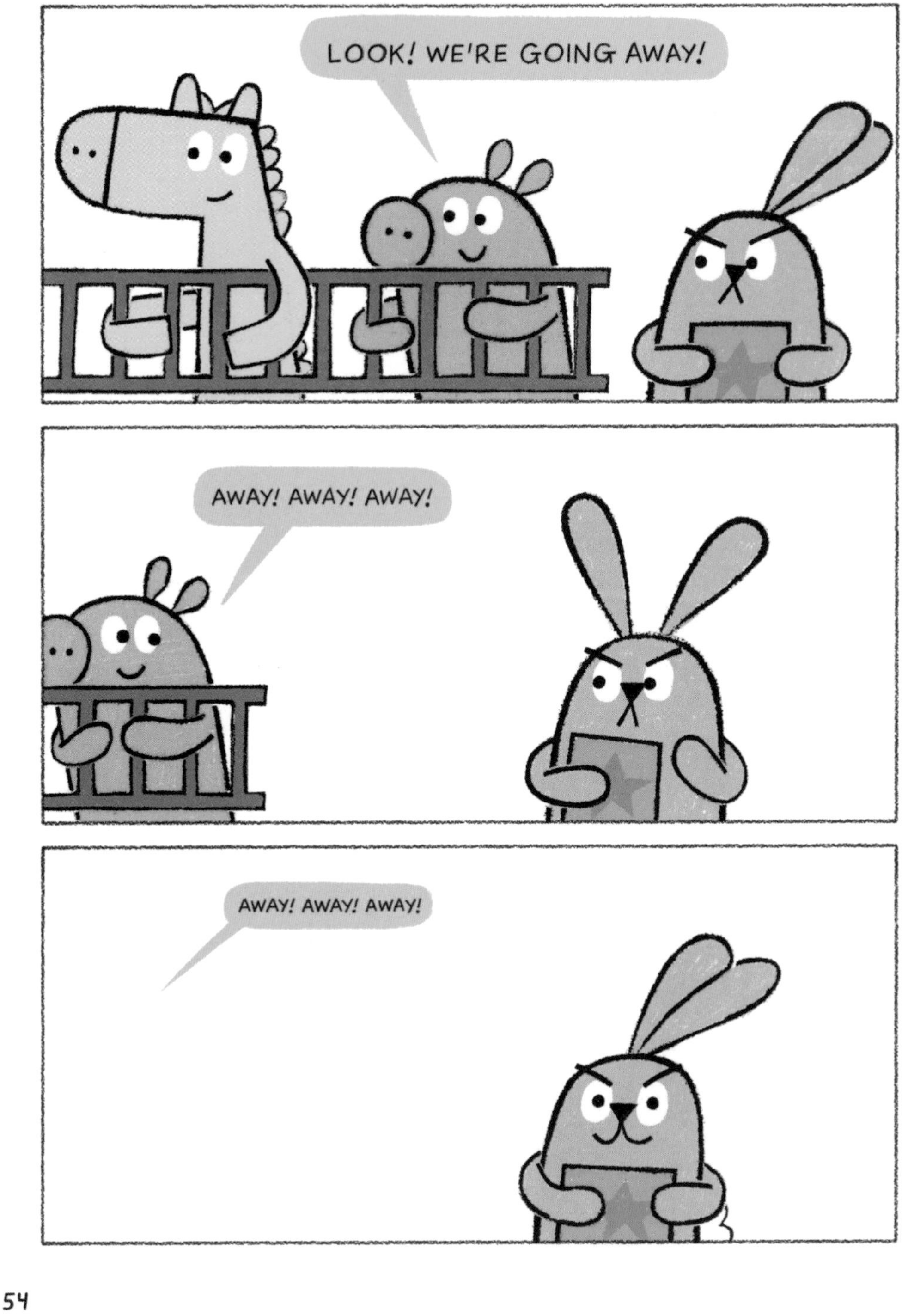
LOOK! WE'RE GOING AWAY!
AWAY! AWAY! AWAY!
AWAY! AWAY! AWAY!

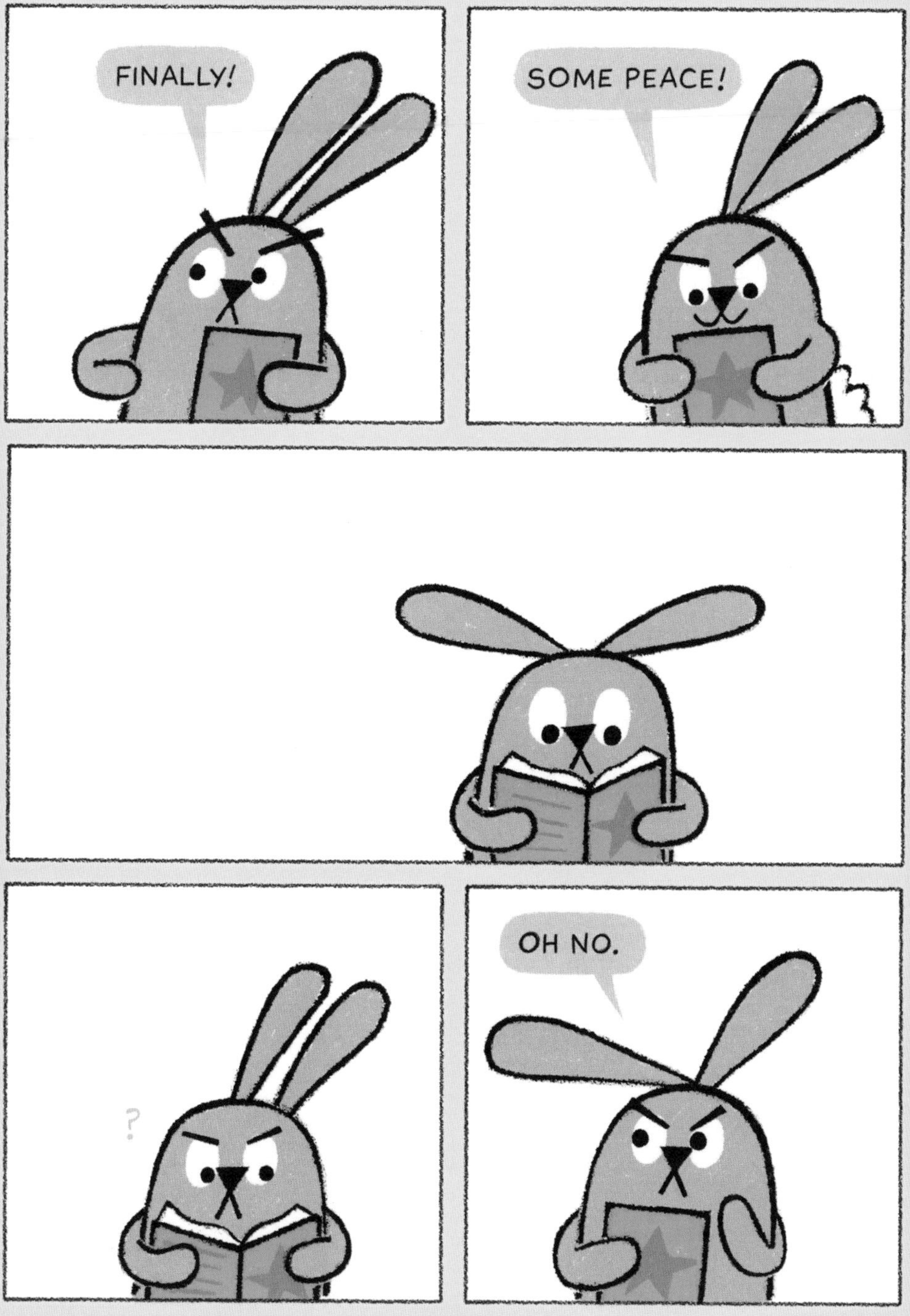
FINALLY!
SOME PEACE!
?
OH NO.

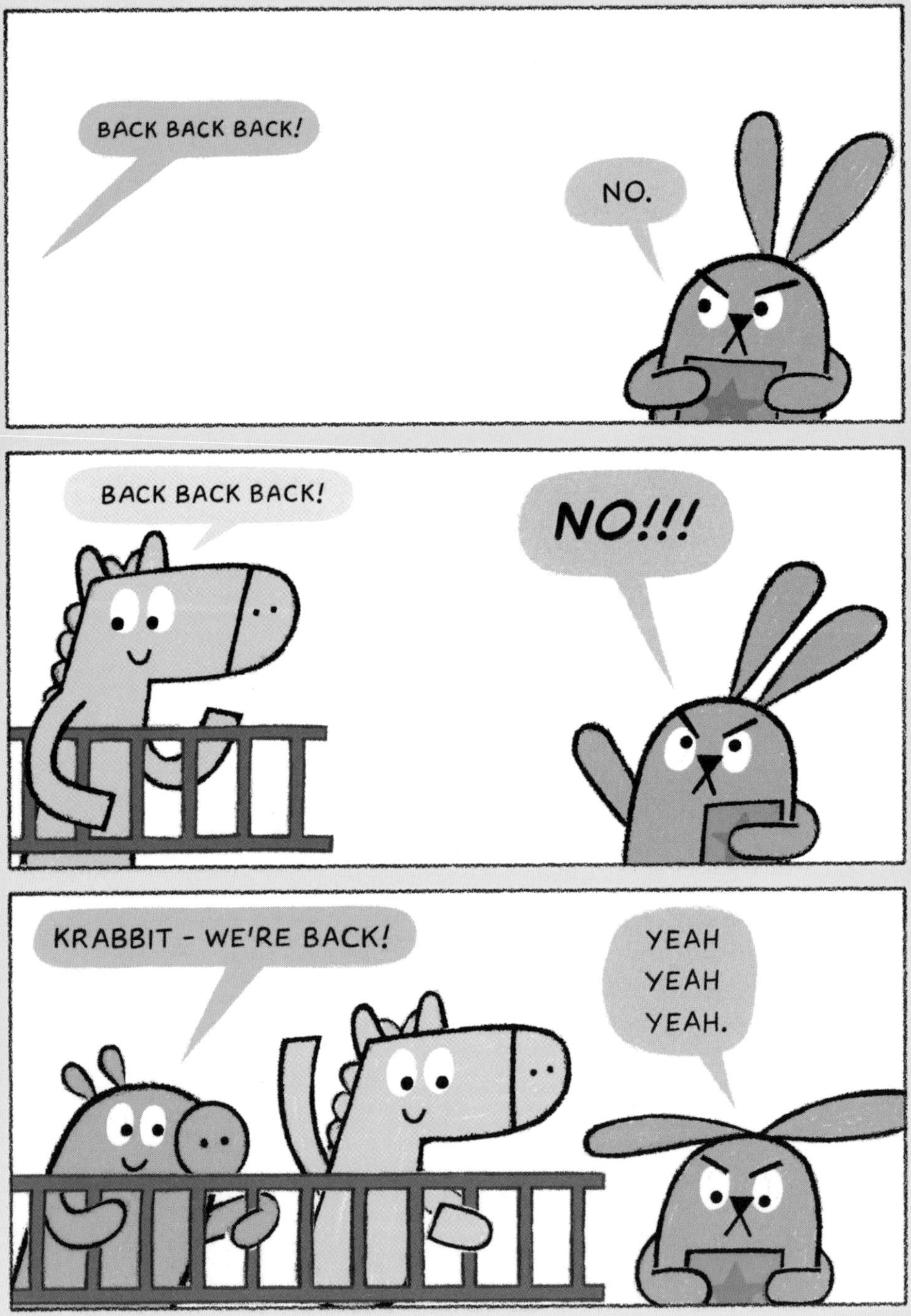
BACK BACK BACK!
NO.
BACK BACK BACK!
NO!!!
KRABBIT - WE'RE BACK!
YEAH
YEAH
YEAH.

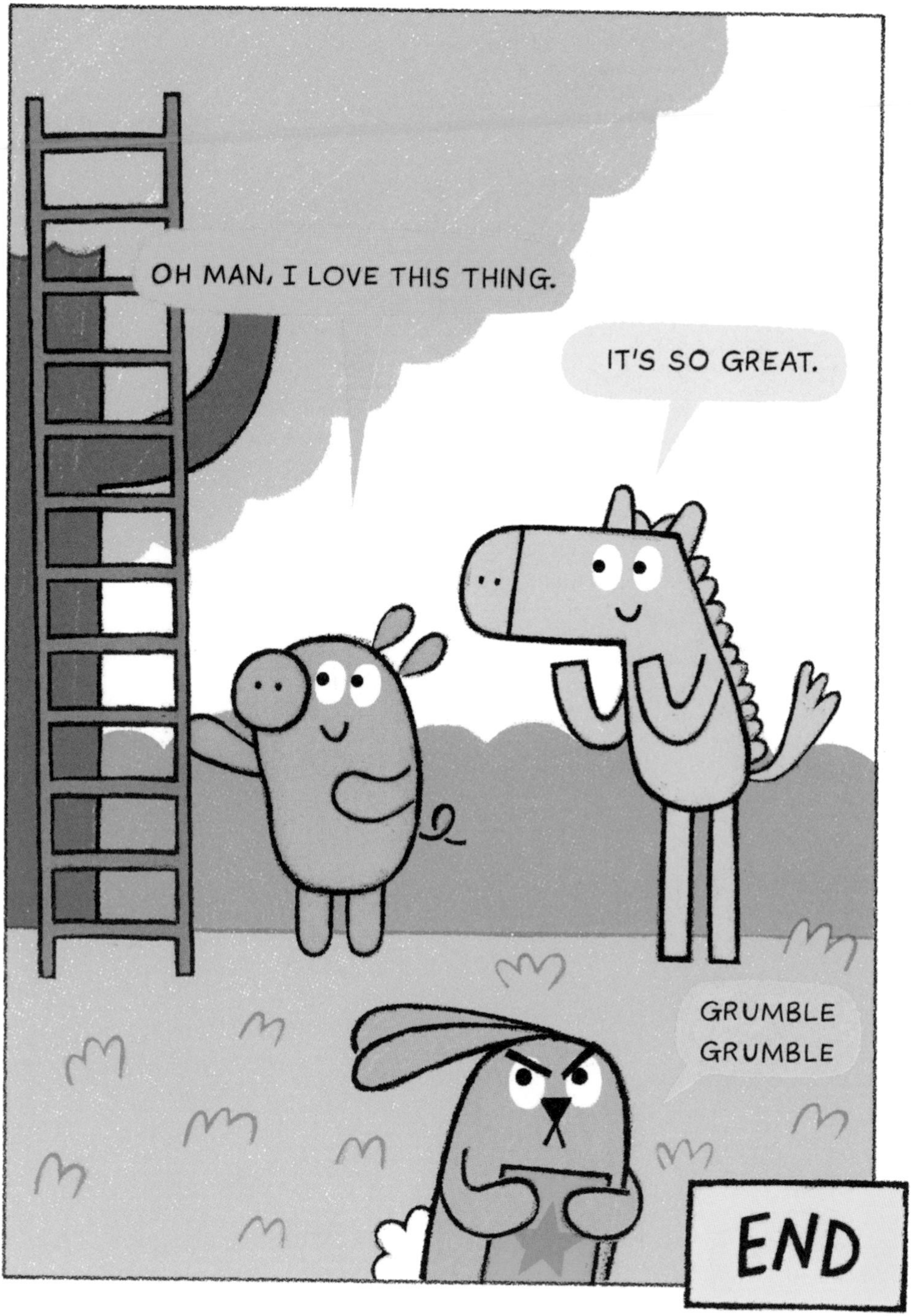
OH MAN, I LOVE THIS THING.
IT'S SO GREAT.
GRUMBLE
GRUMBLE
END

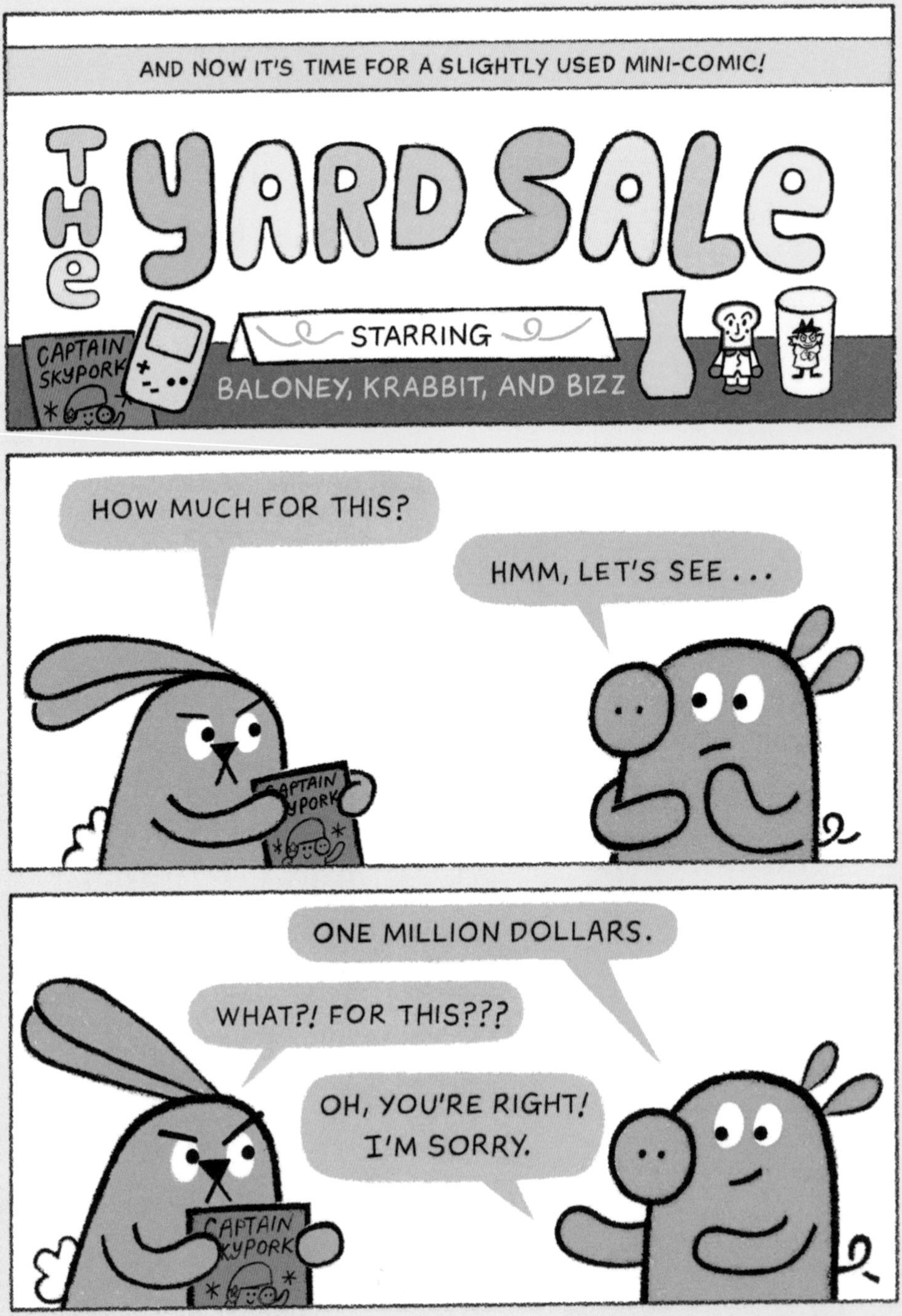
AND NOW IT'S TIME FOR A SLIGHTLY USED MINI-COMIC!
THE YARD SALE
CAPTAIN SKYPORK
STARRING
BALONEY, KRABBIT, AND BIZZ
HOW MUCH FOR THIS?
HMM, LET'S SEE . . .
CAPTAIN SKYPORK
ONE MILLION DOLLARS.
WHAT?! FOR THIS???
OH, YOU'RE RIGHT! I'M SORRY.
CAPTAIN SKYPORK

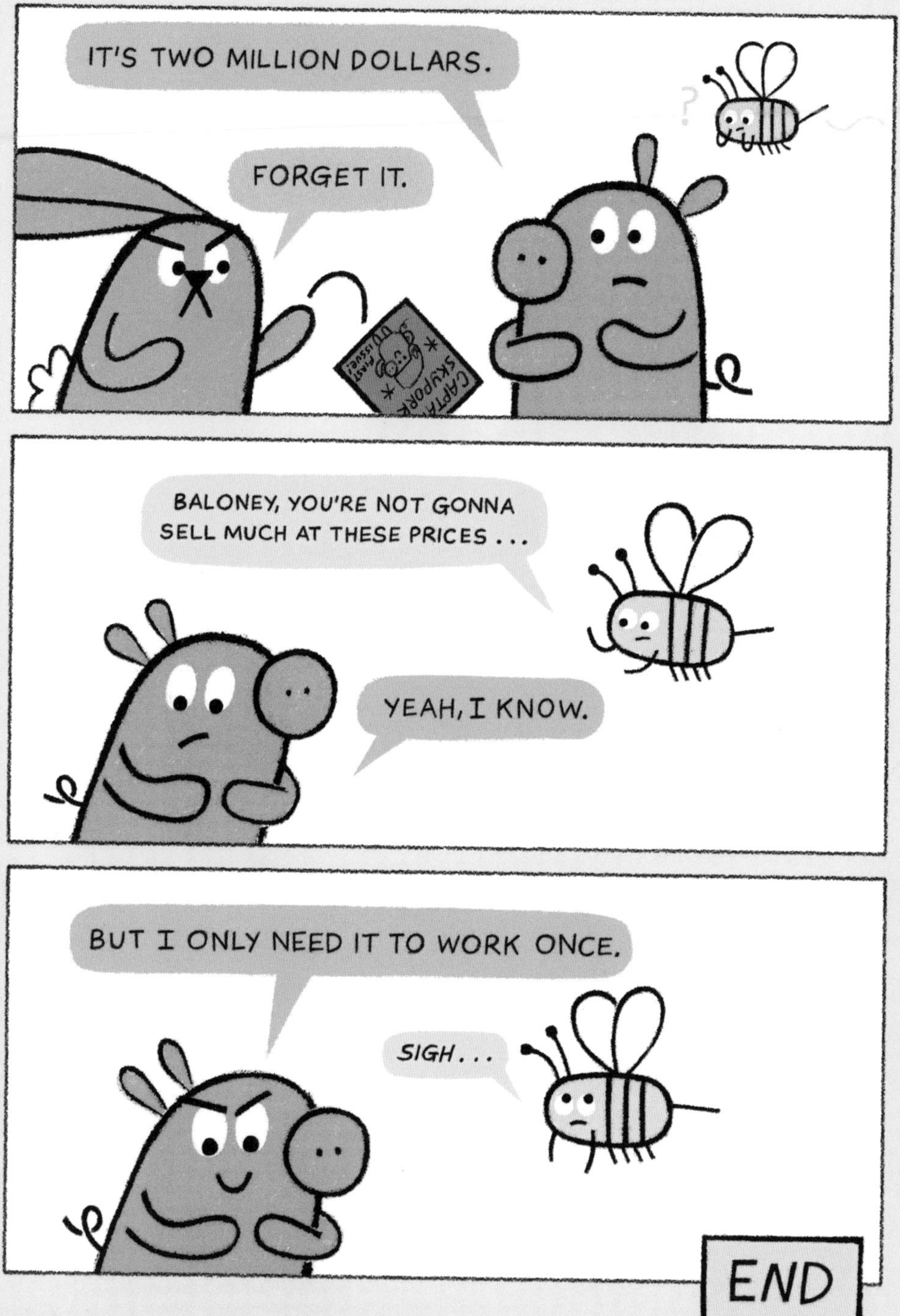
IT'S TWO MILLION DOLLARS.
FORGET IT.
?
BALONEY, YOU'RE NOT GONNA SELL MUCH AT THESE PRICES . . .
YEAH, I KNOW.
BUT I ONLY NEED IT TO WORK ONCE.
SIGH . . .
END

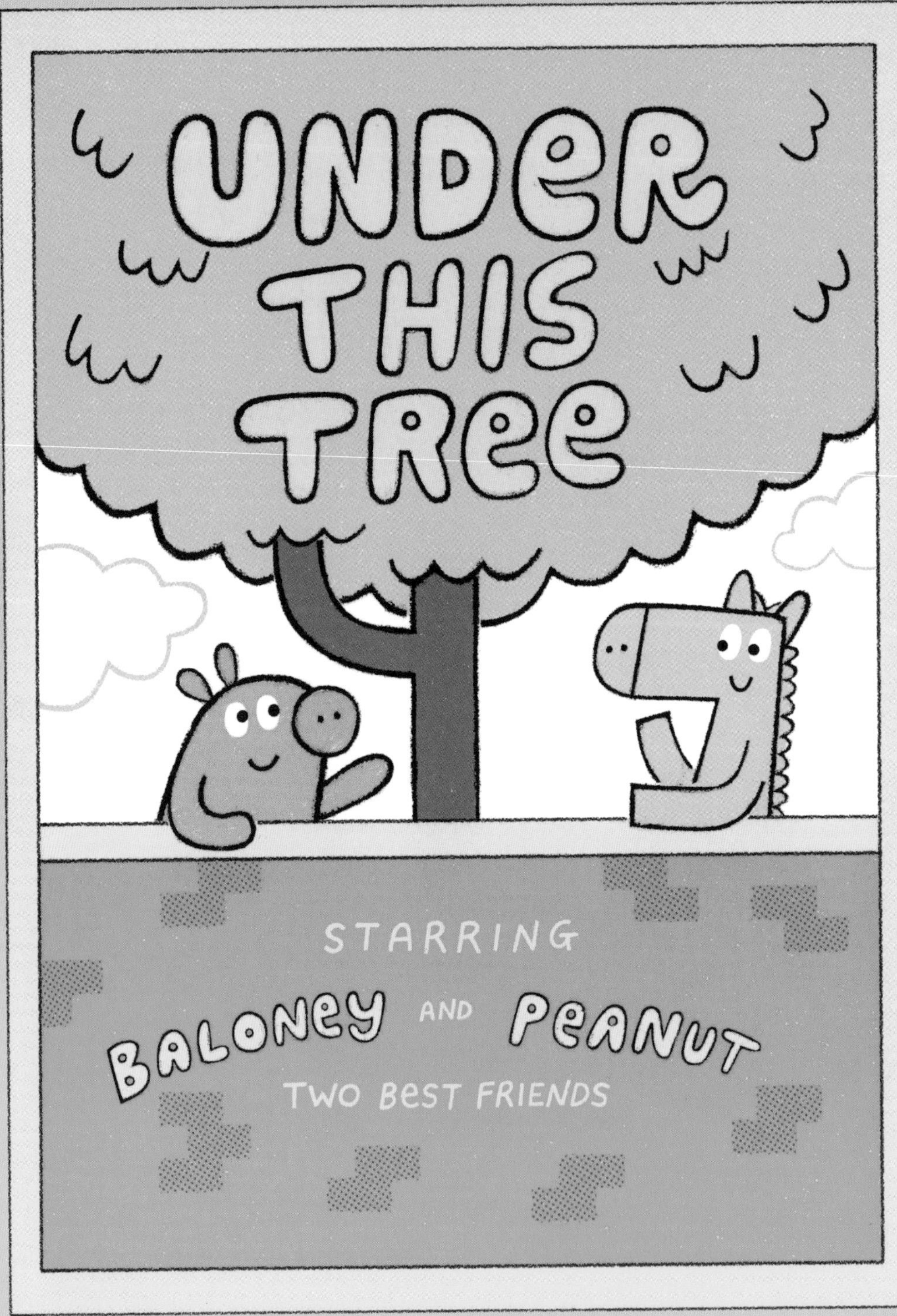
UNDER THIS TREE
STARRING
BALONEY AND PEANUT
TWO BEST FRIENDS

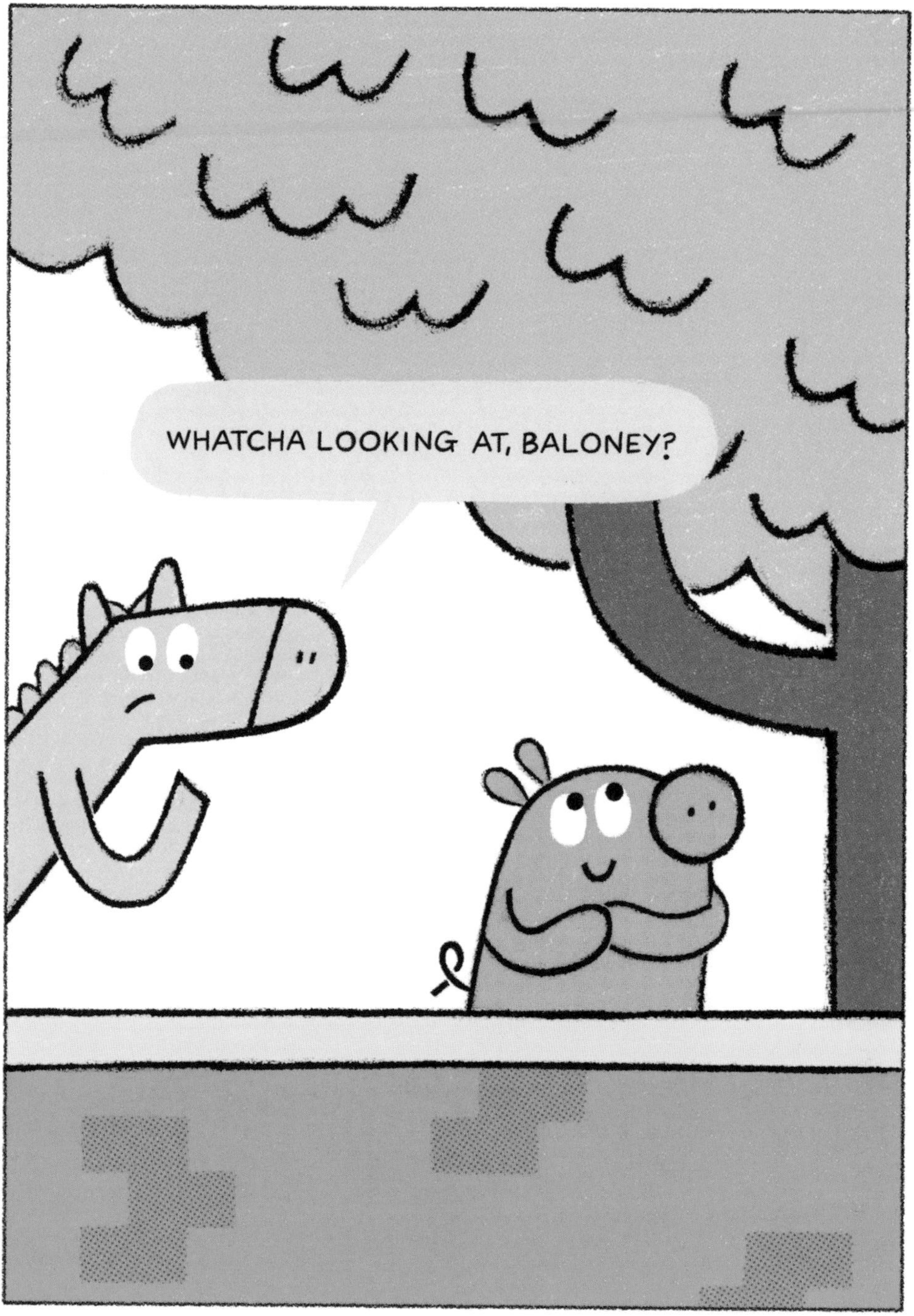
WHATCHA LOOKING AT, BALONEY?

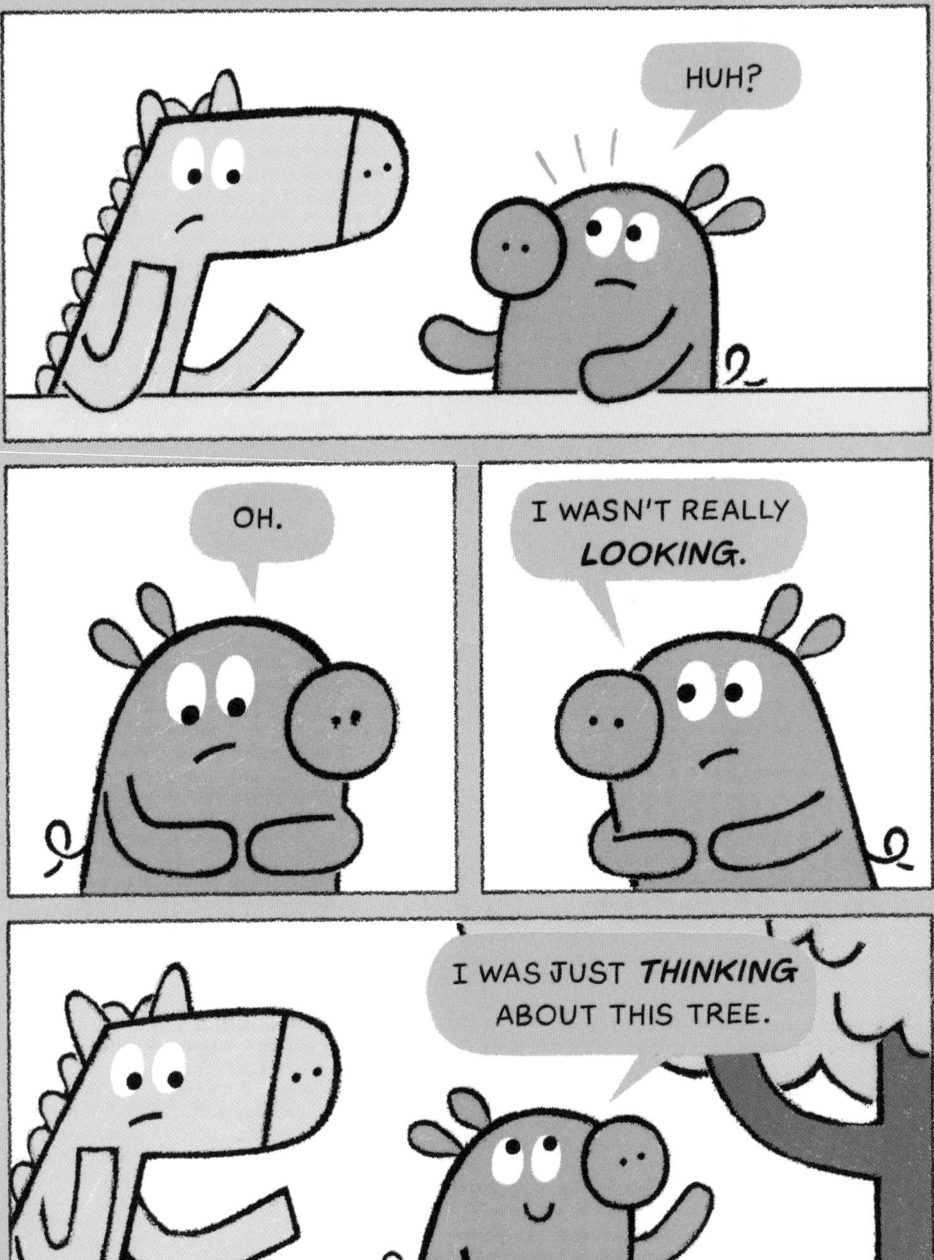
HUH?
OH.
I WASN'T REALLY LOOKING.
I WAS JUST THINKING ABOUT THIS TREE.

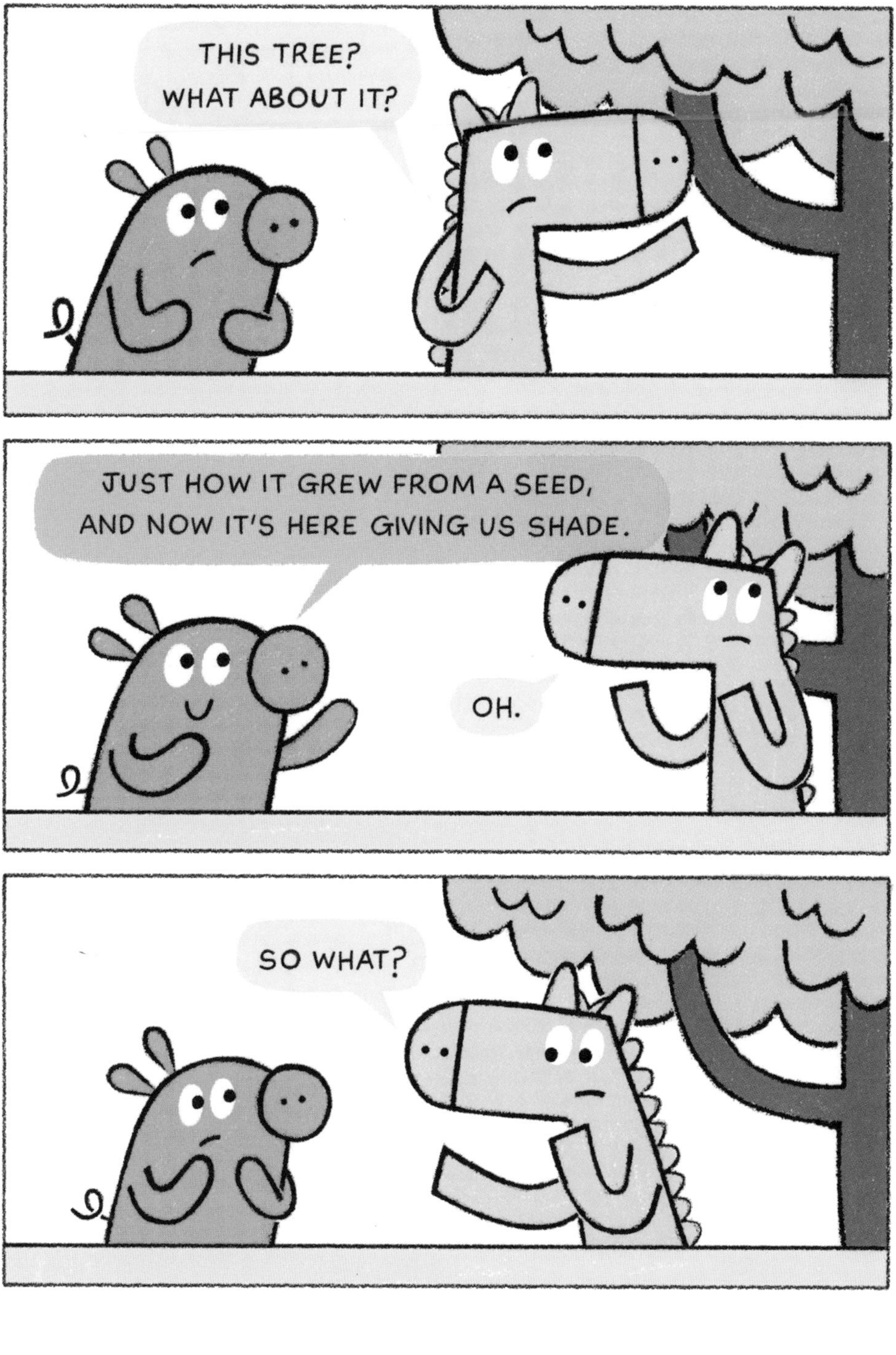
THIS TREE? WHAT ABOUT IT?
JUST HOW IT GREW FROM A SEED, AND NOW IT'S HERE GIVING US SHADE.
OH.
SO WHAT?

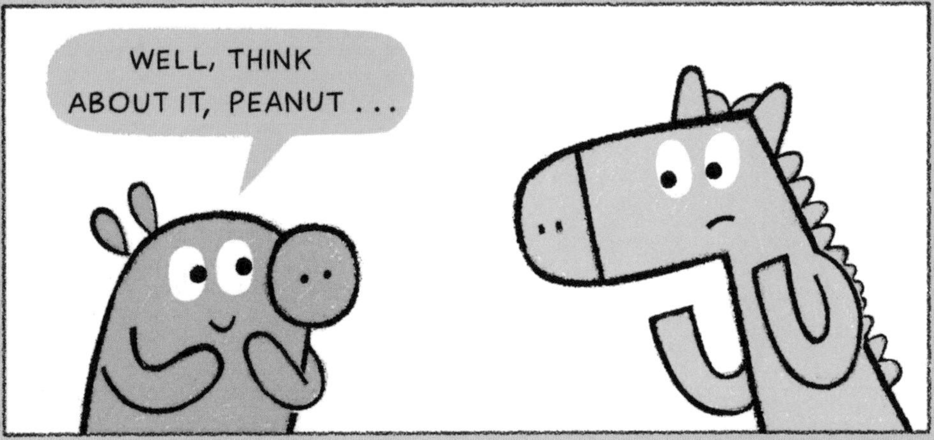
WELL, THINK ABOUT IT, PEANUT . . .

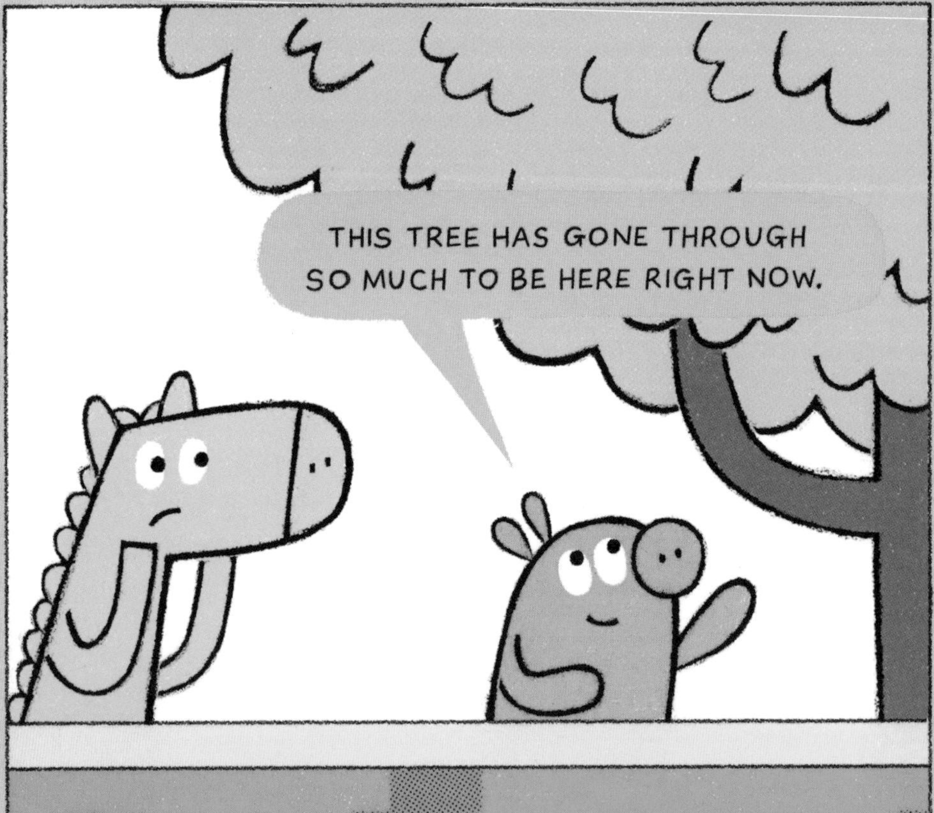
THIS TREE HAS GONE THROUGH SO MUCH TO BE HERE RIGHT NOW.

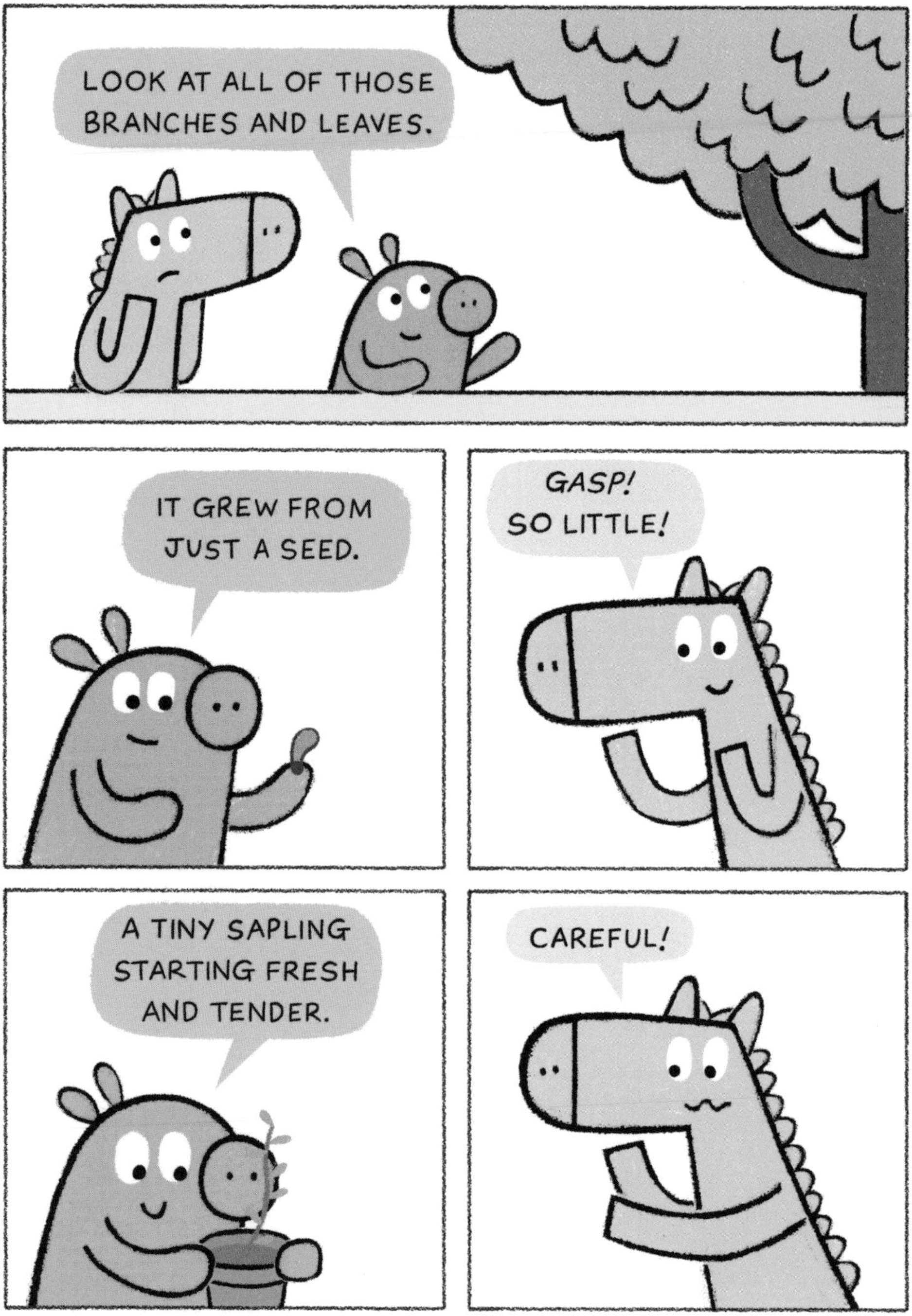
LOOK AT ALL OF THOSE BRANCHES AND LEAVES.
IT GREW FROM JUST A SEED.
GASP! SO LITTLE!
A TINY SAPLING STARTING FRESH AND TENDER.
CAREFUL!

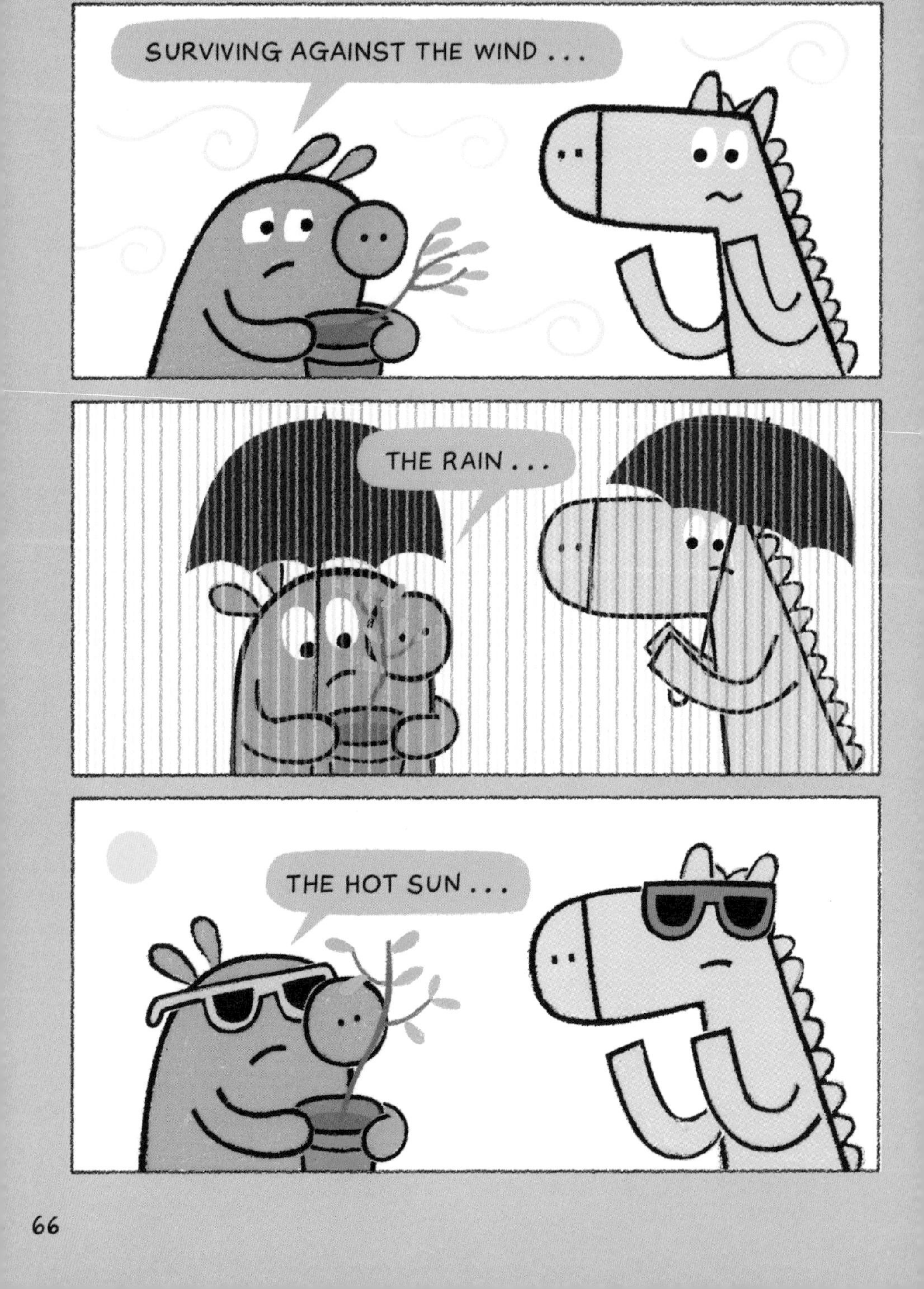
SURVIVING AGAINST THE WIND . . .
THE RAIN . . .
THE HOT SUN . . .

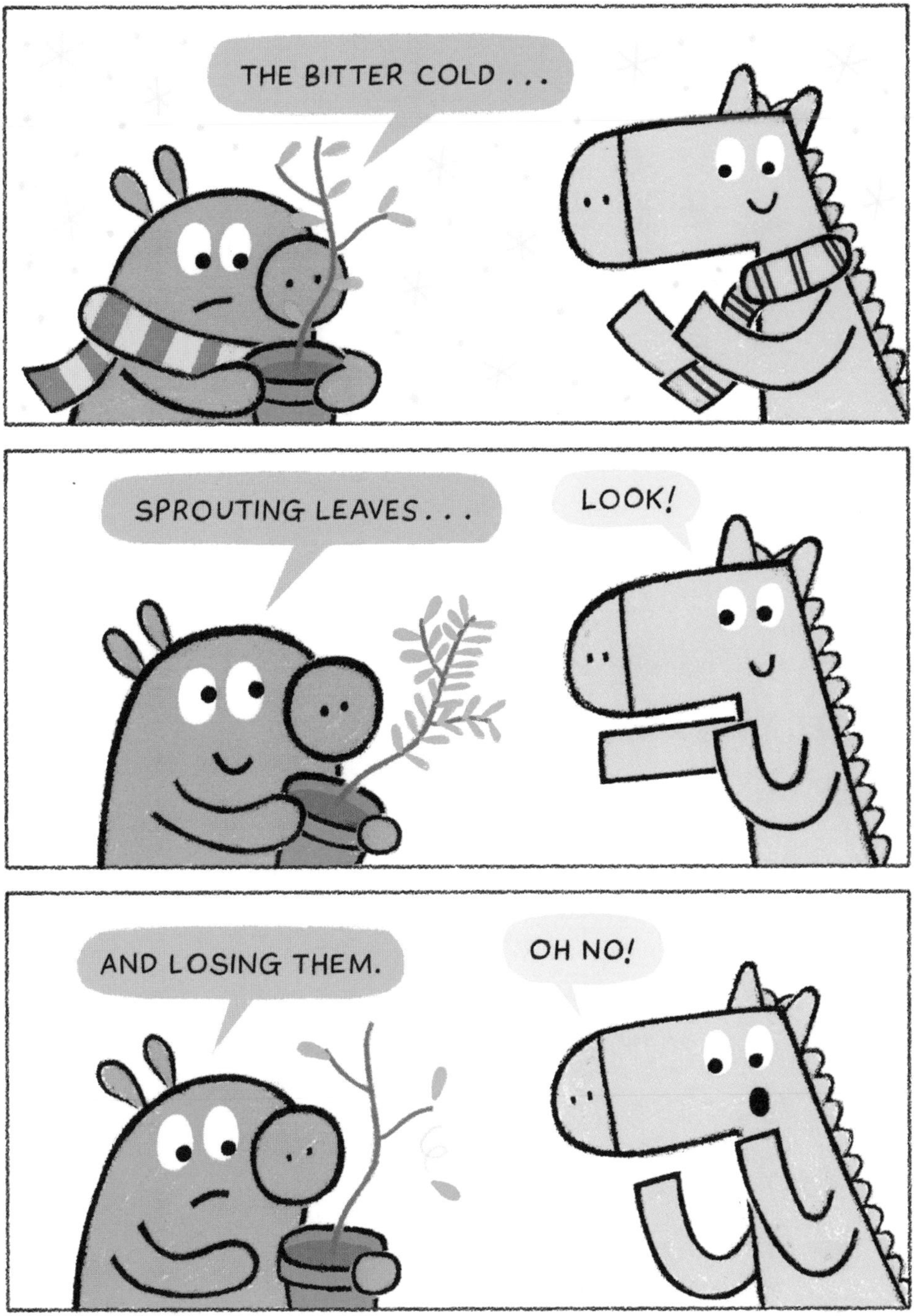
THE BITTER COLD . . .
SPROUTING LEAVES . . .
LOOK!
AND LOSING THEM.
OH NO!

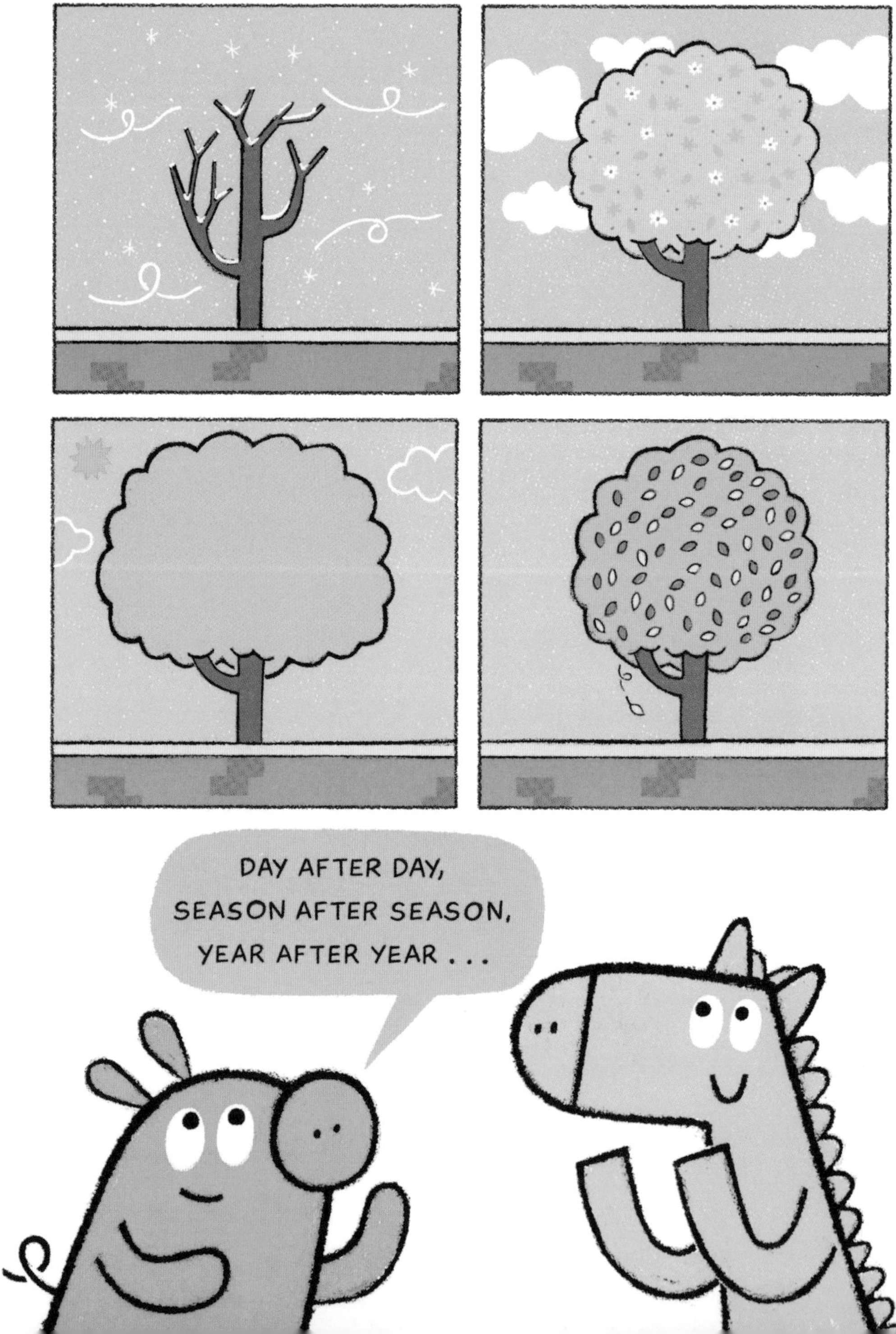
DAY AFTER DAY,
SEASON AFTER SEASON,
YEAR AFTER YEAR . . .

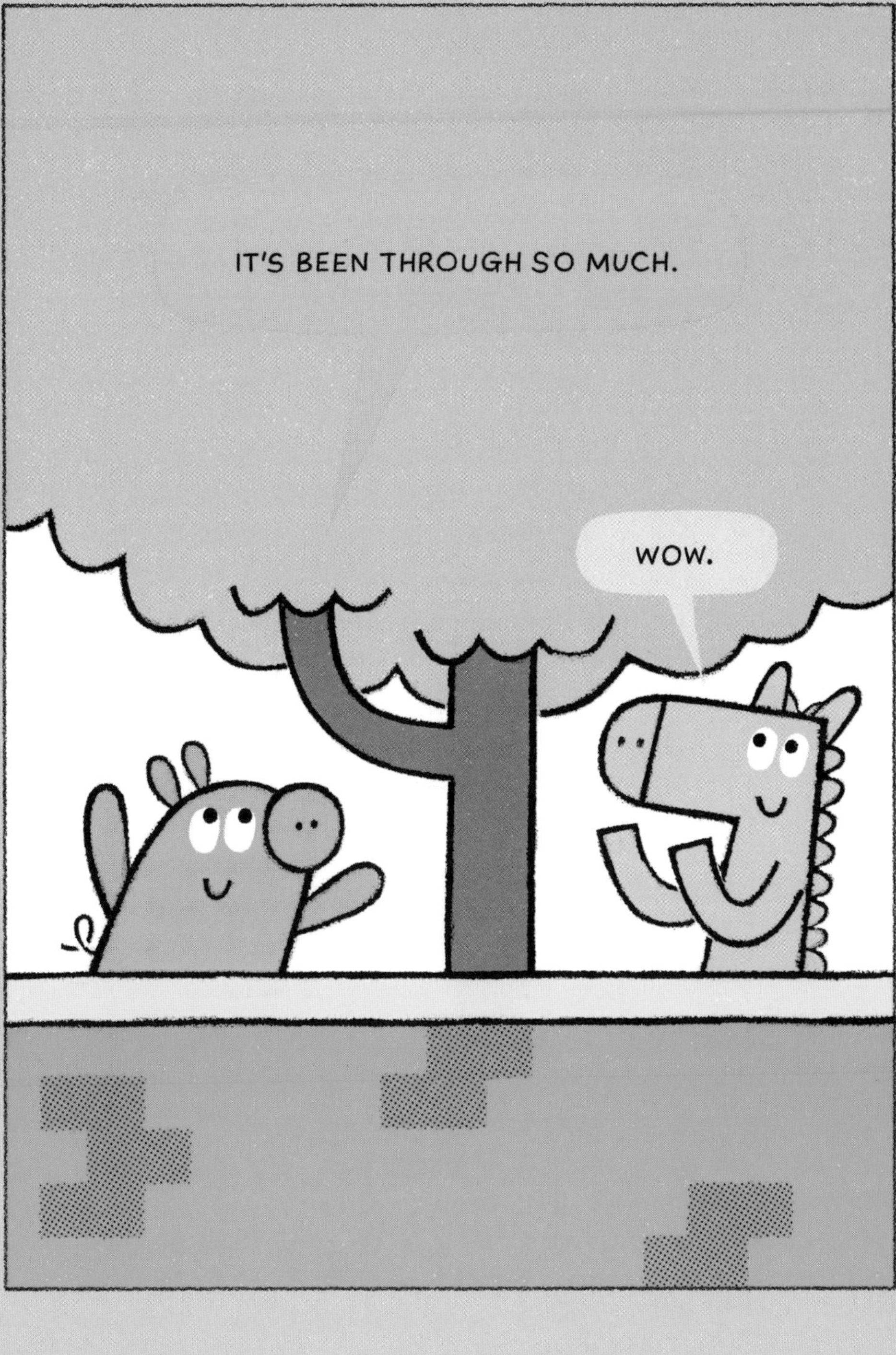
IT'S BEEN THROUGH SO MUCH.
WOW.

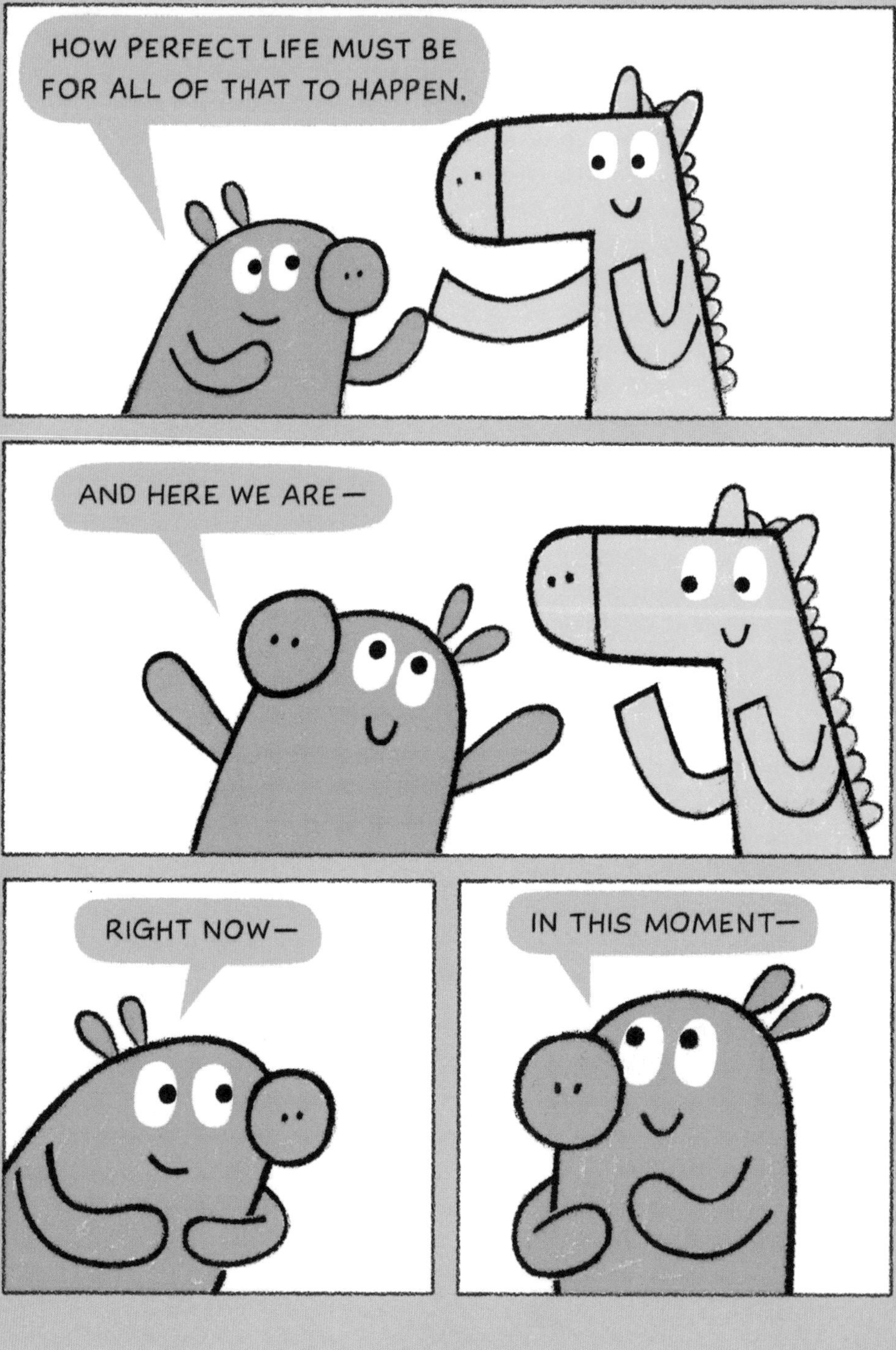
HOW PERFECT LIFE MUST BE FOR ALL OF THAT TO HAPPEN.
AND HERE WE ARE—
RIGHT NOW—
IN THIS MOMENT—

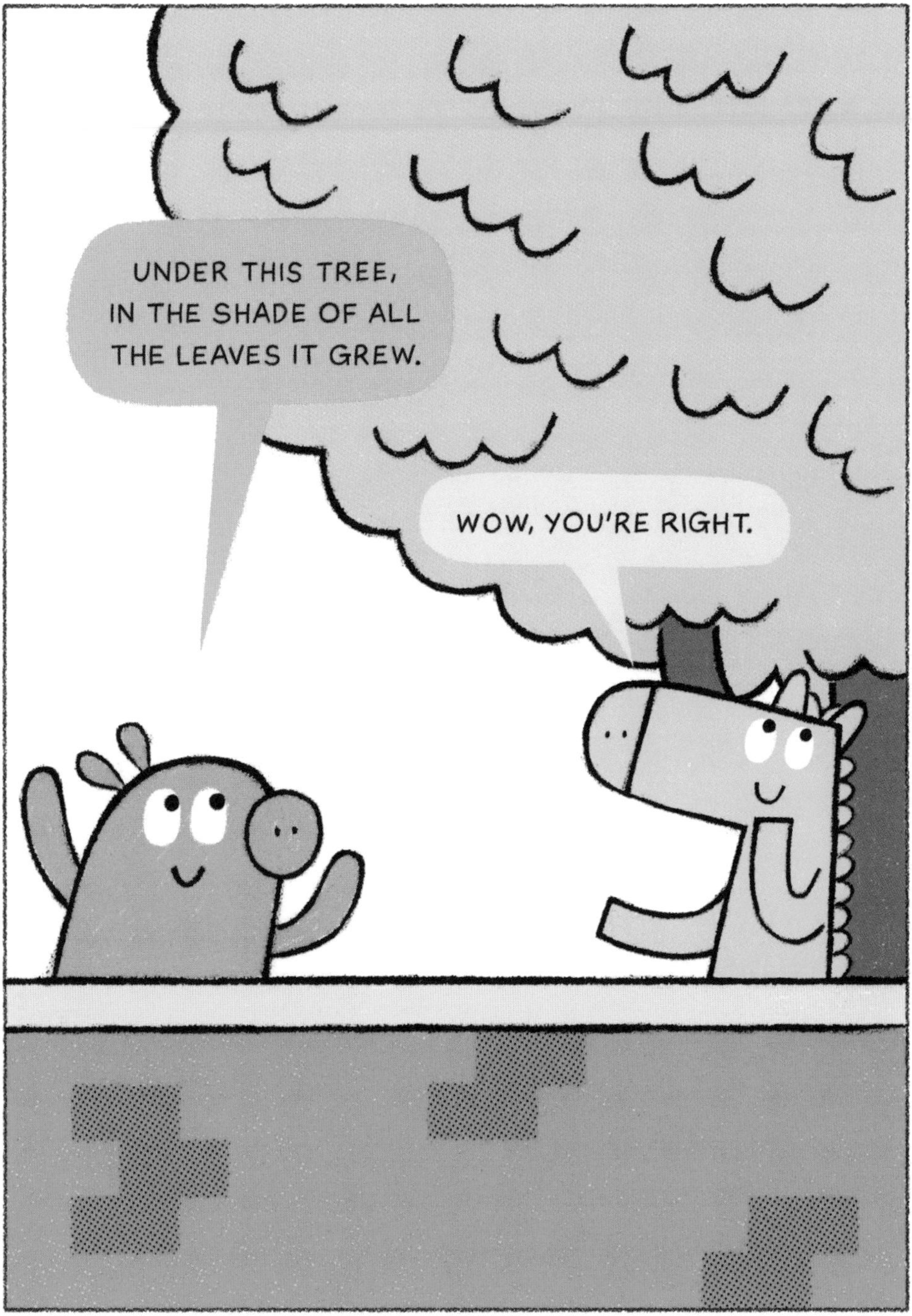
UNDER THIS TREE, IN THE SHADE OF ALL THE LEAVES IT GREW.
WOW, YOU'RE RIGHT.

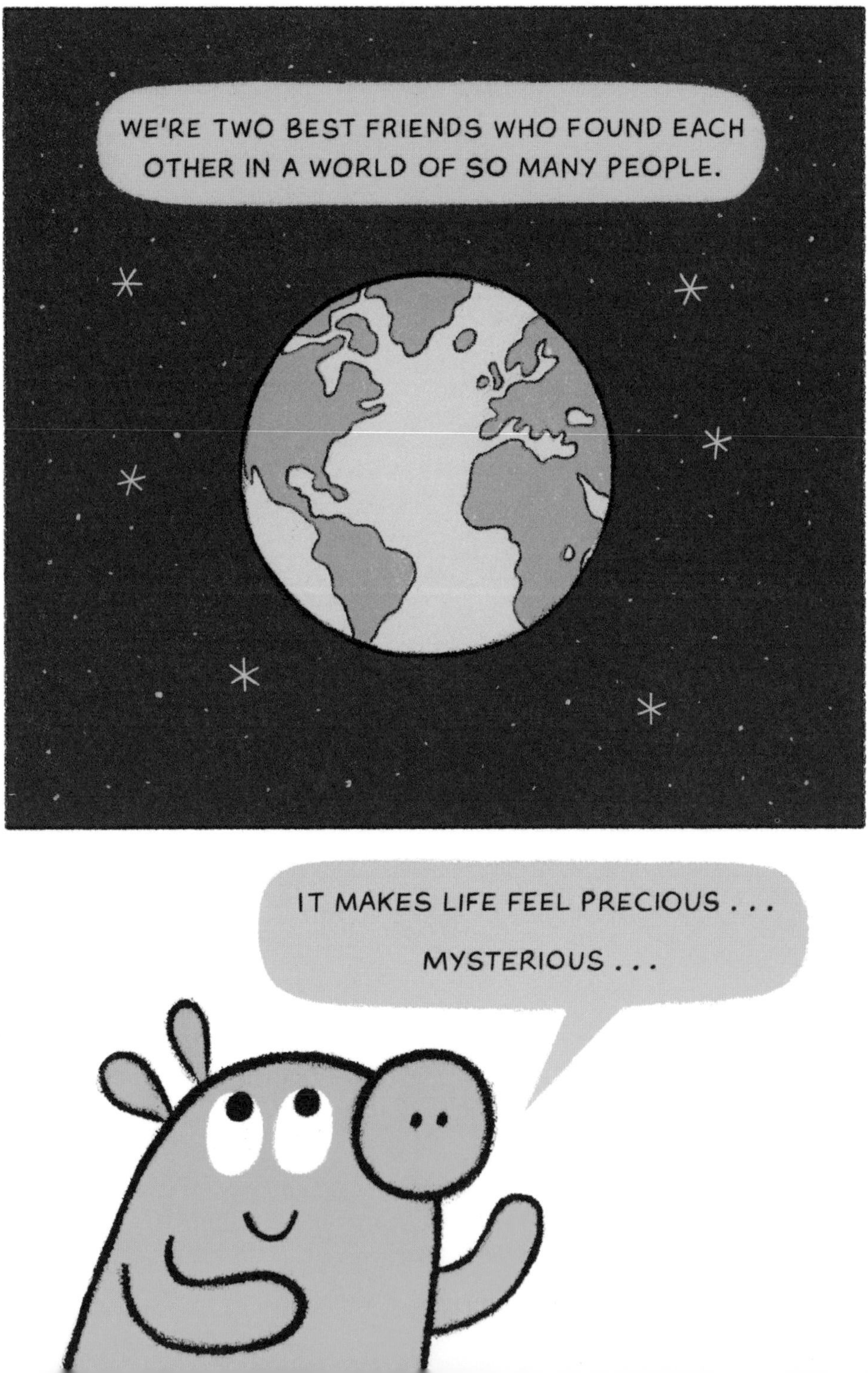
WE'RE TWO BEST FRIENDS WHO FOUND EACH OTHER IN A WORLD OF SO MANY PEOPLE.
IT MAKES LIFE FEEL PRECIOUS . . .
MYSTERIOUS . . .

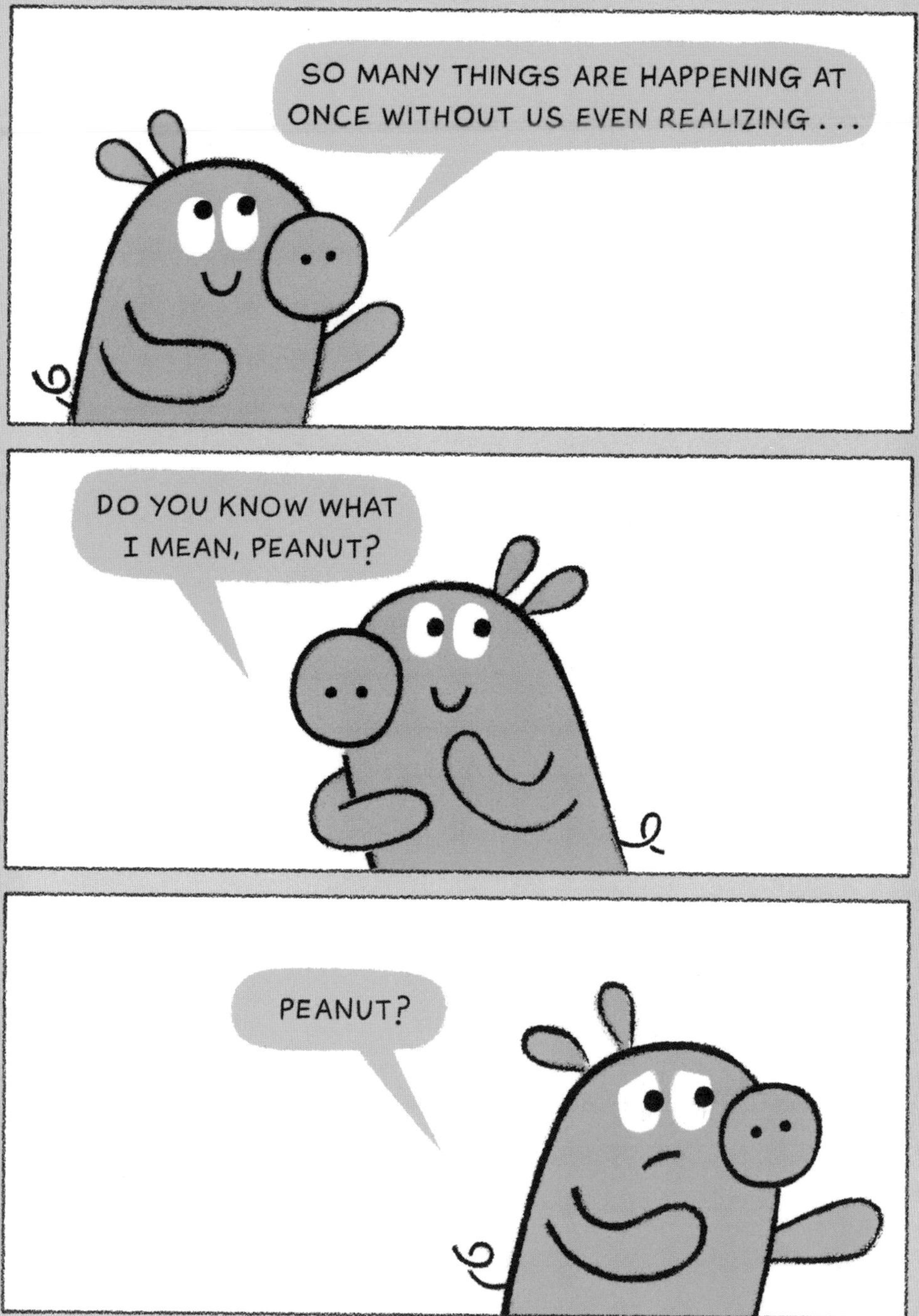
SO MANY THINGS ARE HAPPENING AT ONCE WITHOUT US EVEN REALIZING . . .
DO YOU KNOW WHAT I MEAN, PEANUT?
PEANUT?

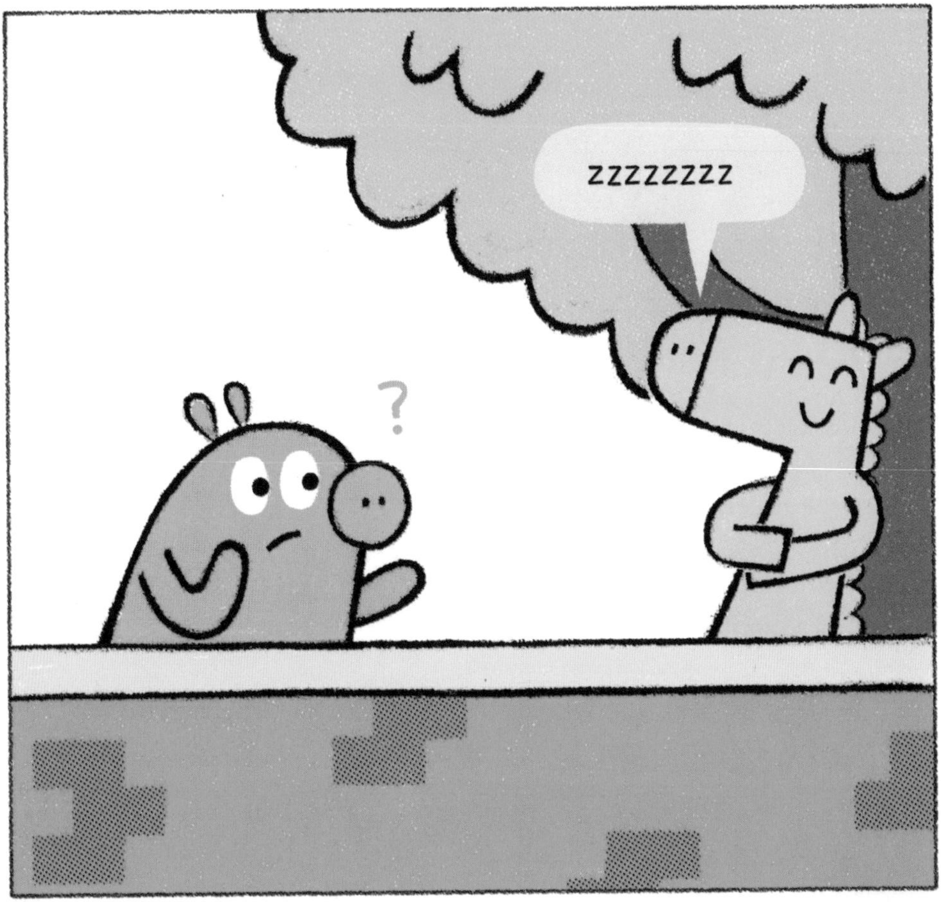
ZZZZZZZZ
?

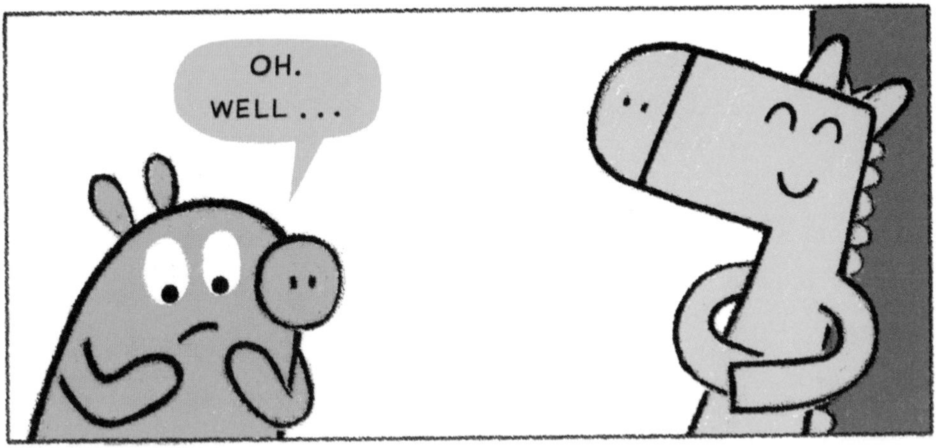
OH.
WELL . . .

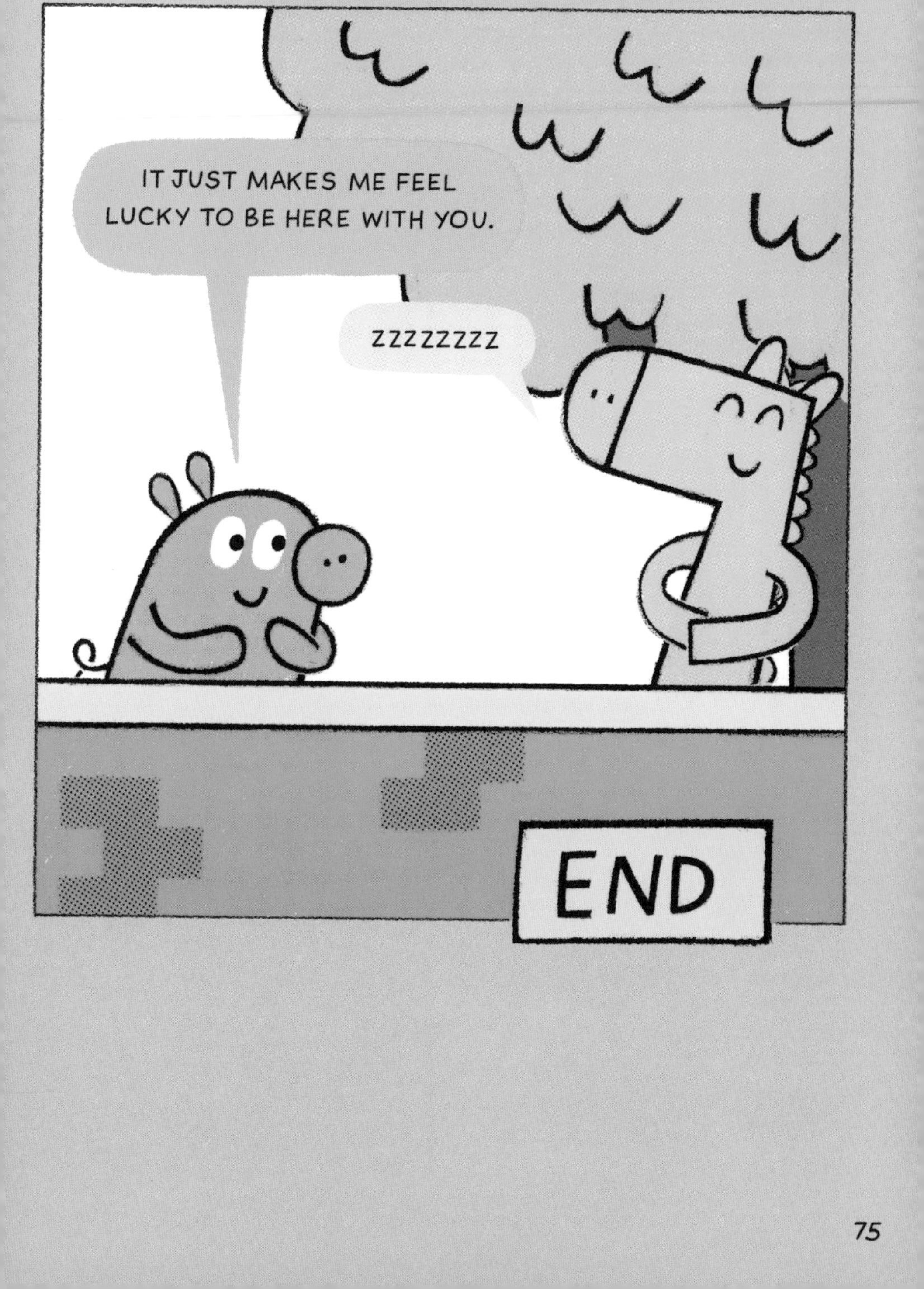
IT JUST MAKES ME FEEL LUCKY TO BE HERE WITH YOU.
ZZZZZZZZ
END

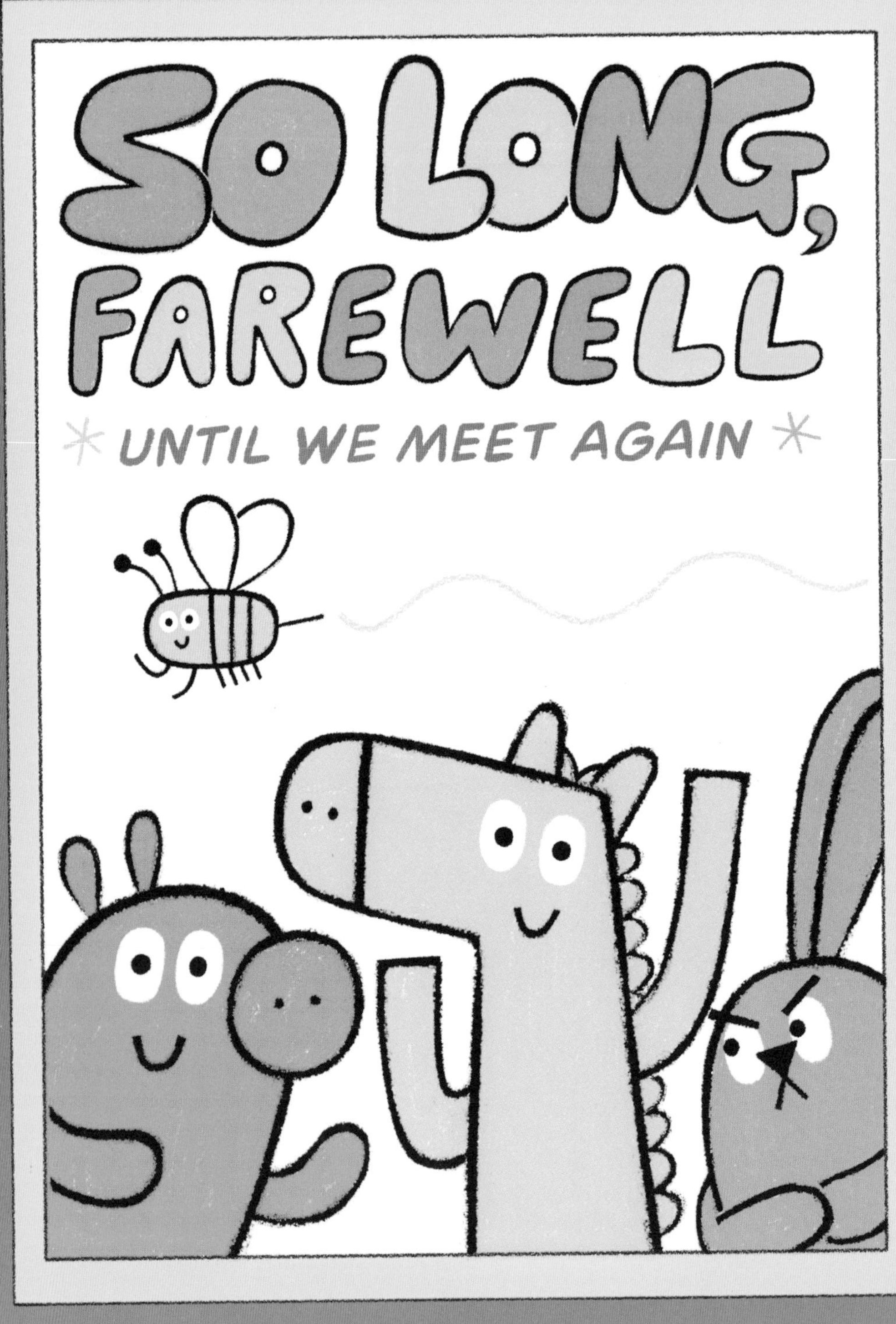
SO LONG,
FAREWELL
UNTIL WE MEET AGAIN

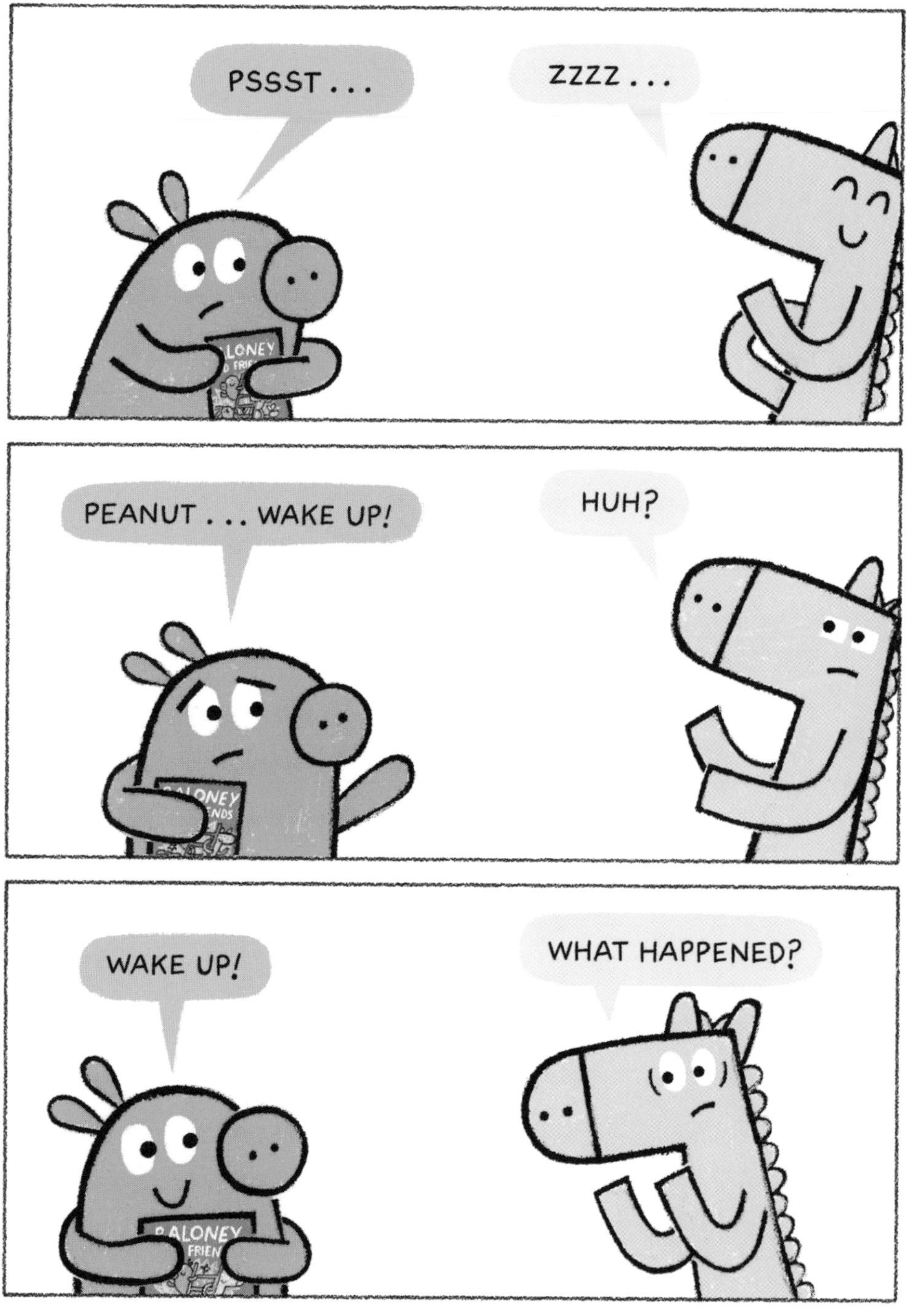
PSSST . . .
ZZZZ . . .
PEANUT . . . WAKE UP!
HUH?
WAKE UP!
WHAT HAPPENED?

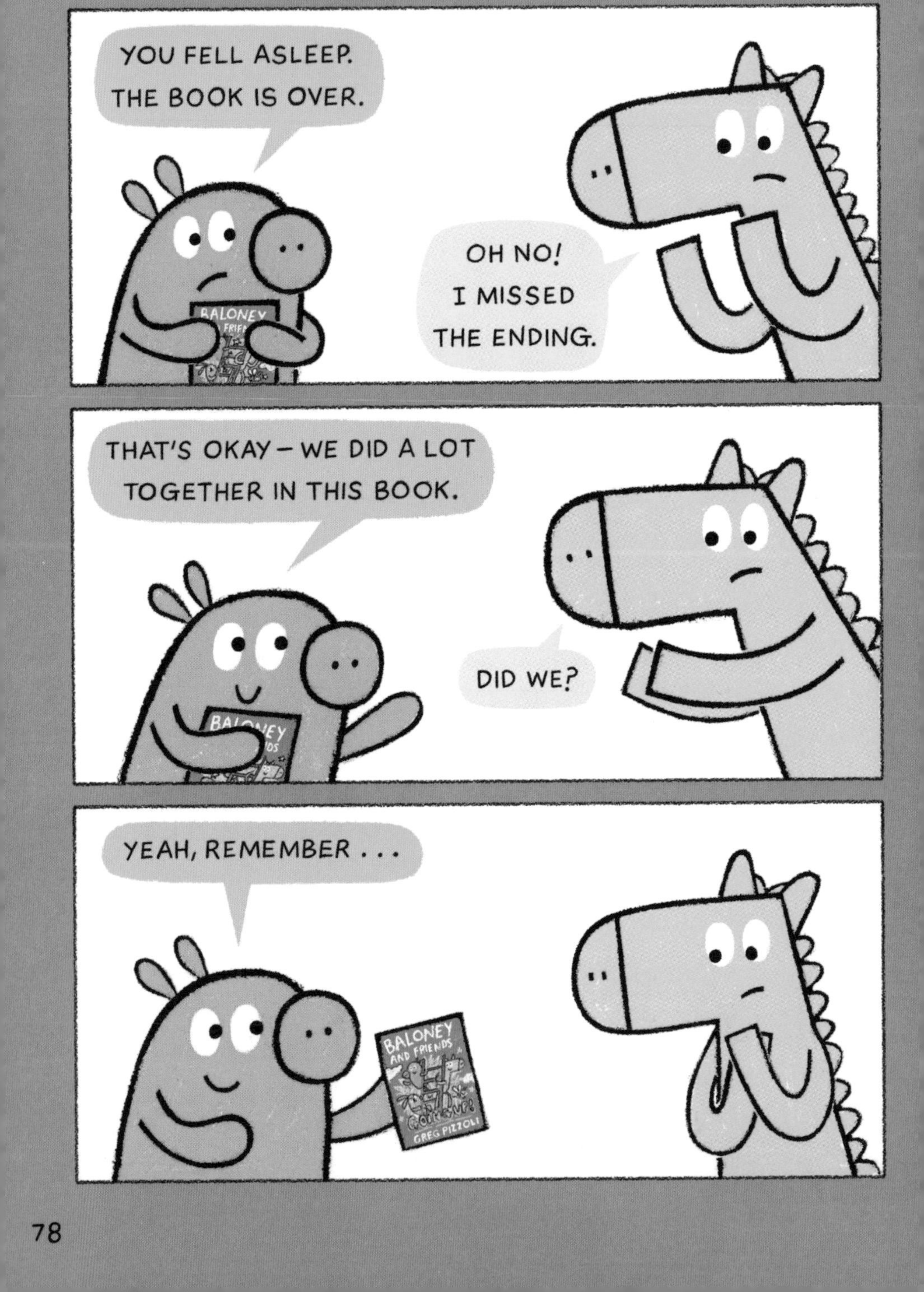
YOU FELL ASLEEP. THE BOOK IS OVER.
OH NO! I MISSED THE ENDING.
THAT'S OKAY – WE DID A LOT TOGETHER IN THIS BOOK.
DID WE?
YEAH, REMEMBER . . .
BALONEY AND FRIENDS
GREG PIZZOLI

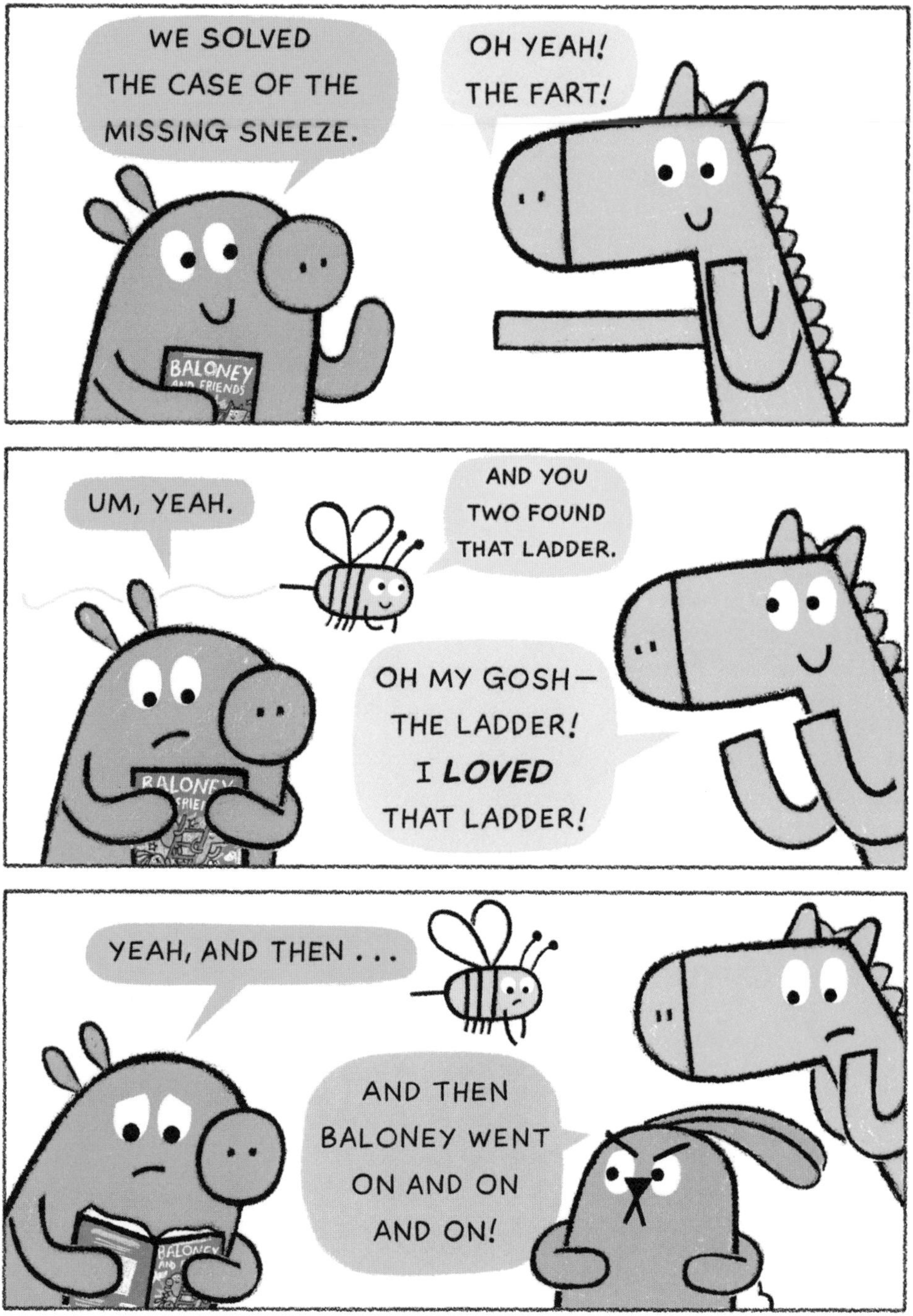
WE SOLVED THE CASE OF THE MISSING SNEEZE.
OH YEAH! THE FART!
BALONEY AND FRIENDS
UM, YEAH.
AND YOU TWO FOUND THAT LADDER.
OH MY GOSH— THE LADDER! I ***LOVED*** THAT LADDER!
YEAH, AND THEN . . .
AND THEN BALONEY WENT ON AND ON AND ON!

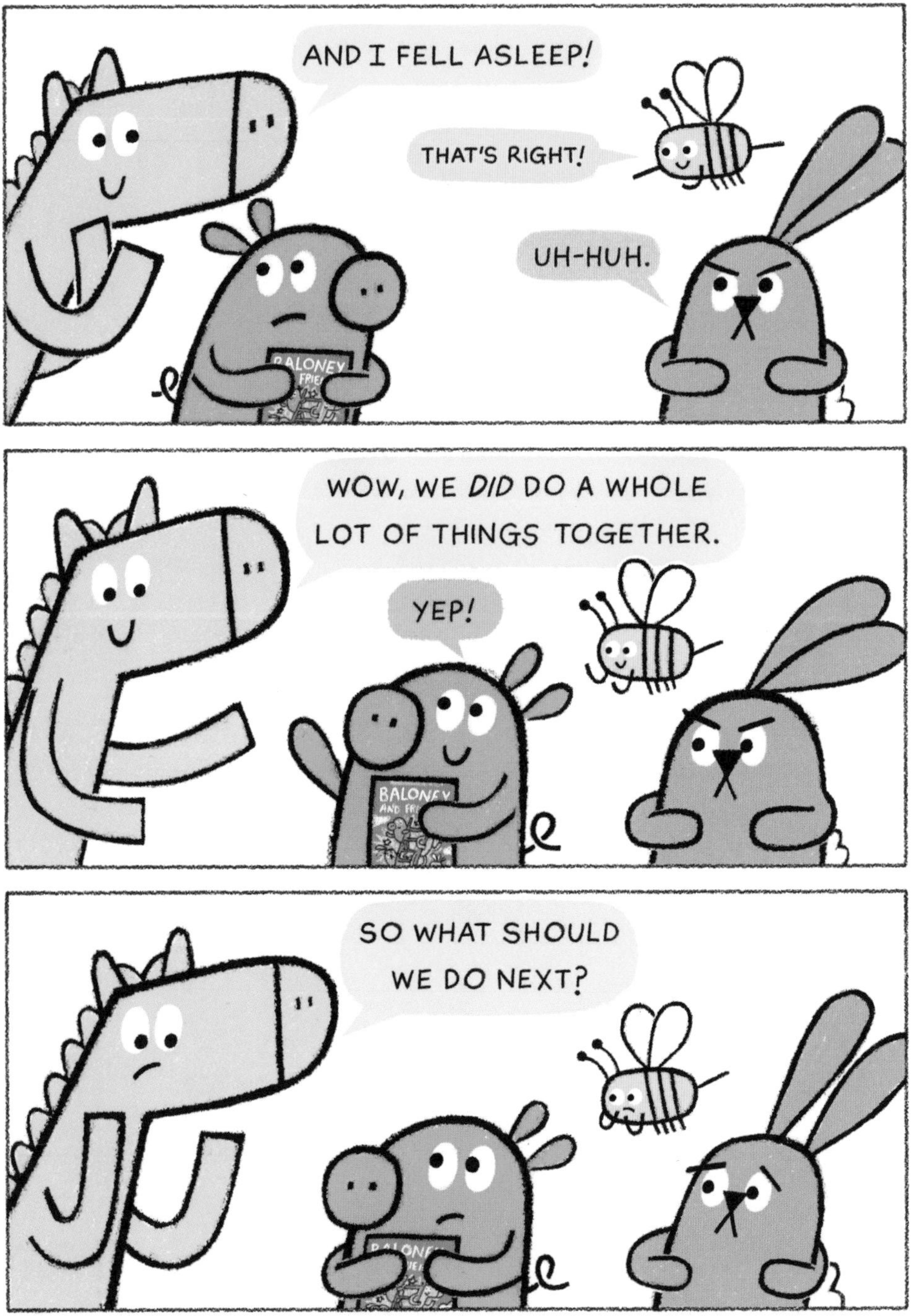

AND I FELL ASLEEP!
THAT'S RIGHT!
UH-HUH.
WOW, WE *DID* DO A WHOLE LOT OF THINGS TOGETHER.
YEP!
SO WHAT SHOULD WE DO NEXT?

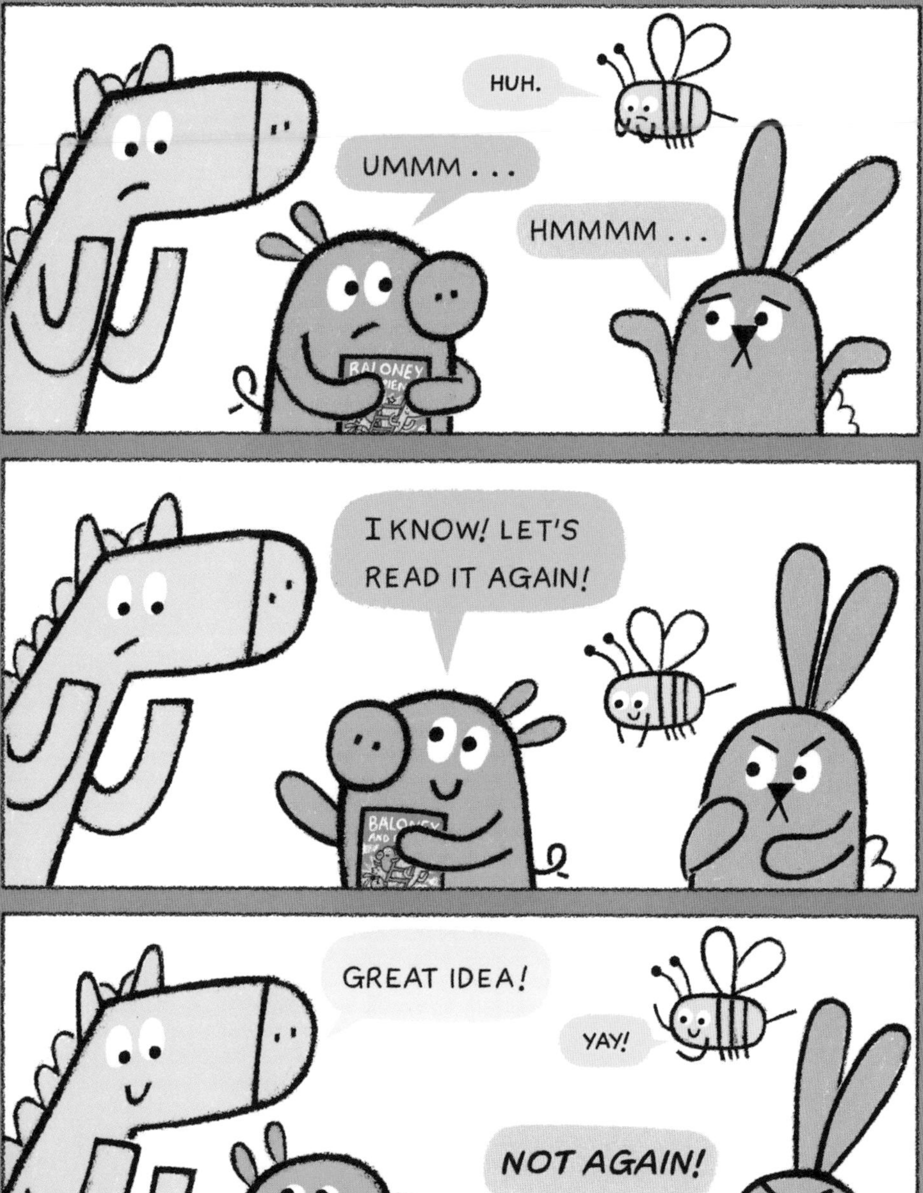
HUH.
UMMM . . .
HMMMM . . .
BALONEY FRIEN
I KNOW! LET'S READ IT AGAIN!
BALONEY AND
GREAT IDEA!
YAY!
NOT AGAIN!
LONEY FRIEND
THE END

DRAWING TIPS
FROM SUPER FAMOUS AUTHOR + ILLUSTRATOR
GREG PIZZOLI

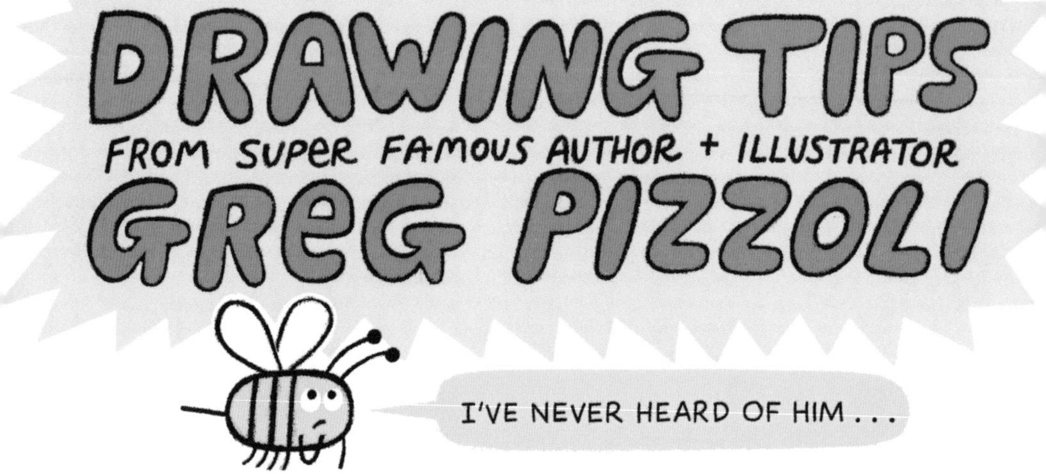
I'VE NEVER HEARD OF HIM . . .

IF YOU ARE MAKING YOUR OWN STORY STARRING BALONEY AND FRIENDS, BE SURE TO GIVE THEM LOTS OF EMOTIONS— IT'S EASY!

YOU CAN EXPERIMENT WITH THE PLACEMENT OF PUPILS, EYEBROWS, SMILES, OR FROWNS— THERE ARE LOTS OF WAYS TO SHOW EMOTION.

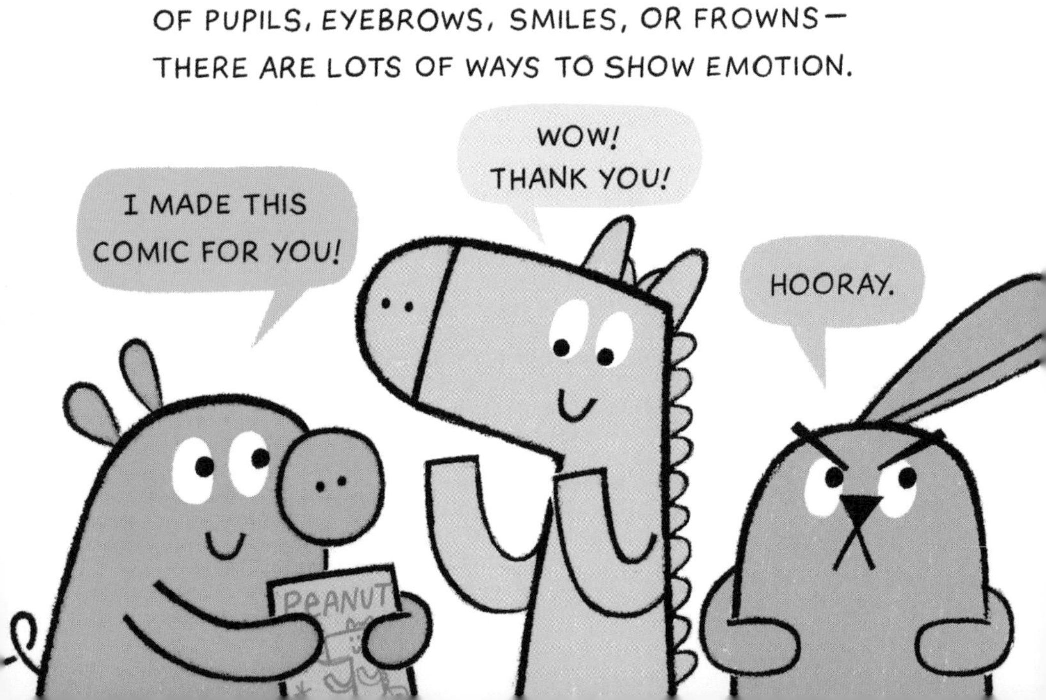
I MADE THIS COMIC FOR YOU!
WOW! THANK YOU!
HOORAY.
PEANUT

HAPPY

CHEERFUL • GLAD • MERRY
DELIGHTED • PLEASED • JUBILANT

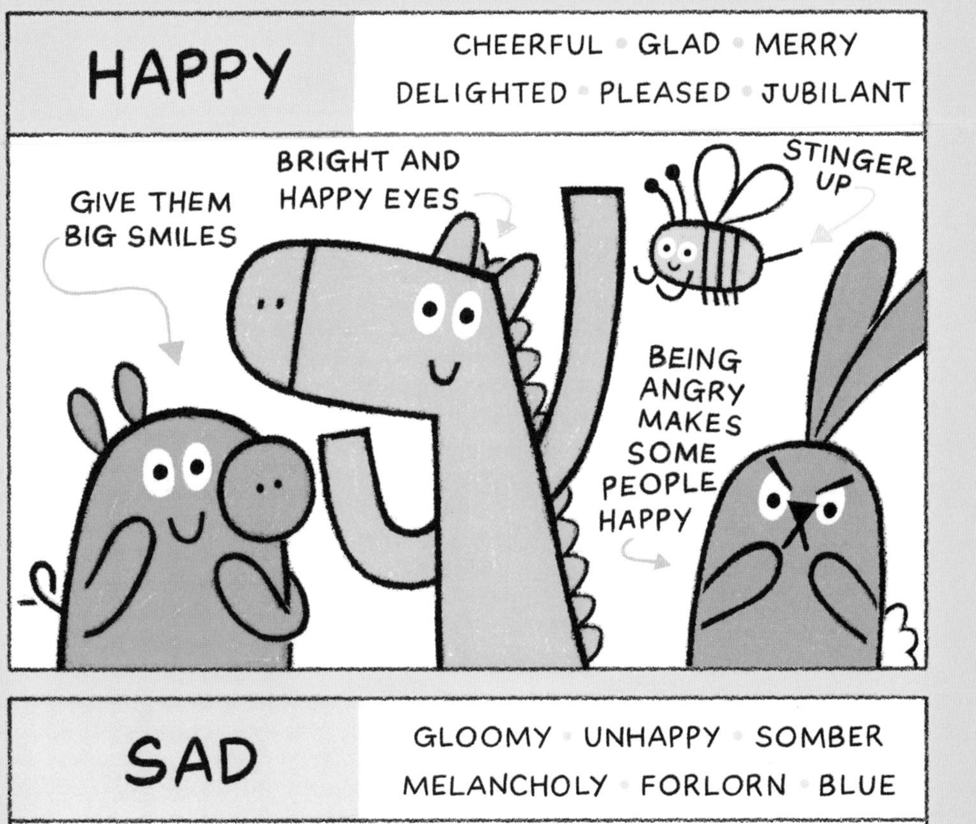
GIVE THEM BIG SMILES
BRIGHT AND HAPPY EYES
STINGER UP
BEING ANGRY MAKES SOME PEOPLE HAPPY

SAD

GLOOMY • UNHAPPY • SOMBER
MELANCHOLY • FORLORN • BLUE

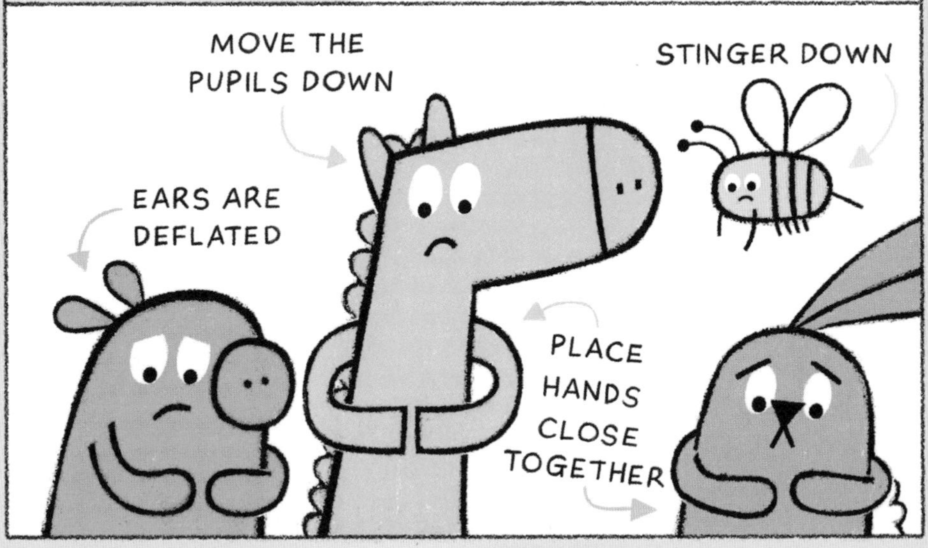
MOVE THE PUPILS DOWN
STINGER DOWN
EARS ARE DEFLATED
PLACE HANDS CLOSE TOGETHER

ANGRY

FED UP • MAD • FURIOUS
ANNOYED • OUTRAGED • IRATE

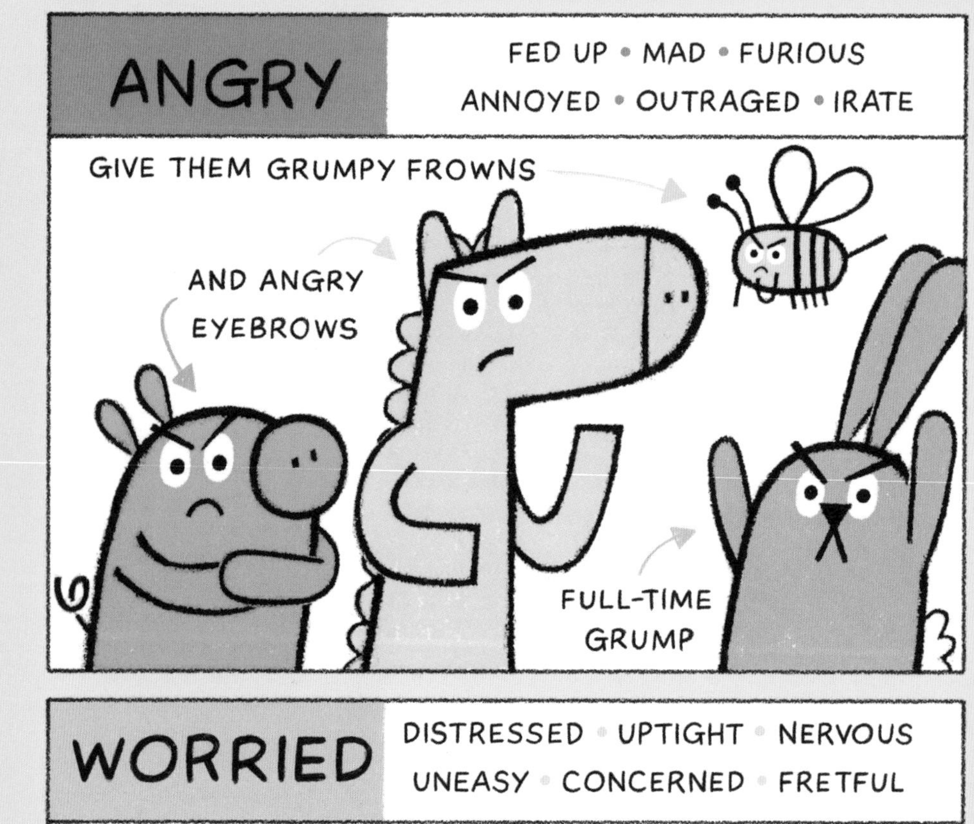
GIVE THEM GRUMPY FROWNS
AND ANGRY EYEBROWS
FULL-TIME GRUMP

WORRIED

DISTRESSED • UPTIGHT • NERVOUS
UNEASY • CONCERNED • FRETFUL

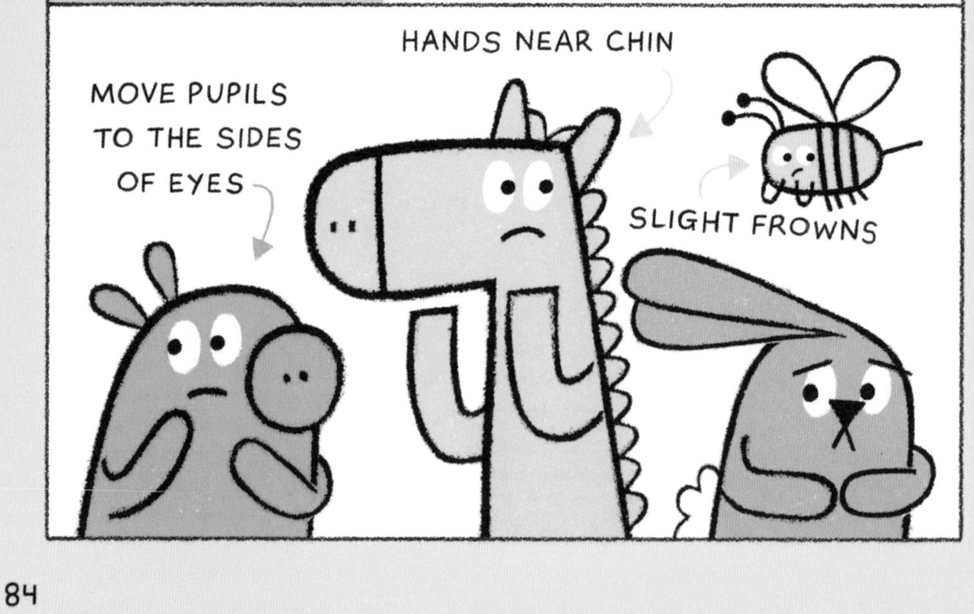
HANDS NEAR CHIN
MOVE PUPILS TO THE SIDES OF EYES
SLIGHT FROWNS

SUSPICIOUS

CAREFUL • CAUTIOUS
DOUBTFUL • SKEPTICAL

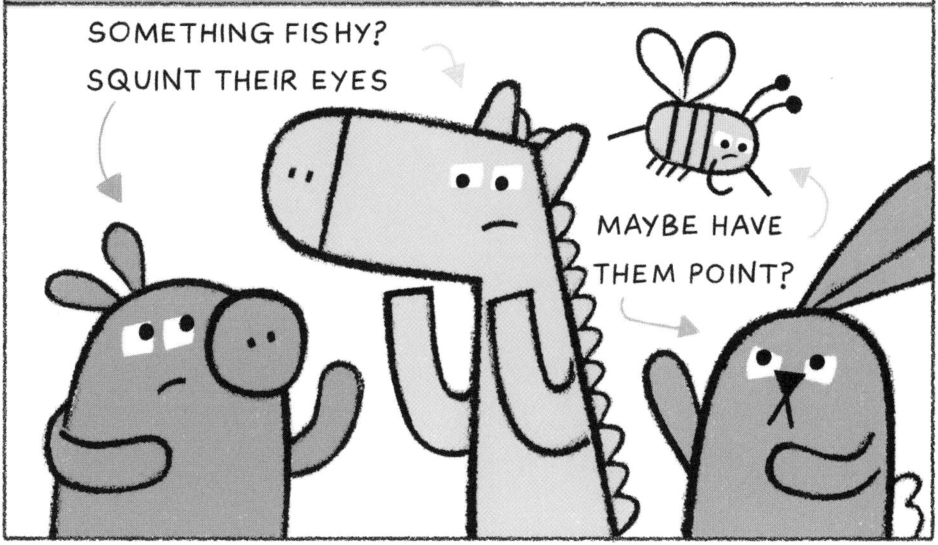
SOMETHING FISHY?
SQUINT THEIR EYES
MAYBE HAVE
THEM POINT?

NOW GO AND MAKE YOUR OWN COMIC!

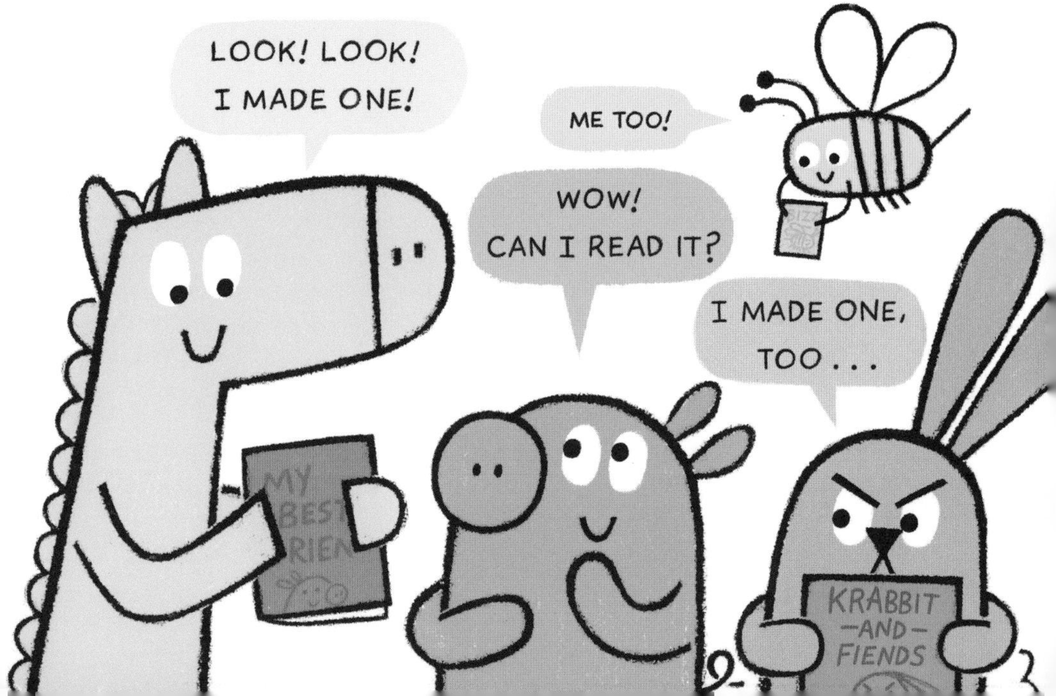
LOOK! LOOK!
I MADE ONE!
ME TOO!
WOW!
CAN I READ IT?
I MADE ONE,
TOO . . .
MY BEST FRIEN
KRABBIT
-AND-
FIENDS

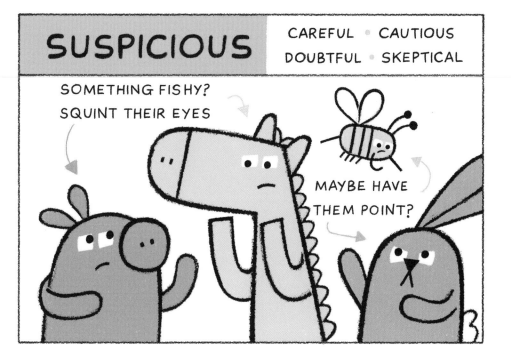

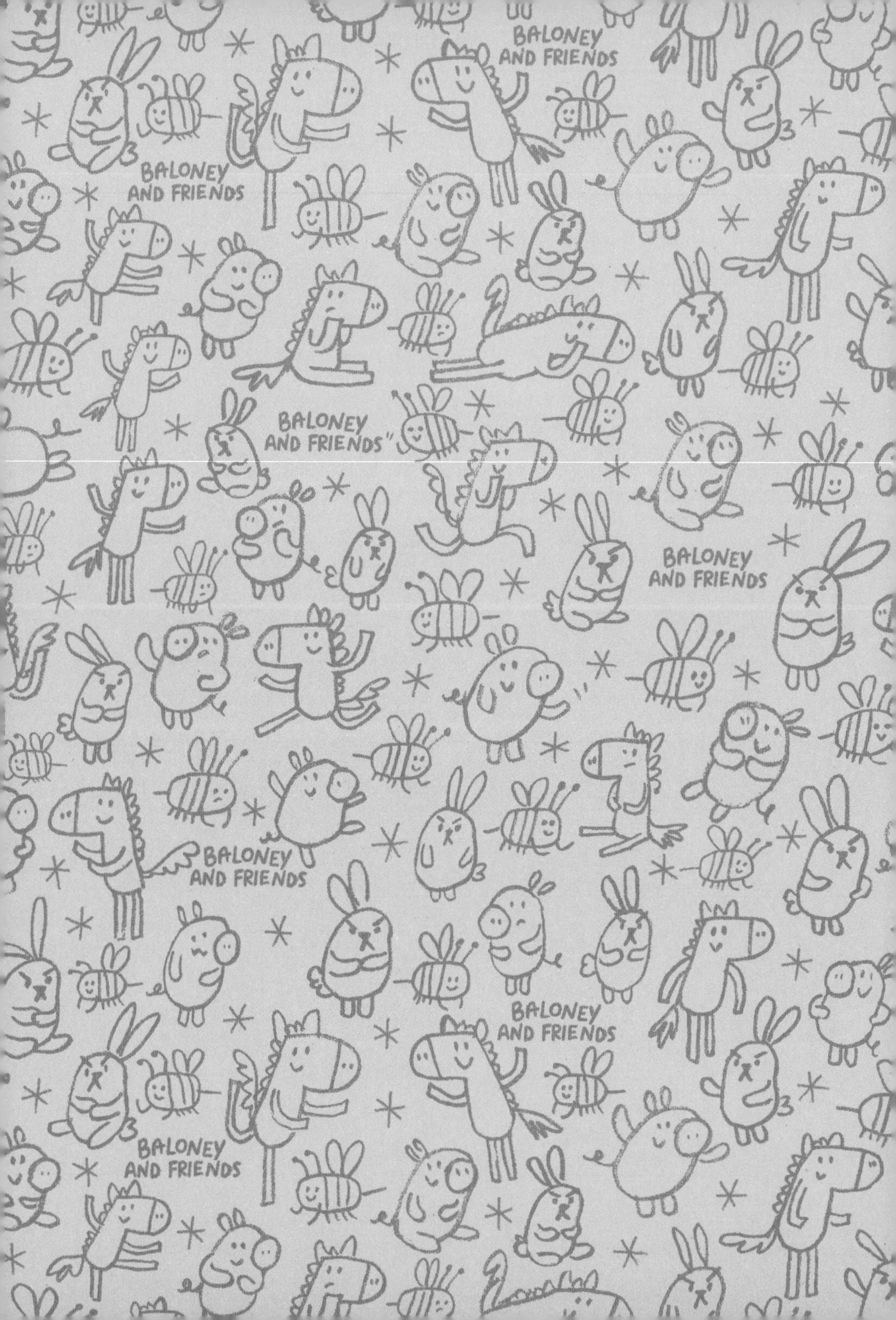
BALONEY AND FRIENDS
BALONEY AND FRIENDS
BALONEY AND FRIENDS
BALONEY AND FRIENDS
BALONEY AND FRIENDS
BALONEY AND FRIENDS
BALONEY AND FRIENDS